SEEDS OF FEAR

THE HOT BLOOD SERIES

EDWARD LEE
BENTLEY LITTLE
J. N. WILLIAMSON
AND OTHERS

EDITED BY JEFF GELB AND MICHAEL GARRETT

PINNACLE BOOKS
Kensington Publishing Corp.
http://www.kensingtonbooks.com

PINNACLE BOOKS are published by

Kensington Publishing Corp.
850 Third Avenue
New York, NY 10022

All Kensington Titles, Imprints, and Distributed Lines are available at special quantity discounts for bulk purchases for sales promotions, premiums, fund-raising, and educational or institutional use. Special book excerpts or customized printings can also be created to fit specific needs. For details, write or phone the office of the Kensington special sales manager: Kensington Publishing Corp., 850 Third Avenue, New York, NY 10022, attn. Special Sales Department, Phone: 1-800-221-2647.

Pinnacle and the P logo Reg. U.S. Pat. & TM Off.

First Pinnacle Books Printing: April 2005

10 9 8 7 6 5 4 3 2 1

Printed in the United States of America

PRAISE FOR THE HOT BLOOD SERIES
The Original Anthologies of All-New Erotic Horror Fiction

HOT BLOOD

"One of the best-put-together anthologies I've seen in years. . . . Rush out and buy *Hot Blood*—but don't say we didn't warn you that you'll be up all night reading it. . . ."
—*Fangoria* magazine

"Read *Hot Blood* late at night when the wind is blowing hard and the moon is full."
—*Playboy*

HOTTER BLOOD

"An outstanding collection . . . a daring combination of sex and terror . . . mixed with deadly intent by the best writers the horror field has to offer!"
—*Cemetery Dance* magazine

"*Hotter Blood* really smokes. Every piece of fiction in this anthology is superb."
—*Rave Reviews*

HOTTEST BLOOD

*Winner of the Horror Writers Association
Bram Stoker Award for Best Short Story
for Nancy Holder's "I Hear the Mermaids Singing"*

"An amazing anthology of all-new stories by some of the hottest writers around . . . the kind of anthology every horror writer would kill to crack . . ."
—*2AM* magazine

"Not for the weak-hearted or puritanical . . . Seek out this one (or its predecessors) for some naughty fun. . . ."
—*Booklovers*

The Hot Blood Series

HOT BLOOD

HOTTER BLOOD

HOTTEST BLOOD

DEADLY AFTER DARK

SEEDS OF FEAR

HOT BLOOD XI: FATAL ATTRACTIONS

STRANGE BEDFELLOWS

Published by Kensington Publishing Corporation

Copyright Notices

This book is dedicated to Rod Serling, Richard Matheson, and Charles Beaumont, without whose *Twilight Zone* stories this anthology might never have been born.

CONTENTS

PREFACE   xi
Jeff Gelb and Michael Garrett

INTRODUCTION   xiii
Brinke Stevens

SCREAM QUEEN   1
Ronald Kelly

HIDEYHOLE   18
Billie Sue Mosiman

HIGH CONCEPT   41
J. N. Williamson

JUST A PHONE CALL AWAY   62
John F. D. Taff

BLACK AND WHITE AND BED ALL OVER   83
James Crawford

HANDYMAN   99
Jeff Gelb

AIRHEAD   109
Michael Newton

FIVE SECONDS   122
J. L. Comeau

CONTENTS

SYMPATHY CALL   130
Michael Garrett

OVEREATERS OMINOUS   143
Stephen R. George

GRUB-GIRL   160
Edward Lee

HUNGER   168
Kathryn Ptacek

THE WATCHER   182
Rex Miller and Jeff Gelb

LULLABY & GOODNIGHT   200
Wayne Allen Sallee

I AM JOE'S PENIS   212
Scott H. Urban

WHAT YOU SEE   219
Paul Dale Anderson

THE BEAST   236
Larry Tritten

SEE MARILYN MONROE'S PANTIES!   243
Bentley Little

DEVIL WITH A BLUE DRESS   264
P. D. Cacek

THE CONTRIBUTORS   289

PREFACE

Welcome back!

This, the latest in the *Hot Blood* series, represents the fifth "date" for our blooming relationship.

We're proud that the *Hot Blood* series has proven to be more than a mere one-night stand. We're gratified we've developed an intimate connection with you, the reader. We're happy you've made the commitment, and we hope you'll be with us till death do us part.

Or later.

This time around we're pleased to present a foreword by Brinke Stevens, world-renowned "Scream Queen," who offers her uniquely informed perspective of eroticism and horror. Within these pages you'll also find first appearances in the series by several notable authors, as well as lurid tales by those who have been with us before. All in all, it's another stimulating package of goose bumps and ants-in-the-pants stories in the *Hot Blood* tradition.

So relax and travel with us, from somewhere south of the *Twilight Zone* to your own erogenous zones, through stories that would make even Masters and Johnson blush.

And finally, thanks for making this series such a success. It's been good for us, and we hope our performance has satisfied your sexual appetite as well.

Jeff Gelb
Michael Garrett

INTRODUCTION

Brinke Stevens

A strange thing happened to me during late October of 1993. For two weeks I was staying at a Hyatt Hotel near San Francisco. Every night I was top-billed as a horror movie celebrity at The Scaregrounds, a Halloween theme park. Thus, I obligingly penned my autograph and posed for countless photos. Called a "Scream Queen," I'm a popular, well-respected actress among all those horror B-movies fans. If you like to stay up late watching scary low-budget films on TV, you've probably already seen me at least a dozen times . . . often in steamy shower scenes, or murdered by a crazy driller-killer, or suddenly transformed into a bloodthirsty demoness.

At midnight the crowds wandered home at last. I traded my spike heels for sensible flats, trudged across the empty parking lot to my rental car, and drove too fast up the freeway toward "home" . . . my small hotel room. First, I ripped off my long raven wig and slithered out of my familiar black "Evila" costume, then washed the makeup off my face. Now I looked nothing like the glamorous vamp who'd been worshiped by panting fan-boys. Finally I collapsed onto my bed—deeply exhausted, and feeling an inevitable letdown after six hours of intense admiration. But once the outer public mask came off, I was armed and ready for . . . *my own private fix!*

A dozen or so lurid fiction paperback books filled my suitcase. *Ah, pulp fodder for my secret midnight vice!* Among them were *Hot Blood, Hotter Blood,* and *Hottest Blood.* Really, who could resist such promising titles? Besides, I've known editor Jeff Gelb for almost twenty years—and so I'd dutifully amassed all his anthologies on my dusty library shelf. It wasn't until my Halloween junket that I found enough time in my busy schedule to actually *read* them.

Each night I promised myself I'd just read ONE story and then fall asleep. But by 3:00 A.M. (and five or six stories later), I realized my relaxation plan was self-defeating. The stories were too sexy, too exciting, too scary! The erotica bordered on pornographic *(but that's not necessarily a bad thing!),* and the horror was pure and unadulterated. After two weeks of devouring those tasty *Hot Blood* books, I lost a lot of sleep—but I gained a new obsession.

Often it seems standard B-movie fare involves nudity, terror, sex, and gore—after all, it *is* tried-and-true commercial formula. I've routinely worked with killers, corpses, blood, and guts . . . and loved every minute of it! So saying, my own films might be considered the cinematic equivalent of erotic horror literature. You may enjoy reading my own insights and perspectives on what I do for a living—as a modern woman who's written and starred in dozens of "erotic horror" exploitation films.

I believe that erotic horror stories, for the most

part, are grown-up versions of *Grimm's Fairy Tales* (though the original stories are hardly for children, as you well know). They are little morality plays, revenge stories, tales of what happens when we lose control. Or—more to the point—when we take advantage of something that seems too good to be true. In *Teenage Exorcist* (a screenplay I also wrote), I eagerly rented an opulent mansion at bargain-basement rates—and soon paid the dire consequences for it, when the evil ghost of a dead occupant possessed me. And in *Slave Girls from Beyond Infinity,* my seductively generous host, Zed, later turned the tables on me. An unfortunate case of hospitality turning to homicide!

In a similar vein, the "revenge" factor in horror fiction is a holdover from *Tales From the Crypt* comics of the 1950s, wherein the wronged murdered husband returns to snuff his killer (usually an unfaithful wife, you will notice). It is a zombified "karma" sort of deal, often reflected in cinema, as well. In *Haunting Fear* I clawed my way out of a coffin in the basement while my husband was climaxing with his sleazy blond mistress in our bed. Needless to say, I was slow, brutal, and quite exacting while taking my revenge on them both!

Sex and horror *do* go together. Sex is a one-way door that, once entered, cannot be exited. It is also an imitation of death. The French, after all, call an orgasm "the little death." People don't like to talk about sex any more than they like to talk about death. Sex is a part of that old reptilian brain. Seemingly, the rational mind turns off . . . and Something Else appears. There is a roar of a dinosaur behind every moan between satin sheets. Sex is mythic (and let's face facts, seldom as good as we think it's going to be), just like horror. You know, the truth shattering the fantasy like glass in an automobile accident. Like the supposedly vampish Brinke admitting to a preference for flannel sleepwear rather than silky lingerie . . . as a way of telling the reader that everyone has expectations about sex and eroticism, but they are predicated on images that may or may not reflect reality.

And no one ever tells the truth about sex. It's too personal. It is something that unfolds between lovers. Hence, even more potential horror . . . finding out that your true love is into really odd stuff, or is not exactly what you'd expected. How many times, in erotic horror stories and films, has this theme been a subtext? Just take a look at *Nightmare Sisters,* in which I'm among a trio of hopelessly nerdy college girls who are ridiculed by cruel frat boys. After holding a séance one dark night, we suddenly transform into voluptuous dolls—and then gleefully slay the same would-be suitors who once rejected us. There's a chilling episode of *Dark Romances,* too, wherein I play a gorgeous woman who seduces many great artists . . . and later collects their very souls. A hidden agenda can be a powerfully frightening thing, indeed.

We all have concrete examples from real life, too. For example, did you ever find a partner who liked to be bitten during sex? It may be something you're uncomfortable with, because it's too close to losing control of the rational mind. But you might eventually like it, anyway. *That* is the final aspect of the sex-horror connection . . . finding out things about yourself that you really didn't want to know.

Possibly, it was a bold stroke to write a bondage scene for myself in *Teenage Exorcist.* But you'll also see me tied to a pillar on the video box cover of *Ladies of the Lotus.* In *Slave Girls,* I was chained to a dungeon wall in black lingerie. A year later, in *Warlords,* I was bound topless to a cross. The director, Fred Olen Ray, cocked an eyebrow and queried, "What is it with you, Stevens? Do you *ask* for these parts?" No, it must be a mere coincidence . . . yet I can only think I've come to enjoy it a little too much, perhaps. We naively think we know ourselves, and we do not. The comfort of our identity is twisted by something that's beyond our control. The Beast is always there—it is a wild heat that stays in the veins. And supposedly, we take off our chains along with our clothing. In my business, I apparently look for others to put them on me.

Until about 1980, sex was definitely guilt-free. It was the era of Erica Jong's infamous "zipless fuck." Sex without fear, and often without much emotional commitment. Then AIDS reared its retroviral head. Once described as "the little death," sex could now be death for real. Sex became even more mythic, even more linked with the symbolism of death. All we had to fear before was rejection, or the occasional scary partner (the Date from Hell is another fecund horror theme, right?). Now we had real death confronting the threat of ego-death.

So the concept of a femme fatale—a beautiful, sexually aggressive woman—becomes very important to men. And because it is (quite frankly) uncommon, it makes the mind revolve around such cautionary-tale archetypes as lamias, vampires, succubi, and so on. Writer Hazel-Dawn Dumpert said: "Murderers, vampires, ghosts can be frightening, yes. A crazy dame? Now *that's* scary." She also suggested that family values define woman as a nurturing force. A woman is an element of the earth itself—they don't call it Mother Nature for nothing. She's the link to physical and emotional survival. If a kink throws the womanly works off kilter, if they're perverted in any way, the results can be catastrophic. We all know what horrors are unleashed when bizarre circumstances transform beneficent babes into creatures of evil.

In fiction, a feminine monster is generally not brought into the world in the usual way. Instead, her origin lies in some pagan effrontery—or in the release of an ancient malevolence, now free to violate the nubile bodies of innocent coeds. Consider that disastrous séance wherein I evoked a succubus in *Nightmare Sisters*. And that ugly, vicious imp I accidentally freed from a bowling trophy in *Sorority Babes*. In *Dark Romances,* my own bloodthirsty immortality was the result of a vile pact with a demon.

In movies and literature, it's always a good idea to ask: Why is this gorgeous woman coming on so strong like that? If it's too good to be true, there must be a catch. In real life, I believe this is a major psychological difference between men and women: ego reinforcement. That isn't to say the majority of men will turn down sex when it's offered to them, even by strange women. But don't think men aren't suspicious of the situation. Even for the most testosterone-driven men, sex is scary. You are going off into the metaphorical dark with someone you don't know well, and getting as close to her as is physically possible. *Vulnerable.* Sex and death . . . as in Ramsey Campbell's cleverly titled book, *Scared Stiff.*

That is why sex is always more than simply sex. It ties in with all kinds of issues. It is a *big deal.* Remember what Woody Allen said about sex and death? "Two things that only happen once in a lifetime." We joke about it, but sex is scary. These concerns about sex and death, about the Beast within, are all throughout our popular culture: in songs, books, and films. In this decade of white-trash glamour, we even get it delivered to us daily by *Hard Copy* and *Oprah* inside our own living rooms.

Men's erotica is more broadly humorous, while women's erotica tends to be more philosophical and high-minded. Truism: different strokes for different folks. And it isn't just men, of course. Women have their own kinks in their psychological garden hoses, too. It reminds me a bit of the Victorian female attitude about sex, and why Count Dracula was so appealing both then and now. Victorian women weren't supposed to like sex, or to be wanton. It was control, then as now, that was important. Stephen King described the underlying theme thusly: The vampire was saying to these chaste Victorian ladies, "I will fuck you with my mouth, and you will love it."

He is right, too. For both sexes, the concept of losing control in romance is somehow very attractive. *I couldn't help myself* becomes a catch phrase . . . *I was drunk.* It is the most human of states: to want to feel good, to feel better, or to not feel at all. We learn secrecy, new definitions of the truth. And a certain sense of assault develops in whatever mirror we choose to look into . . . because we take off many thousands of years of civilization when we dive beneath the sheets.

I doubt women can appreciate how scary sex is for men. Perhaps this is why erotic horror pretty much revolves around a male readership. Since much of horror has gone the rather messy splatterpunk direction, that may be a limiting factor for some women's appreciation of the genre. But I think there are a lot of females who, like myself, enjoy erotic horror immensely. What about Camille Paglia, the bogeyman of feminism, admitting to a great love of bodice ripper novels, complete with the bare-chested man bending the gasping maiden near double over a stone bench! And THIS from a committed foe of the paternalistic, woman-bashing status quo?

Guiltlessly, I'll admit my obsession for these wonderful erotic horror stories. So it's my great pleasure to welcome you to another spectacular volume of *Hot Blood*. Right now it is time to dim the lights, pull the covers up to your chin, and delve into these little gems of exotic terror *(and if you're in bed with a significant other, be sure to check for fangs first!)*.

SEEDS
OF
FEAR

SCREAM QUEEN

Ronald Kelly

The images on the screen were black and white, grainy with too many dropouts. The sound was bad, harsh and scratchy. The music was even worse, too melodramatic. The scene was set somewhere up in the California mountains: a lot of boulders, dry grass, and scrubby underbrush.

Ted Culman lay on the full-size bed, naked, his eyes glued to the nineteen-inch TV. The landscape was unremarkable, the backdrop for countless low-budget movies made in the fifties and sixties. The only distinguishing factor about the old flick appeared a moment later, rounding a boulder and walking up a dusty mountain trail.

Ted sunk into the pillows at his back, as if settling into the cockpit of a jet fighter. He was in control now. The hand that rested on his belly crept toward his groin. Soon it was fisted around him, stroking. He was already aroused.

The woman who appeared on the screen was a real beauty. Average in height, but noticeably buxom, her breasts swelling behind the cloth of her checkered blouse. She was platinum blond, much in the same style of Marilyn Monroe or Jayne Mansfield. Her lovely face was partly obscured by too much lipstick, partly by a pair of white-framed sunglasses, circa 1956. Ted studied the woman's lower region: flaring hips encased in skintight white slacks, long shapely legs, and tiny feet slipped inside simple sandals.

The woman on the screen made her way up the lonesome pathway, her hips swaying like a pendulum, her delicate jaw working on a gob of Wrigley's spearmint gum. Ted's hand quickened as a muffled roar sounded from offscreen and caused the woman to whirl in her tracks. An atrocious-looking swamp monster—all dangling latex and bulbous tennis-ball eyes—leapt down clumsily from a neighboring boulder, its thick arms extended in menace.

That was when Ted closed his eyes and let his imagination take over. As his hand went on autopilot, Ted imagined himself to be the shuffling creature. But there was no menace in his monstrous eyes, only desire; a desire shared by the woman he confronted. In a matter of seconds, his claws had torn past her blouse and bra, tossing tatters of cloth and elastic away until her breasts were exposed. The nipples stood out, pink and hard. She reached out for him, and soon they were on the sandy earth. His claws went to work again, hooking past tight cloth, rending it easily. She lay beneath him, completely nude now. They embraced hungrily, a melding of human and alien flesh. Ted felt his bestial member jut from his loins, searching, aching passionately. The woman writhed hungrily against him, then he was there, surrounded by warm wetness.

Ted felt himself quickly reaching the brink. He

opened his eyes. The blonde's lovely face filled the screen, just as he had anticipated. Her sunglasses had been knocked askew and one eye stared straight into the camera. Then those luscious lips parted and a shrill scream powered up from out of her throat. But in Ted's ears it was not the shriek of terror that it was intended to be. Instead, it was a cry of unbridled ecstasy.

Pleasure shot through him, exploding at the base of his spine, causing his hips to buck slightly. Then, a second later, it was all over. The scene had changed. Ted was watching a pipe-smoking scientist explaining a screenwriter's theory of evolution, while Ted's penis shriveled in the palm of his hand.

Ted paused the VCR with the remote control, while his other hand shucked a Kleenex from its box and sopped up the juices of his passion. After the strength had returned to his legs, he hopped off the motel bed and walked into the bathroom. He tossed the damp wad of tissue into the toilet, then cranked up the shower and stepped in.

As he bathed, he smiled to himself, recalling the scream of the monster's blond victim. No one could break the decibel level like Fawn Hale. Oh, many had tried, but none had managed to surpass . . . at least not in Ted's opinion.

Fawn was well-known and appreciated by aficionados of horror and science-fiction cinema, particularly the cheaply made features of the fifties and sixties. Fawn was considered by the majority to have been the premier scream queen of that era, very much the way Betty Page had become a cult favorite in the realm of nostalgic pinups. There had been dozens of others, some even more beautiful and bustier than Fawn. But none had possessed the lungs she had. For sheer expression of horror and vocal power, the actress had no equal. Ted remembered the first time he had heard Fawn scream. He had attended an all-night Halloween fright fest at a run-down theater off campus. Fawn's shriek had overloaded a couple of the theater's main speakers. They had popped with a burst of ozone, incapable of accommodating the high frequency of Fawn's famous cry.

Just thinking about it made Ted horny again, but he ignored the impulse and finished his shower. He had someplace to go that morning, someplace very important. It was so important, in fact, that he had driven nearly two thousand miles just to get there.

Ted toweled off, then dressed. He left his suitcase behind, but unhooked the VCR and took it with him. He didn't want to risk the chance of the maid ripping it off when she came to clean his room. He also took the cardboard jacket of the tape that was still in the video recorder. The movie was creatively titled *Curse of the Swamp Monster* and sported a black-and-white shot of the beast in all its low-budget glory.

He stepped outside and locked the door behind him. Ted looked around for a second. The Days Inn he had checked into the night before was off an exit on Interstate 24 in the heart of Tennessee. There was only one reason why a California grad student would waste his spring break and make a cross-country journey to the land of the Grand Ole Opry and Jack Daniel's, and that reason could be summed up in two words.

Fawn Hale.

Ted walked to his car—a restored '69 Mustang convertible—and opened the trunk. He set the VCR next to a cardboard box full of videotapes. All were the kind of schlock horror flicks Ted thrived on—the outrageously bad classics of Edward D. Wood and Herschell Gordon Lewis. And two out of three of them featured Fawn Hale and her bloodcurdling scream somewhere between the title and ending credits.

Before he closed the trunk, he picked up a copy of *Filmfax* that lay on top of the box. It was an article in the movie magazine that had been responsible for his journey south. The story chronicled the history of a dozen popular scream queens and, in the portion devoted to Fawn, had laid the key to a mystery that had bugged Ted for several years. After Hale had retired from films in 1968, she had left Hollywood and seemingly vanished off the face of the earth. But, according to the article, Fawn had returned to her hometown of Cumberland Springs in central Tennessee.

That single tidbit of information had been a revelation for Ted. Fawn had almost become an obsession to him, creeping into his sexual fantasies lately. His dorm room was papered with posters and glossy photos of the B-movie blonde, while Ted's dreams were filled with bizarre images of Fawn being seduced by the monsters she had shared the screen with. It wasn't long before Ted began to imagine himself inside those garish suits of latex and fur, conjuring screams of pleasure from the actress, rather than ones of horror.

After reading the article, Ted simply couldn't put it out of his mind. The closer spring break grew, the more maddening the knowledge of Fawn's whereabouts seemed to be. Finally the thought of driving to Tennessee crossed his mind, lodging there like a splinter. It was during the day of his last class that Ted had made his decision. He took seven hundred dollars out of the bank, packed up his suitcase and VCR, and hit the road. He knew it was foolish and against his better judgment, but he had still gone. Now, three days later, he was only a short distance from his destination.

Ted closed the trunk, taking the magazine with him. He climbed into the Mustang's bucket seat and sat there for a long moment. Across the main highway—which boasted several other motels, an Amoco station, and a McDonald's—was a post bearing two signs. The upper one pointed west and read MANCHESTER—15 MILES. The one underneath pointed east and proclaimed CUMBERLAND SPRINGS—7 MILES.

Well, what're you waiting for, Culman? he thought, feeling a little nervous. *You came this far. Seven more miles and you'll be able to get this out of your system for good.*

He took a deep breath to calm himself, then put the Mustang in gear and pulled out onto the highway.

The town of Cumberland Springs could scarcely be considered one at all. It consisted of only a church, a post office, and an old-timey general store with a couple of ancient gas pumps out front. A few white clapboard houses were scattered around the main buildings, but that was about the extent of the little hamlet.

Ted stopped in at the general store, which was called Roone's Mercantile, and bought himself a honey bun and a Dr. Pepper for breakfast. After he had paid for the food, he regarded the man behind the register. Oscar Roone was a lanky man of sixty with bushy eyebrows and a perpetual scowl on his weathered face. Ted debated asking the man for directions, then decided it wouldn't hurt.

"Excuse me, but could you tell me how to get to the Hale place?"

The old man glared at the overweight boy with shaggy brown hair and glasses. "Why in Sam Hill would you wanna go way out there?" he asked.

Ted was at a loss for an answer at first. He shrugged. "I just have some business there, that's all." Nosy old bastard.

Roone looked like he'd bitten into a green persimmon. He opened his mouth to say something, then changed his mind. "You go on down the highway here about a half mile, till you pass the Knowles farm. You'll know the place. The barn's got 'See Rock City' painted on its roof. Well, you take the next turnoff, a dirt stretch called Glenhollow Road, and head on that way for three or four miles. The Hale place is the first house on the right."

"Thanks," said Ted. He gathered up his purchases and made his way past the tightly packed aisles of canned and dry goods, eager to be out of the shadowy store and back into the sunshine. He glanced back only once and saw the old man staring at him peculiarly. As if he wanted to ask Ted something . . . or maybe tell him something.

He quickly gobbled down the honey bun and chased it with the soda. Then he started his car and headed farther southward, trying to keep Roone's directions fresh in his mind. He found the Knowles farm without any trouble and turned down the dirt road, even though there was no visible sign marking it as being Glenhollow.

Ted drove down the rural road, his hands clenching and unclenching the steering wheel. The day was beautiful, and the dense woods to either side of him were green and cool. Birds sang in abundance from overhead and the air was rich with the scent of honeysuckle, but those things failed to soothe his frazzled nerves. He felt none of the control he had felt earlier that morning, when he had masturbated to the monster movie.

It seemed like an eternity, but he finally reached the first house on the right side of Glenhollow Road. Ted parked the Mustang next to a drainage ditch, a hundred feet from the structure. It was a simple, two-story farmhouse that looked as if it hadn't been treated to a good roofing or paint job for ten or twelve years. Tall oaks surrounded the house, and the yard was knee-high with weeds. Standing at the side of the road was a single mailbox with the name HALE painted on the side, nothing more.

It was at that moment that Ted Culman wondered exactly what he was doing there. Exactly what had he had in mind when he left California? Had he come to simply tell her how much he appreciated her movies and ask for her autograph? Or was there more to it than that? Ted thought about the fantasies he had been indulging in lately, but they concerned the Fawn Hale of the past. The woman had been nearing her forties when she retired. She would be in her sixties now, drawing Social Security and soaking her teeth in a glass by her bed.

The thought made Ted feel a little nauseous. He had the sudden urge to make a U-turn in the country road, retrieve his suitcase from the motel, and head home. But he knew if he did that, he would always wonder about Fawn and the meeting he had aborted out of sheer panic. He took a deep breath and, climbing out of the car, started up the road to the Hale residence.

As he crossed the unmowed yard, he began to

wonder if anyone even lived there anymore. The front porch was littered with dead leaves, and many of the house's windows were broken, most notably those of the upper floor. The steps creaked beneath his feet as he approached the front door, and beyond the storm door he could only make out darkness. From the other side of the screen drifted a scent of mustiness and decay, the odor of a house that had not been aired out in a very long time.

Nervously he raised his fist and knocked on the doorjamb.

At first he didn't think anyone was going to answer. Then a form emerged from out of the gloom. "Can I help you?" asked a feminine voice with a soft southern drawl.

Ted stared at the woman on the other side of the door, and at first, the mesh of the screen caused an unnerving illusion. For an instant it was like looking at a freeze-frame of a grainy black-and-white film. A frame of a buxom blonde, minus the sunglasses and fifties clothing. The resemblance was uncanny, almost frightening.

"Fawn?" blurted Ted, even though he knew that the woman couldn't possibly be the one he had come to see. She was too young; a little older than him, maybe twenty-six or seven. And her hair wasn't platinum, but a more natural shade of strawberry blond. But the eyes were identical to Fawn's, and that mouth . . . There certainly was no mistake that it had been derived from the same voluptuous gene pool.

The girl smiled. "No, but I'm her daughter, Lori," she said. She stared at him for a moment, waiting. "Uh, can I do something for you?"

"My name's Ted Culman," he said, still stunned by

how much she looked like Fawn. "I'm a big fan of your mother. I wonder if I could talk to her for a minute, if it wouldn't be too much trouble?"

The smile faltered on Lori's face and she looked a little sad. "I'm sorry, but that's impossible."

"Please," said Ted, sensing that something was wrong. "Just a couple minutes and I won't bother her again."

"You don't understand," said Lori Hale. She hesitated for a moment, her eyes full of pain. "My mother . . . she's dead. She passed away about a year ago."

Ted felt as if someone had sucker-punched him in the gut. "Oh, no," he muttered. "But . . . how?"

"Cancer," she told him.

Ted took a step back, his face pale. For a moment he felt as if he might pass out.

He heard the girl unhook the screen door and open it. "Are you all right?" she asked, concerned.

"I . . . I don't know," he said truthfully. Even though Fawn Hale had died in practically every movie she had been featured in, Ted had a difficult time accepting the fact that she was actually dead in real life. "Could I sit down somewhere for a minute?"

"Sure," said Lori Hale. "Come on inside."

Ted accepted her invitation and was soon sitting on a threadbare couch in a dusty parlor. The room was decorated with antique furniture, and the walls alternated between old family photographs and glossy eight-by-ten stills of Fawn in her prime, most of them showing off more of her teeth and tonsils than anything else.

When some of the color had returned to Ted's face, the young woman seemed to relax a little. "Are you sure you're okay?" she asked again.

"Yeah," replied Ted. "I was just surprised, that's all."

"And disappointed, too," said Lori. "I see it in your face. Just how far did you come to see my mother?"

"San Diego," he said.

"California? No wonder you're so upset." She started toward an adjoining hallway. "I'll go to the kitchen and fetch us something to drink. I just fixed a pitcher of iced tea. How does that sound?"

Ted's throat felt parched. "Great," he replied.

A minute later, Lori returned with a tall glass of iced tea in each hand. When she entered the room, Ted couldn't help but admire the girl's figure, clad only in a halter top and a pair of denim cutoffs. She possessed practically the same body that her mother had in her youth: perfectly formed breasts, graceful hips, and long, muscular legs.

Lori seemed to sense his attention, but didn't seem to mind. She sat down next to Ted and slipped a cold glass in his hand. "There you go," she said. She watched as he gulped several swallows of tea. "So you were a fan of Mama's?"

"Yes," said Ted. The tea was a little strong for his taste, but it seemed to calm him down. "I have about every film she ever made on video."

"Really?" asked Lori, impressed. "Even *Demon Conquerors from Mars?*"

Ted laughed. He knew the film she was talking about. It was a dreadful science-fiction flick made on a shoestring budget of two thousand dollars and featured some really horrendous special effects, such as a sinister robot constructed from an oil drum, and a magnified iguana attacking a shoddy model of a small town. If there was one shining point about the movie, it was the appearance of Fawn as an unsuspecting diner waitress who falls victim to the Martian robots and their oversized lizard.

"I do have that one," he said.

"That was one of my favorites," said Lori. She smiled. "You know, I do appreciate you coming. Mama would've appreciated it, too."

"I'm just sorry I couldn't have met her," he said. Ted thought of the way he had exploited the actress in his own sleazy fantasies and suddenly felt ashamed.

"She would've enjoyed talking to you," Lori told him. "She liked talking about her career." A strange expression surfaced in the woman's eyes. "Well, most of it, that is."

Ted drank his tea, a question suddenly coming to mind. He wondered whether he should ask it or not, then figured it was safe to do so. "Exactly why did your mother retire, Lori? I've read about everything I could dig up on her, but I've never been able to find out the reason."

Lori avoided his gaze at first. "There was a scandal."

"Scandal?"

"Yes," she went on. "It happened during her last picture, *Night of the Jungle Zombies*. They had finished up a day's shooting on location near Los Padres National Park. It was after dark and Mama was walking through the forest back to her trailer. Before she got there, someone jumped out of the shadows and attacked her." Lori paused for a moment. "She was raped."

Ted couldn't believe what he was hearing. "Did she know who it was?"

"Yes, although she never told anyone," said Lori. "It was a bit player in the picture. A guy by the name of Trevor Hall."

"Trevor Hall," repeated Ted. The name sounded familiar, but Ted had difficulty matching it with a face. There had been hundreds of bit players in the industry back then, some only lasting a picture or two.

Lori stared at Ted for a long moment, watchful. Then she continued. "After the attack, Mama found out that she was pregnant," said Lori. "She decided to leave Hollywood and come home, to this house that once belonged to my grandparents. She had dreams of going back to California and taking up where she left off, but she never did. I was born and that was the end of it."

"Oh, I see," said Ted. He raised the tea glass to his lips, but it seemed strangely heavy in his hand. "You know, it wasn't your fault," he assured her. "It was that Hall jerk who screwed it up for her."

Anger suddenly flared in Lori's eyes. "My father was never as bad as folks made out," she snapped. "He was just . . . misunderstood."

Ted was surprised. He couldn't understand the outburst, especially considering what the man had done to her mother. Ted couldn't figure out why he was beginning to feel so exhausted, either. He guessed the long drive was catching up to him.

Almost as quickly as her anger had surfaced, it was gone. She smiled, eyeing him in that odd, attentive way of hers. "You haven't told me about yourself, Ted," she said. "What do you do for a living?"

Ted's head began to swim. His eyelids felt heavier than lead, as if they could hardly stay open. "Uh, what did you say?" he asked.

"I asked what you do for a living," she repeated. Her smile was fixed, unwavering.

Ted had to think for a moment before he could answer. "Nothing yet," he said. His words seemed to flow as slowly as molasses. "I'm still in college." He looked over at Lori. Two of her wavered before his eyes. "What do you do?" he asked softly.

"I make movies," she said.

Before he knew it, Ted could no longer sit up. He slumped forward and rolled off the sofa, onto the parlor's hardwood floor. He looked up at Lori, expecting to see a look of alarm on her pretty face. But it wasn't there. Instead there was a peculiar look of satisfaction.

"I make movies," she repeated, as if making sure that he had heard. "Just like my mother." Her smile broadened a little, curling wickedly. "And my father."

Then her face turned into a blur and faded to black.

Ted was in the midst of a dream. One of the dreams that starred Fawn Hale.

He was on a big round bed that seemed to take up the entire room. He was naked, except for his glasses. Even then, his vision was a little hazy, like a camera fitted with a soft-focus filter.

The mattress sagged a little as someone joined him. It was Fawn Hale, also naked, her platinum hair gleaming in the harsh glare of a klieg light. She wore the sunglasses she had worn in *Curse of the Swamp Monster*, the ones with the white frames. The lenses were pitch black, impenetrable.

Without a word, she crept across the bed toward him with the predatory grace of a cat. He moaned when she reached him and her flesh touched his. A tiny grin crossed her lips as she moved over his midsection and mounted his hips. Ted stared up at those wondrous breasts. They stared back at him, transfixing him, like the eyes of a Svengali.

Fawn purred down deep in her throat, then lowered herself. Ted groaned. They joined effortlessly.

The platinum-haired beauty seemed to ride him forever, her head thrown back, her huge breasts bouncing in time to the rhythm. Ted found himself to be powerless. He simply lay there and let the actress have her way with him.

Eventually Fawn could contain herself no longer. Her thighs tightened around his waist and her pace began to quicken. Ted felt himself begin to climax, too. The mounting pleasure in his groin seemed to clear his head a little and the sluggish, weighty feeling began to lift.

That was when he saw the black object at the far end of the bed. It was a video camera on a tripod. Aimed straight at him and Fawn.

Ted remembered something Lori had told him. *I make movies.*

Suddenly he knew that he wasn't dreaming.

And there was something else. Something that he had failed to recall before. Trevor Hall. He knew who he was now. Hall had not been a bit player, but a stuntman. A hulking stuntman big enough to play a convincing monster. And he had played them, too: werewolves, robots, swamp monsters. But that was not all that Ted remembered about Hall.

The stuntman had been a serial killer. In the early seventies he had been convicted of brutally raping and murdering several dozen women over the span of two decades. The evidence had been what had bought him a seat in the electric chair: an entire library of sixteen-millimeter reels Hall had filmed himself. Snuff films of those he had violated and slaughtered.

Ted stared up at the woman on top of him. He

reached up slowly, his arms as heavy as concrete. He removed the white-framed shades. Lori's eyes sparkled down at him. They looked as crazy as the photos Ted had seen of her father. Gleaming with a fiendish satisfaction that was a mixture of ecstasy and bloodlust.

He reached out for the platinum wig, but it was beyond his grasp. Lori leaned in closer, smiling. Her shoulder flexed as she brought her right hand from behind her back.

"Scream for me," she whispered.

Ted felt the coldness of steel against his throat. He opened his mouth, perhaps to reason with her. But just staring into those lovely eyes and seeing the legacy of darkness that danced beyond them, Ted knew that any attempt would be futile.

As the edge of the knife stung his flesh, he braced himself and, regretfully, gave her what she wanted.

The images on the screen were color. Sharply defined, perfectly lit. The sound was minimal. The creaking of bed springs and the low murmurs of passion. There was no music. No sound track was necessary.

Lori Hale lay on the round bed, naked, her eyes glued to the television at the far side of the room. She watched as the image of a platinum-haired beauty straddled the hips of an overweight boy with brown hair and glasses.

She watched the scene unfold, slowly snaking her hand past the flat of her stomach to the cleft just beyond. Soon her fingers were at work, stroking.

The video—one of many—continued at a leisurely pace; finely orchestrated and leading toward a familiar finale. Lori watched as the woman reached beneath the edge of the circular mattress and withdrew a long-bladed butcher knife.

As the scene reached its climax, Lori found herself reaching her own. Her fingers worked furiously as she awaited the command she had given more times than she could remember.

Waves of ecstasy gripped Lori, washing through her, giving way to abandonment. Gritting her teeth, she clutched the bedcovers and felt the stiffness of dried blood in the fabric of the sheets.

Then she closed her eyes tightly and listened for the sound of the scream . . .

HIDEYHOLE

Billie Sue Mosiman

At the entrance into the restaurant area, a girl dressed in skinny black jeans and matching black tank top waited for Bastine Rendeaux to open the door. She smiled, lips full and new as red smoky moons. He smiled back. "Eating alone?" he asked, feeling especially horny and turned on by how her breasts rounded the material of her shirt and how her hips swelled the jeans. "Want company?"

"Sure." She fell into place at his side as he went for a back booth.

She didn't say much. For a Lot Lizard, she sure didn't fit the stereotype. She was much too pretty, for one thing. All the curves were in the right places, her clothes were of good quality, and she wasn't too heavily made-up. She didn't look like any Lot Lizards he'd met before. *This* girl didn't need to waste herself on truck drivers.

"What's your name?" he asked, lighting her cigarette, fantasizing about taking it slowly from her sensuous lips and taking a puff, one puff, then placing it back in her lips.

"Shaw."

"Oh. Nice name. How'd you get a handle like that or is it a professional secret?"

"You could call it a secret if you want to."

She was intriguing, the type who liked to play games with him. All the dark sweaty games.

"You free tonight, Shaw? Want to keep a lonely trucker company?"

"I wouldn't mind spending some time with you." She blew out a cloud of blue smoke that he leaned over and inhaled as if it were exotic perfume. He closed his eyes as he did this, and when he opened them again, she displayed a mysterious smile playing around her satiny lips. "You like it different, don't you?" she asked.

"Not so much," he said. Blood thudded in his temples so hard, his vision blurred. To think he hadn't wanted to take this load of chemicals to Tallulah, Louisiana, for his dispatcher. What if he'd missed this opportunity? It made him sickly faint to consider it.

God. He had to get her outside *now*. He had to have her *immediately*. He'd explode if he didn't. He said in a voice gruff with lust, "Come with me."

Shaw shrugged and let him move her along to the glass exit door. Outside in the neon night of the truck parking lot she crooned his name. "Bastine. Bastine. Don't hurry so. We have all night, Bastine."

This only served to make him hustle her faster across the macadam to his idling truck. Diesel fumes filled the air. Noise from the dozens of truck engines created a thumping roar that echoed in his head. "I have to hurry," he said, unlocking the driver's door. "I'm so nuts for you, I can't wait."

Her laugh tinkled around his head like silver dimes falling onto a metal counter. Bastine climbed down again and lifted Shaw onto the first step to the open cab. "C'mon, baby, I'm serious now. You can't keep a guy like me waiting. I might get dangerous."

By the time Bastine entered the cab with her, he saw she had pulled the tank top over her head, the sunglasses tumbling behind her. He caught his breath. She was fleecy white as a sheet washed until it is see-through-thin, even her nipples hardly discernible because they were soft pink and small. She wasn't scared, she wasn't the least bit anxious.

"How you want to do it?" she asked.

"Any old way is fine with me, girl. Just anything at all." He fumbled, unbuckling his belt and stripping off the faded Lee jeans into a heap that he had to fight off his feet. His organ tapped at his belly when he leaned way over to push the clothes into the front of the cab. He almost laughed, giddy with excitement.

"Whatever *you* want, sweetcakes. I've been waiting a long time for it, Bastine. I won't give you any trouble."

Bastine mulled over her confession and found it tasted of the truth. "Want to tell me what this is gonna cost me?"

"Nothing. Absolutely nothing."

But Bastine didn't believe that. He knew the lay of the land, and in that land nothing came free, not life or pretty women either. He'd settle with her later. If she squawked on her pay, that was her own damn fault for not getting the matter over with in the beginning.

All thought of money fled once he was completely nude and had climbed into the sleeper with her. It smelled like old socks and dirty sheets and nights of unfulfilled passion back there, but he didn't want to think about that. The one small reading light above and to the left of them inset into the cab gleamed down onto her marble flesh. She looked as bright to him as a sunny beach resort billboard caught in the glare of headlights.

He kneeled between her upraised knees. His hands clenched and unclenched. To mold and manipulate that perfect skin. That's what drove through his mind. To make her want him as much as he wanted her. To make her cry out and plead with him never to stop, never to release her.

"Go ahead," she whispered. "Don't hold back. Don't think about it. Make love to me, I want it, Bastine, I've saved myself for it, I really have."

He didn't know what she meant. She was not a "saved" kind of woman. Not a virgin by any means. Not inexperienced.

Suddenly he lowered himself and the warmth of her thighs embraced his hips like clamps and then fury came, possessing him, robbing him of all sense. She wept silently in climax, and then again, her tears rolling past tightly closed black lashes. She begged, but not for him to stop. She prayed for more, *More, Bastine,* until exhausted, he fell across her sweat-drenched body. She cursed and said, "You're not done, I'm not finished, I require this just once more, you can try. Once more."

"I'm sorry," he said, panting and trying to still his breath.

"Use your hand," she whispered into his ear. "You must do it. With. Your. Hand."

Bastine roused himself throughout the night to take her brutally and then fell dead each time into mindless sleep, something akin to unconsciousness. Each time he woke to her proddings and began again until morning came when they both collapsed into sleep as still as corpses in the dark coffin of the sleeper.

The next morning Bastine, more fatigued than ever before in his life, eyes gritty as ground glass, body weak and bruised-feeling, wanted only to be rid of Shaw. She might protest. She had been special, they both knew that, but this was the part he truly loved the most, his leaving. He planned to unhitch his load and drive into Tallulah for a movie.

"Shaw, baby, what do I owe you?" He was dressed and had his wallet out. Shaw still lay in the bunk, naked, glowing, sleepy-eyed.

"I told you. Nothing. My treat."

Man, she must have *really* liked it. "Fine. Then how 'bout I buy you breakfast before you go."

"Hmmmmm." She stretched and sat up, her breasts bobbing like frosted apples. There were blue marks that tracked her arms where he'd held her down. He was sorry about that. "Where am I going?"

Bastine turned slowly in the truck seat. "Well . . . uh . . . wherever you go to, I guess. Home. On down the road. Wherever."

"I'm not going anywhere." She gave him the smile, the one that had so fascinated him when they first met.

"But you have to."

"Why?"

"Well, I sure as hell can't take you with me. I drive all the time. I don't even have a house! I live in this truck. I can't take you with me." She had him repeating himself. It wasn't like she was stupid. What was wrong with her thinking he'd want her along *permanently?* That wasn't in the game plan. He hated explaining these things to women. She didn't seem bothered that he wanted her gone because she wasn't going. This wasn't how it was played.

"I'm yours now, Bastine. I belong to you. The thing is, it's always been meant for us to be together."

"Hey, wait a minute, wait one goddamn minute. What kind of horseshit is this? I don't own nobody. I don't want to own nobody. You don't belong to me, okay? I'm perfectly willing to give you a couple hundred to help you out, but no way do you go with me. I don't have meaningful relationships and all that silly yuppie shit. This was just a one-night stand, you understand? Shaw?"

She was dressing, pretending to ignore him.

"Shaw? Did you hear what I said? *You can't go.*"

"I can't go, you can't go," she said conversationally. She pulled on black suede slippers and crawled into the passenger seat. She looked at him and there wasn't a trace of humor on her face now. "I'm yours, Bastine. I'm yours forever."

Bastine mumbled, "I can't talk to the bitch," and flung open the cab door. He jumped down to the pavement and stalked to the café for breakfast. He'd deal with her later when he had a full stomach and four aspirin for the headache she'd caused to bloom over his temples. Crazy woman. Forever? Nothing was forever, and if she was old enough, she'd know that. His sexual unions—for that is what they were—never turned out this way. They cried sometimes and they begged, but they never acted so cool and in control this way.

When he came back after eating and brushing his teeth in the men's room, he found Shaw sitting right where he'd left her in the passenger seat of his truck. He took a deep breath and got into the driver's seat.

"This ain't gonna work," he warned. "I don't want you along, you got that? I didn't sign up for a lifetime of crap from some woman. I didn't put a ring on your finger and waltz you to the church. Now, you're gonna have to get out of my truck or I'll call the cops. You know how long they stuff you in jail for prostitution in a truck stop? You got any fucking idea how much trouble you're gonna be in?"

"You do that and I'll have to hurt you, Bastine."

He laughed and it wasn't even funny. He lowered his voice. "You don't want to threaten me, kid. I'm a mean son of a bitch when I want to be. You oughta know that already. Look at your arms! Look what I already done to you."

Shaw lifted a small handgun from her lap and pointed it at him. "I go with you or you don't go."

"Jesus H. Harrowing Christ. What do you think you're gonna do with that peashooter? Don't make me laugh." Though he talked tough, Bastine felt his insides quaking and his breakfast wanted up and out. If she shot him, he might live through the gunshot wound, but he'd die on the spot of a heart attack. Guns scared hell out of him. He had a brief crazy urge to leap through the truck window.

Shaw leaned over the console and pressed the barrel end of the gun against his thigh. "Bastine? You believe me, don't you? I don't want to hurt you, but I will, I swear I will."

Bastine sucked air over his teeth and let it out slowly. "Okay, okay. I'm laid up here the weekend. I dump this load Monday in Tallulah. We'll talk this over until then."

"Good," she said, removing the pistol and slipping it into a small black purse. "Now, how would you like to go inside the truck stop with me so I can eat *my* breakfast."

Bastine nodded. The whole bizarre incident was clicking fast into place in his mind. The girl who called herself Shaw was a psychopath, unlike himself, who he considered, in contemplative moods, as nothing more than a little warped out of the normal pattern. Shaw was the real thing. She was the walking, talking embodiment of Loony Tunes.

She slept most of the day while he read a Louis L'Amour western. They ate a spare dinner, he picking at his food, she nibbling at a chicken salad sandwich.

"Why are you so quiet, Bastine? Don't you like me anymore? I don't want this silence between us."

"Tell me, Shaw, what this is all about, can you? I mean, I'm not a prize or anything. I make lousy money. I live on the road. Why me?"

Shaw leaned her head to the side to study him. "I'll tell you later. As a surprise. It'll be lovely."

"Is it the sex? I mean, hell, lots of guys will give it to you rough, if that's it. You'd be surprised how many guys will do what you want. You're a *damn* pretty girl." Maybe a little flattery would get him off the hook.

She simply smiled her mysterious smile and returned to her sandwich.

Bastine hung his head, thoughts black, the anger coming from nowhere to press against the tight, hot band of his skull. "Let's go to bed," he said, standing with the meal ticket, taking out his wallet to pay the bill.

Shaw slipped on the sunglasses. She took his arm and he let her, though he felt like breaking her fingers one at a time.

Hours later, orgasms later, Bastine hovered above Shaw's sweat-slathered body. "You know I don't want you," he said. "You know you can't stay with me."

She moaned and pulled him down onto her breasts, holding him tightly in her arms. She moved her hips until his limp organ swirled inside her, then began to harden. Again.

"Oh, Bastine, you're like a wild beast. I always knew you were. I saw it in you even when you were young . . ."

Her words turned Bastine to granite. He felt a shock travel down through his arms into his frozen hands. "What are you talking about? Who are you? What's your name?" With each question his voice rose until he was shouting. "*Who are you?*"

Shaw rolled from beneath him and drew the crumpled sheet between her breasts. She gnawed on the tip of the sheet, her eyes like coals in the dark. "I should tell you the secret now, yes, Bastine, it's time."

"What the hell is this all about? Where did you come from?"

"I'm from here, from the same parish as you. I grew up not far from your house. Remember the old Clancine place? I was Sandy then, Sandy Clancine. I went to school with you. But I was younger . . . oh, I was so young and I was always trying to catch up with you, Bastine."

He sank back on the mattress, pressed his hands together in his lap. She was someone from his past. He hazily remembered the Clancine family. They lived as poorly as he, half a dozen kids running around barefoot in rags. He hated Louisiana. He should have known nothing good could come from it.

She continued in a dreamy, detached voice. "I used to sneak out to your place and watch your daddy. He hurt you bad, I saw him. And your mama, she was almost as terrible. That time . . . that time she helped your daddy with the rope in the backyard . . . I saw that, Bastine. I prayed for you, that they'd let you down before you strangled. I would have attacked them if they hadn't let go of the rope. But I was so little. When I was ten you were already in your teens. But I knew all the secrets of everyone in the parish. I spent all my time hiding out so I could learn everything I could. Especially about you."

"What else did you see?" Bastine covered his face with his hands to keep the memories from flooding his head. Already the sleeper smelled of the outhouse to him, the air scented with a miasma of dirty, rotten things.

She rolled onto her back and reached out to touch his arm. "I saw you take out your hate on the animals, the wild things. How you went hunting, but you maimed things, then slowly killed them. I saw you turn on your brothers and devise new tortures for them. I saw you with . . . girls. When you started dating, I would follow you out on the dirt paths into the forests, and I saw how you talked them into things, how sometimes it got out of hand, and you had them scared of you. I saw how you mastered them, how you controlled them.

"I wanted to be those girls, Bastine. I wanted to be your one girl. I had to wait until I was old enough to attract you, but you left. That day you packed your things and fled the parish, I cried for a week. My folks couldn't do anything with me. I stopped going to school. I started thinking about you day and night. I knew we belonged together."

"So our meeting wasn't accidental?"

She shook her head. "I've been coming to this truck

stop every night or so for a long, long time, Bastine. I knew what company you worked for. I've been waiting. All this time."

Understanding made Bastine raise his face from his hands. "You brought the gun because you knew I'd try to make you leave."

"Yes. I didn't want to, but I couldn't take a chance of losing you again. You understand, don't you, Bastine? You forgive me, don't you? You may punish me if you want. I know I haven't any rights . . ."

"I don't know about this, Shaw. I . . . no one's ever . . . all that stuff that happened when I was a kid . . ."

"Shh." She reached up and touched his lips with her own. "Take me with you, Bastine. Don't make me go away. I'll die if you do. Please. I've waited so long, all my life."

Bastine wanted to punish her for insinuating herself into his life, and at the same time he wanted to hold on to her to keep her from leaving again. He'd never had anything of his own except the truck. "Let me think," he said. "I can't promise."

She brought his left palm to her face and pressed it against her lips. "You can't live without me any more than I can live without you. We belong together."

He cradled her in his arms and tried to imagine the future. There would be a thousand secrets they could share, a thousand nights they could make electrifying.

On Sunday he and Shaw spent most of their time together reminiscing. The lengths she had gone to in order to shadow him as he grew up in the parish were beyond anything he thought possible. That's when she'd changed her name, she told him, using "Shaw," the shortened form of the word "shadow."

Near sunset Shaw leaned forward and peered out the windshield. "See that girl?"

Bastine stared. It was a Lot Lizard crossing the back lot. She was scanning the cabs, waiting for a signal of headlights to indicate the offer of a job. "Sure, I see her. Disease carrier."

"Oh, you're a cruel man. They're not all so bad. I even did it now and then to keep body and soul together while I waited for you to come through. I know these girls. And I have an idea for tonight if you're willing."

"Yeah? Like what?" Just the thought of a new sexual game made the blood rise to his head.

"Let's take her to your old place."

"What?"

"Let's offer her some money and drive her out to the swamp. We can have some fun and we can kill some ghosts at the same time. You *do* feel the ghosts out there, don't you? We shouldn't leave here and take them with us. It'll spoil our future together."

Bastine shivered where he sat. "I don't wanna talk about that. I don't think about . . . them . . . if I can help it."

"But you could go back if I was with you, couldn't you? It would be fun, Bastine. We'll play with the girl. Chase her. There's so many places there she can get lost and so many places I know where to hide. It would be terrifying!"

Bastine considered the proposition. Ever since he'd walked into the truck stop his entire life had taken a decided tilt. He felt he was moving on a conveyor belt on a slight angle up to the top floor of a malevolent fun house. What Shaw proposed scared him, but at the same time it thrilled him to imagine the things they

29

could do. And he *did* need to slay, for all time, the lingering, tormenting visages of his mother and his father.

"She looks sweet and vulnerable," Shaw said. "We'd better hurry."

Yes, he thought. Yes, yes, oh Christ, things were different now. He could have Shaw and the girl too, he could make them his slaves for the night, send them with torches to light the forest like nymphs dispatched by a god. They could be his audience while he spent his rage on the land that stole half his life.

"Yes," he said, climbing from the cab. "I'll get her. Wait here."

"I'll pay extra because it'll be a threesome," Bastine told the girl, holding her around the waist as he walked her to his truck. She was slim with small breasts, short bleached hair, a dimple in her chin. She made him think of a cured ham, plain, bony, but sturdy, enough meat for a meal.

"I don't mind anything if there's enough money," she said. Her voice was high and piping, the trill of a monkey. An annoying sound that Bastine immediately decided to tune out as soon as he had the preliminaries completed. Let Shaw talk to her.

"And you don't mind we drive out to my old home place, huh? It's not far. We'll have room there. Can't move around much, not three of us, in my goddamn sleeper."

She laughed easily enough. "Naw, I don't mind. We don't wanna crowd each other, hon."

Shaw had moved into the sleeper and let the girl take the passenger seat. Bastine unhitched his load and slid the rig from beneath it. He bobtailed it out of the truck stop while the girl, who called herself Dory, babbled in her tinny voice to Shaw. He wished he could erase her dimple. And he had to silence that noise coming out of her mouth.

He had not forgotten the dirt and mud back roads that led to the old house. He'd dreamed of it often enough since he'd left.

When he pulled into the bare ground of the front yard, mud clung to the rig's wheels and coated the mud flaps. The headlights outlined the leaning porch, the grimy windows where curtains had never hung.

"Bitch of a place," Dory said. "Creepy."

"Let's go check it out." Shaw pressed the girl through the door and crawled out behind her.

Bastine picked up his flashlight and turned off the motor. He couldn't stop shaking. They were plunged into darkness unrelieved by starlight. Bare trees hung with Spanish moss circled the yard like hairy skeletons, and above their heads the sky was black as the oil in his truck's crankcase.

He heard Shaw calling him and swung the light toward her. "I'm not sure this was such a great idea," he said. A burning tenseness bunched the muscles of his neck as if to ward off a blow from behind. He fiercely controlled the idiotic urge to turn and check for an assailant. He made sure Dory stood next to Shaw. He must keep them in sight at all times. That's what he had to do when he was at home. Keep them in sight. Never let them get the advantage. They were always sneaking up and surprising him, grabbing his collar and hauling him off his feet, the willow switch swinging in that blurred arc to sprinkle his back and legs with furious sparks of pain.

"It's going to be all right," Shaw said. She gestured toward him, pulling him forward with invisible strings. "It's going to be fun, Bastine. Remember? We can kill the fear. We can murder it here where it was born."

"What's that mean?" Dory's high-pitched voice rose another register. "What's wrong with him anyway? Why's he acting so funny?"

"You just do as you're told." Shaw's harsh retort shut the girl up. "This is our night and you do what we want you to do, you got that?"

"Sure. Whatever you say."

Bastine lifted the light beam to the porch steps. He watched the two girls climb them, testing each riser before treading on the next. The creaks were loud and grating.

Creaks. His father approaching. When he was hiding in the cubbyhole beneath the kitchen sink. He could hear him, feel his imminent presence through the bare floorboards. There was always something he had done or hadn't done, something he'd forgotten or something he'd ruined, for which he was to be punished. Holding his breath didn't work. Begging for mercy made it last longer. Nothing saved him, ever.

"Come, Bastine. Come with us inside."

He settled the light beam on Shaw's face and did not recognize her for several seconds. She was fiercely ugly. Her face was all stark planes and protruding knobs.

"Come, Bastine. Don't be afraid."

Oh, that's what they always said, the motherfuckers, the cocksucking bastards. Don't be afraid, we won't hurt you, we just want to talk to you, Daddy's not going to use his belt, Mama's not mad at you, you didn't do anything wrong, Bastine. They lied!

"Liar," he whispered.

"No, Bastine. Don't get upset. Come inside first. We

have Dory with us, remember? Dory, go get him. Take his hand."

"I'm not sure . . . uh . . ."

"Do it!"

The girl skipped down the steps and grabbed for Bastine's free hand. She turned to pull him up the steps. He resisted. She tugged, grunting.

Bastine finally relented and let himself be led up the steps that creaked, across the porch boards that threw him off balance, and to the door where Shaw ran a soothing hand down his chest to cup his crotch. "Soon, Bastine. Inside. Push the door open for us."

Bastine turned his shoulder in to it and the door gave with a sharp crack, then stuck. He had to push again, wood scraping wood as they walked single file into the big dusty room.

Though it was empty except for beer bottles and trash left over from squatters, Bastine watched for someone to slither from the darkness. Every time he swung the light, the dark followed and swallowed the area again. They could be there. Dead or not, they could certainly still be waiting and watching just as always. He hadn't any evidence that they couldn't. Or they could be through the doorway, hiding in the kitchen. Or in the pantry there. Or in the hall closet. Or in one of the two bedrooms. They could even be in the room with the tub, hiding in it. They *had* to be somewhere because he felt them.

"You're shaking, sugar," Dory said, taking his hand again. "Maybe we should go back to the truck. There's a mattress there and there ain't nothing here. This is one spooky trip."

"Shut up," Shaw said. "We want to do it here. In this house. You'll just have to accept that."

"It's pretty dirty. There might be snakes . . ."

Bastine couldn't take the banging pain of her voice any longer. He reached out reflexively with the flashlight and smashed her in the mouth. Oh God, he hadn't meant . . . he really didn't mean . . . She screamed and that anchored him to the present long enough to know what he had done.

"Easy, baby," Shaw said. "Go slow now. We want a long night, don't we?"

Dory was on her knees, hands to face, blood dripping onto the floor. She was moaning and swaying. Bastine leaned down and laid his hand on her hair like a benediction. "I didn't mean it."

He told his mama and daddy that so often, it was a litany he repeated silently in his mind sometimes for days on end. *I didn't mean it. I didn't mean it. I won't do it again. I didn't mean it.*

Dory spluttered through her torn mouth, "You hith me, you prickth. You hurth me bad!" She was crying now, loudly, and spitting rusty sputum on the floor.

"Shut up," Shaw said. "Come on, Bastine, let's look through the rest of the rooms while Dory takes care of herself. Stay put," she said to the girl.

Bastine followed docilely behind, the light moving just ahead of Shaw's feet, now and then coming up to outline a doorway, a cabinet with a hanging door, a sink with rust stains, a bedspring sitting alone in the center of a bedroom. Dust filled his nostrils and made his throat feel raw. He kept jumping at the screech of rats that clawed and raced across the floor. Far off, he heard bits and pieces of what Shaw said to him during the tour.

". . . saw you through that window at night . . . there's the door to the back . . . the stove's still here . . . the flue in the fireplace is probably full of bird nests . . . got to kill off the past . . . get rid of it for good . . . if you murder her, then maybe . . . I thought you needed that gift . . . that release . . ."

Was she . . . could she be talking about murder? Crossing the line. Killing the Lot Lizard. She couldn't possibly mean it.

"I can't do it," Bastine murmured. "I don't want to do that." They stood close together at the window of the bedroom. The flashlight glinted from the black pane, a spear of yellow radiance.

"But you must."

"No," he said. "I can't go that far."

Shaw moved closer to him. "Then I'll do it," she said. "For you. I want to. I've always dreamed of taking revenge on your behalf, Bastine."

"Should we?" he asked. "Can we? But I can't, I said that. It wouldn't be right." He followed her to the open living room. He moved the light around looking for Dory. She was gone.

"She's hiding," he said. "She's scared too."

"Like you were. Like I was for you."

"We ought to let her go. We have to leave here. Now."

"I can find her. I know all the secret hiding places."

Bastine knew them too, but they never saved him. Nothing ever, by God, saved him. He was as shriveled inside as he had been as a kid in this house. Why had he thought he'd be excited and could enjoy some nutty sexual escapade of this magnitude? It was a terrible mistake, maybe the worst one he'd ever made. Shaw was stimulating that dead part of him and making it walk. But she could not make it kill; she could not make it free, either.

While standing, considering his options, he had not

noticed Shaw's disappearance. He moved through the house, trembling uncontrollably, calling for her. "Shaw? Please come out. Don't leave me here alone like this."

He searched for them. The cubbyhole under the sink was empty. The closets smelled of mildew and old coats soaked with body odor. He left the house, skirted the porch, looked in the mud holes beneath it. It looked as if dogs had wallowed there.

"Shaw? Dory? Let's go now. I don't want to stay any longer. I hate it here!"

He heard the rasp of crickets and throaty bullfrogs that leaped and slapped standing water. He heard a breeze ruffle through the silver moss. "Oh shit," he mumbled. "Y'all come on back here."

He circled the house and headed down the worn path to the outhouse. The door was missing. He glanced inside, but couldn't bring himself to go near the hole in the boards or to gaze into the old pit there. He pushed aside brambles and searched behind the outhouse. He was coming around again to the back porch to check an old refrigerator lying on its back when he heard a gunshot shatter the still night. He halted. Let a whimper escape his lips. He'd forgotten about Shaw's gun. He expected to see her any moment come dragging the body of Dory from the woods. He waited, holding his breath. Dew soaked into his shirt and chilled him. He tried calling again, but couldn't speak above a whisper. A fearful idea took possession of his fevered brain. What if it wasn't Shaw? What if Dory possessed the gun?

What if Dory now stalked *him* and he was to be her next victim? He was the one who hit her, wasn't he? She might think he sent Shaw after her.

He must hide. He had done something dreadfully wrong this time. He was involved in a death dance.

He dropped the flashlight in his terror and scrambled up the back steps. The middle step gave way and sent him sprawling onto his knees. His pants tore, his knee bled. He went up the next step on hands and knees, splinters lodging painfully, pulled himself up with the help of the rail, and lunged toward the back door. The hinges gave and the door fell inward as he turned the doorknob. The crash made him scream, his legs wobble. He stumbled over the door and looked wildly around, the darkness impenetrable. Where? Had to find a hideyhole. Where?

He got down on the floor and tried to squeeze into the space under the sink, his favorite childhood cubbyhole, and found he was too large to fit. He had to hold back hysterical laughter welling up at the sight he must make with his ass sticking high in the air and his head lodged next to the drainpipe. He wasn't little anymore. He couldn't fit, he had so few places left for hiding.

He backed out, could now see gray shapes in the black. The doorway. He could find a closet. Or lie down in the old claw-foot tub. He'd seen it was a place where someone had defecated, but that didn't matter. He'd lie in shit if he must. Would the girl look in there? No, no, no, she'd never find him there.

He came to his feet and felt his way through the door to the living room, kicked trash out of his way, gaze skittering to the windows, and the front door that stood open to the night. He felt along the wall, the wallpaper peeling, the grit of old dried glue beneath his fingertips. He found the hallway and crept toward the bathroom.

His father hauled the tub from a junkyard and they filled it with water heated on the stove when they bathed, then he had the job of carrying out the dirty water bucketful by bucketful. His father made the bath by sealing off one end of the hall and installing a door. It was a stupid thing to do, but now it might afford Bastine sanctuary. It *must*.

He turned his back, slid into the tub, lowered himself the way he might have had it been full of warm water. He felt the hard crusts of someone's feces under his hips and grimaced. He slid farther down, knees up and to the side, hands crossed on his chest. The cold porcelain cooled his skin through his clothes and then seeped into his muscles. He bit down on his tongue until he drew blood to keep from whispering that he didn't mean it, he didn't mean it, wasn't anyone, goddamnit, listening to him?

He stared across the rolled white rim of the tub at the door. He willed it to stay closed.

He heard the creaking boards of the front steps first. His heart trip-hammered him half to death. He shut his eyes so tight, tears were squeezed from the edges. His fingers clutched at one another, nails tearing at the skin of his knuckles.

If he were on the road, the cities flying past, the miles rolling behind him, he'd be safe. If he hadn't been dispatched to Tallulah where Shaw waited for him, he would never be here after all these years. *If he weren't so goddamned fucked-up, he'd never have left the truck stop.*

Oh God, oh God, let it be Shaw, he prayed. Let her find me and take me away from here, please God. She is by far the cruelest of the two of us. Punish *her*.

The doorknob slowly rotated. Bastine's eyes

stretched wide open. His breath caught in his throat where he swallowed it.

I didn't mean it.

The door opened without a sound, swinging back by increments.

Don't hurt me. I don't like being hurt. Daddy, please . . .

He could see her now in the doorway, but who was she? Mama? Shaw? Dory? He tried to find his voice, failed.

Her dark shape came toward him, arms hanging at her sides.

I'm hiding, she can't see me, no one can see me.

His legs twitched, his fingers tightened, his teeth closed harder on his tongue until they touched and blood filled his mouth. He must breathe. He must cry out for mercy as he had always been forced to do.

The right arm of the shape came up and he saw something in it. The barrel of the gun pointed at his chest. His vision narrowed into a tunnel that drew him into the cylinder. It was death he faced, that one true monster he had always feared and managed to outrun. He gagged on his own blood, jerked forward, hands coming up to stop the inevitable.

"Shaw!"

The gun blast lit the room and Bastine fell back against the tub as if a sledgehammer had been swung by a giant arm, slamming him in the chest.

"I'm no fuckith thaw." Dory wiped the back of her hand across her split lips and broken teeth.

Bastine tried to rise again, to push away from the cold porcelain of the tub, but his arms would not obey him, and now he felt it. The zone of pain began in his right side and spread out a carpet of fire forward to encompass all the ribs on that side and to the back. It felt like someone with a burning razor ran through his lungs, hacking, hacking.

"What have you done?" he murmured. "Why have you done this?"

"You busth my teef! You and your girfren tried to kill me!"

But no, he wanted to say and couldn't, thought he said and didn't. But no, it wasn't me, it was Shaw, it was her, and she's crazy as hell, don't you see, couldn't you tell, couldn't you just help me now because I'm dying here, I'm dying now, this is no game, girl, that gun's no toy, this was the worst idea, the all-time worst thing ever happened that shouldn't have, but if you'll take my hand, I'll . . .

His thoughts ran down like a weak truck battery without enough juice to start the engine, and he knew finally that she hadn't heard his pleas. She was gone, the doorway empty, the door swinging lazily on its hinges, quietly now shutting by itself, sealing him in the little old room in the little old house that had never once afforded a proper sanctuary for victims who meant to hide away.

HIGH CONCEPT

J. N. Williamson

She wasn't necessarily the tallest woman in the world, Andy Chalminski told himself, gaping at the lady in question with scarcely concealed fascination, but it would definitely take someone special to top her—

Which was exactly what Andy meant to be and intended to do: the first man to climb the human alp named Donna Callaghan and plant his flagpole at the top of the mountain. Or more specifically, wherever his personal survey indicated Ms. Callaghan would prefer the flagstaff to be planted.

For an ambitious guy to get ahead, Chalminski thought as he studied the enormous woman at her solitary table across the restaurant, *sometimes he has to get a little behind.* The crude observation was not original to him but a rule of thumb in the dog-eat-dog business in which the slum-born Andy had struggled for the dozen years of his manhood. Hell, there was absolutely nothing personal about his plan for bedding the current object of his attention.

Truth was, the midwestern giantess quietly eating soup and minding her own business had no more appeal to Chalminski than the zucchini his waitress brought along with his small steak. Her face was probably not as homely as the dictionary definition of zucchini ("a squash shaped like a cucumber")—he couldn't see much of it with that straight brown hair drooping over her ears and temples—but Andy had seen a picture of her in the newspaper before flying to Columbus, and her glasses were as thick and heavy as World War I flyers' goggles.

That photo had lured him to Ohio, or, more exactly, a caption beneath it reading: 6' 10" WOMAN REFUSES DATE WITH NBA STAR. Eddie Burgess, who'd appeared in a few of Chalminski's ultra-low-budget porn flicks before losing his ability to get it up on cue and retiring to the Midwest, had spotted the picture and sent the clipping to Andy. The local story with it—very short because Donna Callaghan was said to be excruciatingly shy—made it clear that six ten was just an estimate of her height, and she might clear seven feet. "I feel awkward enough around people without letting anyone measure me," Donna was quoted as admitting. "Besides, I don't much care for tall men." All that in response to the local press's smart PR move of trying to arrange a date between her and one of the Cleveland Cavaliers.

The second thought crossing Andy Chalminski's mind had been *I'm only five six when I really stand up straight!*

And his first reaction had been the instant awareness that a thirty-two-year-old virgin who had to stoop to enter a room—assuming she didn't look too damn awful with her clothes off—was possibly the only person alive who might save his sagging career as a movie producer!

It had started going bad when schmucks with their own cameras began making "home video" porn and marketing them with the notion that these were "real people in action," maybe the neighbors down the block. So a lot of potential customers of Andy's had decided to watch ol' Bob and Suzy get it on. Well, fuck, did they think actors in a professional flick were androids?

Worse, it had gotten harder and harder to create gimmicks that made some jack-off at an adult vid store grab a box and run to the register to take it home. Every combination of gender, position, and racial mix was *already* on film! Even Eddie Burgess had said, before Andy hung up and came to Columbus, "Unless you can talk some aliens from another planet into screwing our girls on camera, Andrew, skin-flick folks are going to be the blacksmiths of the twenty-first century."

Since Andy privately thought Eddie Burgess was right, he had immediately seen the latent potential in a seven-foot-tall babe—he'd definitely claim she was that tall, right on the box—and instantly other exciting promotions swarmed through Chalminski's mind. Just glancing at Eddie sitting next to him now—the actor'd come to McGarrett's Restaurant to introduce him to Donna—was a reminder of how Burgess was hung. There'd been females who were turned off by the sight of him naked, and not every actress had been able to accommodate "actors" like the guy.

But with a *seven-foot dame*—the hell with anatomy experts who'd say Donna's size made no difference; studs with dongs like Eddie could be billed as "Finally

Meeting Their Match!" Shit-fire, flicks with her in them would go like hotcakes to broads as well as guys!

Now, persuading titanic Ms. Callaghan to earn a mint of money seemed to pragmatic Andy Chalminski the most down-to-earth and easy proposition.

"Not so, Andrew," Eddie said softly. He had nodded in the giantess's direction and hadn't looked at her again. "I've come to know her and she is shy as hell. Probably a virgin, as I said, and definitely a lady."

"I never met a woman who hated the idea of big bucks," Andy argued, and forked steak into his mouth. "All I need t'do is make my pitch and be first to break her in." Suspicious, he glowered at the still handsome Burgess. "How the fuck did you meet Madam Amazon, anyways?"

"It happens Donna and I belong to a local amateur writers' club."

"You?" Andy nearly choked on his steak. "You and the female Lurch are budding Shakespeares?" He tried to regain his control. "Sorry, babe, I just can't picture you romancin' the muse. Fucking the bitch, absolutely, but not in your mind!"

"Listen." Eddie clamped a hand on Chalminski's forearm. He had the first serious expression Andy'd seen since Burgess began his career twelve, thirteen years ago and wondered if he could have sex with a stranger and a film crew watching. "I like Donna, but I haven't touched her."

"Bull hockey."

"Andrew, she's written the story of a girl as tall as her dad by the age of ten; she was through puberty before she was eleven. Other kids saw her as a freak, so she couldn't relate to anyone. She's all alone in the world."

Andy squinted his surprise. "She's doin' an autobio? I don't see how that—"

"A retired actor moves to town," Eddie went on relentlessly, "and listens to what the tall girl reads to the class." His fingers on Andy's arm tightened. "He tells her," Burgess whispered, "he knows a film producer who's interested in finding hot properties, and he himself might introduce her to the noted Andrew Chalminski."

Andy whistled low. "Whew, that's smart! But, Ed, I don't wanta buy no fuckin' disease-of-the-week story. I wanta buy the use of her body! So how am I gonna—"

"I said," Eddie went on, his grip bringing pain, "if the famous movie guy *wants* to film her story, he will have a tough time finding an actress *tall enough* for the leading role!"

"Brilliant!" Chalminski exulted. Could Eddie-the-Meat-Man actually have a brain? "It's a great setup. But what do *you* expect t'get out of this, old buddy?"

Eddie's forever-photogenic eyes opened widely. "After explaining that producers are quaint fellows who enjoy testing would-be actresses who double as screenwriters, I mentioned the possibility that I, her new confidant, might be willing to serve as her . . . *costar.*" He smiled. "Being timid, she liked that idea very much."

"You want a *comeback?*" Chalminski demanded incredulously.

"She's waiting for *us,* Andrew," Eddie said quietly, "so I hope you'll listen to me very closely: I didn't become an addict or spend all my money, and I didn't get any nasty diseases that will kill me. I just got out of the sleaze biz before it devoured me. I find I like a normal life, writing, and Donna—even if she is as tall as the Chrysler Building." He sat straight across from Andy. "I want you to think seriously about *decently* producing her life story. You might begin a chapter in your life you'd really enjoy. Even people like you, and I, can go straight."

Andy was badly shocked by what had happened to Burgess. But he considered the request, lips pursed, and nodded. "I'll think it over. But as for usin' you as a real actor, with his *pants* on——"

"Let me finish," Eddie interrupted. "If and when you choose to pass on doing the right thing, Andrew—if you score with the lady and get her to sign a contract—*that's* when I intend to collect. *That's* when I want my comeback to take place."

"With her," Chalminski said slowly, getting it. "You—*want* this broad!"

"Just this one time, in one film," Burgess said with a nod, "that I can watch over and over when I otherwise can't get Herman up even for my own pleasure. Besides," he added a bit smugly, "I think we could make a classic with a good girl like Donna."

Andy stared at him as he stood. Then, chuckling, he followed Eddie to Donna Callaghan's table. "You got a deal," he said under his breath, clapping the taller man's back. "You actors!"

Donna raised her head, and till then, Chalminski had forgotten how different she would seem to him. But at first she didn't appear extraordinary except for how she blinked repeatedly. The nearsighted eyes behind massive glasses were an oddly innocent light blue, and Andy remembered how much Monroe's eyelashes batted due to vision problems. Donna's brown hair was as straight as he'd expected, but the girls he used frequently wore wigs, and contacts would take care of the blink. On the other hand, broads who looked innocent and blinked at the actors' erect members might have considerable appeal to some viewers.

Yet Donna Callaghan, looking up, had not looked *far*—seated alone at her table, she was nearly as tall as Andy Chalminski was, standing!

"Hi, nice to meet ya," he said when Eddie'd introduced them. Speaking triggered his autonomic, charming smile and he sat down even as he shook her hand. Wishing he had worn a less showy sport jacket, he reminded himself Donna believed she was a writer. "Eddie says he's pretty impressed with your book."

She smiled, slouched back to minimize her height. "You two must be very good friends for you to call him 'Eddie' instead of 'Edward.'"

"Yeah, well, we go back." He'd liked the feel of her hand even if her thumb had reached around his paw to her other fingers. They wouldn't exactly feel bad on a guy's cock. She had a generous mouth (a matter of some importance in Chalminski's line), and one chipped tooth could be capped. "You're kind of young to have done an autobio."

Donna answered carefully. "It's not so much autobiography as, well, the story of any woman who learns she's going to be different. From other girls."

Andy wished she'd sit up so he could get a clue about her build. The top of her huge sweat suit was so big, he couldn't make out her tits at all. "I mentioned your youth just because I'd want ya to do a lot of TV. Interviews with Oprah and Geraldo; a ton of publicity." That was a surefire come-on, and Andy was rewarded by a flush of color in her cheeks. "I need a way, to . . . well, gauge whether we should shoot for feature flicks or the tube."

"I must get back to work on my current story," Eddie interjected before Donna could speak. He gave Chalminski a familiar, man-to-man studied stare they'd used before, one that meant he had done his part and now he was clearing out. "I live right around the corner, so here." He produced two car keys on a ring, dropped them in the producer's palm. "You'll want to read some of Donna's writing, so bring my car back when you two are through talking and you can stay the night with me. I'll drive you to the airport in the morning."

"You'll want to see my work," Donna asked Andy, "tonight?"

"A movie guy's work is never done," Andy said, and shook Burgess's hand. "Thanks for the wheels, 'Edward.'"

"Sure thing." Eddie paused, smiled down at Ms. Callaghan. "I left a bottle of bubbly on the front seat in case the two of you close anything. It's for you."

"Oh, Edward, you are so *sweet!*" Donna said, and half stood to give the former porn star an impulsive hug.

Chalminski couldn't believe his eyes. Not even stretched out to her full height, this broad he'd come to Columbus to see was at least several inches taller than Burgess, and he was surely a good five eleven. More than that, Donna's head was larger than his, and she was able to reach the guy and begin the hug from a solid yard away! The arms in the blue sweatshirt were like the branches of a tree covered by some kind of fungus!

Andy bobbed up after Eddie was headed for the door and before the huge young woman could sit down again. The ex-actor had arranged things perfectly—maybe he could get it up for one more movie after resting up more than a year. But probably he'd get the broad who'd do Donna since the studs who screwed her would have t'be in fucking *shape!* Now there was no reason to waste any more time in the crappy restaurant, and Chalminski wanted Miss Amazon to see he was short, no conspicuous threat—and he wanted out of there! Everyone in the joint was staring at her and how she dwarfed him.

"If ol' Eddie is as sharp a judge of talent as usual," he told Donna, "I'm really anxious to see what you got. *Have,*" he corrected his grammar, taking her arm.

Absolutely nothing happened as he tried to propel her toward the door; she didn't budge an inch. "Well, if you're *truly* interested in my work—I mean, I haven't been published anywhere." She took a wary step, so long a one, Chalminski had to skip to catch up.

"Look," he said, speaking straight ahead instead of craning his neck to see her face, "I flew in from Jersey to check you out, so it's now or never." They were already at the door, he couldn't recall when he'd walked so fast, and the sweat running into his collar told him he needed to exert his masculine sense of authority or he wouldn't be able to do anything with Lady Kong if he *did* get her in the sack. "Who knows, maybe what you've written so far is such terrific raw material, we can get 'Edward' to do the screenplay."

He let her think about that while he tried to remember where Eddie'd parked the car. Finding it, he was glad it wasn't a compact job. Holding the door for her and watching her squeeze inside was like seeing the shadow of a skyscraper folding itself into the front seat of the full-sized Buick.

Donna realized she had to provide him with her address and, because he was an out-of-towner, directions for getting there. She told him as if passing along state secrets.

"Why would an important man like you be interested in my life?" she asked, crammed into the seat beside Andy. Her voice was unaccented, husky enough to make him wonder suddenly if she could be a transsexual with a bad case of self-delusion. But she added, exhibiting more emotion than he had heard up to then and sounding as bitter as a babe who found less in her paycheck than he had promised, "I wouldn't mind genuine publicity, but I d-don't want to be anybody's freak-of-the-week!"

He turned right when she remembered to point, used the turn to stall. "In case you didn't notice, Donna," Andy said softly, "I'm a little guy. A *real* little guy."

"Around that corner, the third apartment on your left," she said. Her face turned to him and he caught a glimpse of it thanks to a streetlight. Seen that way, without considering her height, she was definitely pretty—and feminine. "I suppose you are, Mr. Chalminski. I don't understand the connection."

He had it now, and her! "We're two of a kind—and make it 'Andy,' awright? We're birds of a feather, Ms. Callaghan. Don't you get it?" He pulled into a space at the curb in front of her brown-brick building, switched off the ignition.

"Not wholly," she confessed. She opened her door but made no move to get out.

"I'm the freak here," he explained, "'cause the whole world wants guys who are six feet tall, six five—and showers goodies on them, honey; didn't you know that?" To his surprise, he heard emotion creeping into his voice—that, and a ring of honesty he hadn't heard in it for a long while. "All my life I've had t'be smarter and quicker-thinking—*better*—than other guys, because I sure as hell can't lick 'em!"

Donna actually laughed. And it was pretty to hear; it gave him hope she might look okay under those loose-fitting clothes. "I never thought of it that way."

"See, we're like two peas in the same pod, just at different ends." He snatched up the brown bag with the champagne Eddie Burgess had left on the seat. "You think of yourself as too tall for anyone to like, right? And I've thought of ways t'*make* people give me what I got a right to, 'cause I feel the same way." Boldly he put out a hand to touch her knee. It quavered but didn't pull away. "I got things t'teach you, Donna. Listen to me and you'll have half the men in the world on their *knees* to you!"

"I always thought I'd like men who aren't tall, like me," Donna confessed. Then, though, she was uncurling out onto the sidewalk and leading the way to her apartment.

Once inside the place and seated in a comfortable chair, Chalminski tried to remember all the polite things guests were supposed to do in a nice girl's home. When nothing much came to his mind, he studied her as covertly as possible and tried to form an opinion about her attractiveness. Meaning, by and (very) large, her body.

Through the open doorway to the kitchen he was able to detect a rising bosom as Donna brought down two ordinary water glasses; and when her back, briefly, was to Andy, her sweat-suit-concealed tush looked sort of cute. But then he was strangely relieved to be uncorking the champagne bottle and pouring out bubbly even if she had brought a meaty file folder along that doubtlessly contained her manuscript. As she carried it and her glass to her chair, Andy tried to understand why he'd begun to perspire a lot. Hell, the heat was on her, not him!

Yet it dawned on him when she was seated, crossing her impossibly long legs and sipping champagne, that he was oozing sweat for three damn good reasons: First, Callaghan was the real thing, not on the make, and it might prove harder than he'd imagined to get her out of the ugly clothes and eyeball her the way his audience would. Second, if her bod truly was in perfect proportion, the way he wanted to advertise it, Donna might not represent merely his last chance at another moneymaker, she could just earn him a fucking mint! And third, the primary reason for his sweating like a pig in heat, the biggest woman he had ever put it to was maybe five nine, and she'd been one of the squeezes in a flick he'd produced.

He sneaked out a handkerchief, blotted his forehead. While Donna went through a line of chatter meant to set the scene for reading her manuscript to him—it was obvious she wanted to do it, more obvious he wouldn't be conscious when she'd finished—Chalminski faced the total truth about his state of mind: Until this true midwestern woman was bare-ass in a position where no one was ever taller than anybody else, Callaghan was nothing more nor less than a *possible* gigantic hope—and the most intimidating broad one Andrew Chalminski would ever meet! She had shyly kicked off her shoes, and he decided he actually liked her; but that was not, could not conceivably be, the point.

Just as it had always been for a tough little pink-faced shrimp of a guy from Oceanside, it was up to him to twist Lady Luck like a gawdamn pretzel until she handed over the destiny he had in mind for himself. No way he wanted to hurt this sweet-tempered freak of a dame, and he'd take the responsibility to check out the health of every actor or actress who ever fucked her, but this was ol' Andy's livelihood on the line. Anyone who didn't know enough to cover their own ass was just too ignorant to survive these days anyhow, and it was only a question of time till *somebody* screwed 'em!

"We're interested in high concept, Donna," he broke into what she was saying.

Donna lowered her manuscript, lashes blinking behind the heavy glasses. "Sir?"

"It's a film term," Andy said grandly, waving. He fixed a squint on the ceiling. "Like, can a motion picture be summed up in no more than two sentences. Those are the pictures that sell." He took the champagne over to her, refilled her glass, smiled when she drank most of it immediately. "Movie people, at the buying and optioning level, don't *read* scripts or novels, y'see. Writers and agents come in and explain that concept I mentioned. If it strikes us as a bankable idea, we tell 'em to explain more of the concept to us." He shrugged very, very faintly before retreating to his chair. "Books are for publishers, readers."

"But I thought y-you wanted to know my story." She removed the glasses, rested them on a coffee table. Her blue eyes looked damp and quite pretty. "Why else would you come—?"

"Ms. Callaghan," Andy interrupted, standing as he refilled his glass, "we were discussing the concept for your movie *while we drove here*. And it's a very high one, indeed," he added, retracing his steps to pour more bubbly into Donna's glass. "I got t'tell you, I was very impressed." Instead of smiling, he looked as earnest as humanly possible. He straightened to his full height to appear at least slightly taller than she was sitting. "Once some other matters are cleared away, I'm prepared to write into your contract an authorization for you to do the novelization of your life story."

"A movie *tie-in book?*" she asked in a small, shocked, did-she-dare-hope-for-this tone of voice.

"Imagine the reader potential for a book based on a *real-life* film—*starring the author herself!*" Andy let that one sink in, then adopted an expression of concern. "Our gifted mutual pal Edward did mention that possibility, didn't he?"

Donna gulped champagne and nodded simultaneously, getting the tip of her nose wet and evoking an excited, embarrassed giggle. "He did—but I'm no actress, Mr. Chalminski, and Edward is the only one who's said my wr-writing is good enough for a book."

Andy patted her shoulder, smelled a pleasant perfume lofting to his nose. "You ever hear of editors, Donna? And I insist, I'm *Andy.*" He put his glass next to hers, refilled each of them. "Of course, even with the finest acting coaches, there are some questions I must answer before we can go to the next step."

"I'd try to answer them, Andy," she said quickly, drying her nose.

Chalminski inhaled, shook his head slightly. "Donna—I don't even know what you *look* like!" He decided to let himself look as troubled as he really was. "We can use ten-year-old girls t'play you when you were five. But what about the later scenes?"

"B-b-but this *is* how I look!" she blurted. Whether she realized she was starting to slur words occasionally or not was hard to tell because she was so swept up in their discussion. Again she reached for her glass, sipped from it. "I don't understand—Andy."

He took two quick steps away, patted his own face to dry it of sweat before turning back. It was time to move forward swiftly, surely, like a basketball point guard taking charge of a close game. "Donna dear, how many motion picture actresses under the age of fifty do you see in sweat suits? Not t'be rude, but I can't even see what your legs look like! It ain't necessarily a case of sex appeal; but *men* go to movies, rent videotapes, and they like to see actresses who look—do forgive me for this—as attractive and as, well, *female* as possible." He edged another inch toward the goal, cautious as hell about how he worded it. "I think you may be pretty—but even as much as an admirer of feminism as I am, I got to have a gander at how you look."

She hesitated for such a long period of time, Chalminski nearly forgot to breathe. At last, nodding, she got to her feet, her proximity—and height—once more amazing him. "I have other clothes," Donna said shortly. She went on nodding as she headed toward a hallway of the apartment. "I do see what you mean. I guess it's only fair and reasonable."

He watched her leave, noticed she staggered just a little despite the effort she put into walking with dignity. Chalminski's heart leaped with joy—

Until she added, possibly speaking as much to herself as to him, "I have a nice sweater and some hiking shorts. 'Scuse me." A door banged against a wall seconds later.

Andy clapped his forehead with his hand. A sweater? Hiking shorts? What—a sweater large enough for a baby rhino, and shorts that went down to calf-length socks? Gawd, every other broad he'd ever given that speech to had gotten the drift immediately, and half of 'em had started stripping on the spot!

He gulped down the rest of the champagne in his glass and Donna's too. At least she'd swilled it away pretty good; *that* would help!

Without hesitation, he strode down the carpeted hallway to her bedroom and threw the door open.

Donna Callaghan, no more than six feet away, was the most naked human being Andy Chalminski had ever seen. His eyes, his mind, and his glands described her that way to him and couldn't have listened to any quibbling about degrees of nudity if Andy's life had depended on it. There was just so much *more* of Donna than of any other woman he had even heard about that the sight of her simultaneously supercharged all his senses and threatened to short-circuit them—and the almost seven-foot giantess certainly fulfilled the little Chalminski's fondest hopes of being well-proportioned for her size. Gaping up at Donna, he discovered fat only where fat was supposed to be, and he was reminded of old *Playboy* pictures he'd seen of Jayne Mansfield—except Mansfield probably hadn't broken the tape bustwise in the low to middle fifties!

"I was lookin' for the b-bathroom," Andy stammered.

"I was trying to d-decide," Donna said, waving an arm longer than some women's legs at a sweater and pair of shorts on her bed, "whether to put these on. Or n-not to wear anything." Her words were still slurring on her, but she was definitely aware she was naked even if she made no move to cover herself. Instead she was taking a somewhat off-balance step forward, standing at the foot of the bed, raising her arms to

Andy. She wasn't remotely crude about the way she added, "I definitely do like men who aren't as tall."

This was the producer's cue to produce, Chalminski knew—the time any man worth spit encircled the bare-ass girl with his arms and kissed her lips. But there was no way possible for him to wrap his arms around the part of Callaghan facing him, and—

Donna caught the small-man's hands in her enormous ones, fell back on her bed and took Chalminski along with her. One of his wide-open eyes wound up staring into her navel, and the incredibly generous breasts above him, standing straight up without a bra, made it impossible for him to see her distant face. He thought for a moment she'd passed out. That, combined with his total awareness of where his hands had fallen when they landed hard on the reinforced and ultra-king-sized bed—between her beautiful and impossibly long legs—finally directed a completely uncluttered message to Andy's brain and his body.

He got out of his clothes in record time thanks to the easy way one button on his sport jacket and two on his shirt popped away, and he didn't look down again at the warmly furry place where his hands had been. If she was virginal and everything he had read about feminine parts proved to be wrong, he might have to be Superman to help Donna Callaghan complete the rest of her audition.

After climbing her and resting with a blend of near overawe and definite readiness on Donna's impressive bosom, Andy craned his neck in order to kiss her and also learn if she was conscious. Her eyes were closed, but when he pressed his lips to hers, her tongue shot out of her mouth like a projectile at the identical instant her heavy-thighed legs ascended from the bed and crossed Andy's ass. *She may be a virgin,*

Chalminski thought, mouth full of exploring female tongue that might become the most famous one in the world, *but her instincts work like a fuckin' computer*—

But he also realized he was what seemed like three miles too far north to do what she suddenly wanted him to do!

"Andy, Andy," she moaned, opening her marvelous blue eyes and staring myopically at the way he was pinned to the upper half of her body like a teddy bear in some little girl's dream of tomorrow, "go ahead! Do it! *Do* it to me!"

The circulation in Andy's ass, legs, and other parts was being shut off, and the passion that had let him overcome his initial sense of inferiority was slipping out of him like air from a balloon, but Chalminski was game. "I'm willing, babe," he managed, struggling against her gorgeous and powerful legs, "but you're gonna have to let *go* of me a minute."

Instantly helpful, Donna dropped her legs and also wriggled quietly out from under—throwing Andy heavily to the mattress on his back—and sat up straight above him, straddling his body but not touching him. She cupped her ideally proportioned breasts in hands that could palm basketballs and threw her head back as she licked her lips. They weren't yet in any contact, but Donna's girlishly pink nipples seemed nearly the size of erect boys' penises. Chalminski's organ promptly showed signs of life but primarily in the sensations he began experiencing in his mind. Callaghan's body tapered to a waist that was trim for her if wider than Andy's, and the hips swept out to the sides just as suitably and meatily matching the rest of her as he had hoped. Best of all, the sexual center of the lady giant was detectable in a modest, moist tangle of attractive light brown pubic hair and unmistakably female of nature.

"Am I pretty at all?" she asked softly, breathily. Her eyelids blinked and he wondered how drunk she was. "No one has ever seen me this way. Please, Mr. Chalminski—do you approve of what I look like?"

She was squinting down at him—at his face—in the nearsighted manner she had without her glasses, and he felt himself stiffen enough to know he was almost ready again. Andy wondered if she even knew what that long tongue of hers could do to a man, and decided that this amazing squeeze who was soon to become a money train with him playing engineer even while he rode in her caboose was definitely cherry. "Well, Donna," he grunted, reaching down to make them both ready and help her ease it down sweetly on him, "I'll know for sure in just a few minutes."

Donna rose up from the bed a good foot and a half—more than enough distance to triple what Chalminski had to offer—and powered herself down at him with the equivalent force of a locomotive crashing through a barricade of Swiss cheese. Andy had just enough time to wonder if his wrist had been the first thing to be crushed, and to know that one or more parts of his body would never function normally again.

"You bastard!" Donna said, rearing away from the producer a second time and thrusting herself down on him again—and *again,* till the groans she heard gave way completely to the bubbling of blood dribbling quietly from the corner of Andy's motionless mouth and onto the sheets beneath him. "Everything Edward said about you was right." She turned her head to see Eddie Burgess, video camera in hand exactly as they had planned, walking in from the bathroom with a smile. "After the ghastly life this little pipsqueak lured you into in your innocent youth, darling, it's a wonder you were able to make such pure, sweet love to me these marvelous weeks we've had together."

Eddie wrapped his arms around her from behind. It was a reach, but he did it with tenderness. He'd left the camera on her dresser. "If our Andrew had listened to what I said about your story being interesting enough to tell straight, we wouldn't have had to send him to the Big Set in the Sky—or of course, if *he'd* had a big set himself."

Donna giggled and let Burgess kiss her neck, then help her off the heap. "You got it all on videotape?"

"Yep, in tight close-up just like the bastard would have wanted it. If anyone ever figures out what killed Andrew, and whom, we have a record of his seduction —and your self-defense, if any prosecutor ever had the balls to bring such a *graphic* case to trial!" *And I,* Eddie thought, more or less holding Donna close, *have the makings of a really* different *snuff film if our own collaboration doesn't fly.*

Donna began pulling on a sweater and shorts. "He talked so many young people into turning the act of love—like ours—into cheap entertainment for—for losers like him."

"Yes, but you have to admit sex can be pretty entertaining," Eddie remarked, motioning for Donna to help him bundle the mess on the bed into the several sheets they had thoughtfully added early this morning. Together, they tied them at the top rather like a Hershey's Kiss.

"You're right," she agreed, pausing to lean over, down, and kiss him. Then she slung the improvised sack over one shoulder, and with Eddie opening doors for her, carried the trash out to the apartment Dumpster. "And you're right that times are changing. We'll still find somebody to produce my story, and you will play a true-life role opposite me—in the script we've written together!"

He took her hand as the heavy Dumpster lid clanged shut and squeezed it. He realized she might well fulfill the dream he'd placed in her head, and he hoped she would. He truly did. But if not, there was always the videotape with the close-up of old out-of-date Andy Chalminski's agonized expression at the very end. People today wanted a higher concept than a little guy making it with a big girl. "How many units did you say have access to this Dumpster?" he asked, casually glancing around.

Donna laughed then because her Edward did, and they used his car to drive over to his place for the night. The trash pickup was in the morning.

JUST A PHONE CALL AWAY

John F. D. Taff

*H*ome seemed foreign to Cynthia on a weekday morning, a place she wasn't supposed to be. The small apartment wore the air of a person awakened too soon, groggy and grumpy and put upon.

"Get used to it," she mumbled, shivering in her underwear at the kitchen table. She took another sip from the heavy ceramic mug that said "Don't Ask Me, I Just Work Here," a memento of her recently ex-job.

Cynthia was going on forty. Her long brown hair was worn pulled back, showing off a handsome, if somewhat heavy, face. She wore the best clothes she could afford, but they were old and too tight in some places, too loose in others.

All told, Cynthia was not the type of person one would normally choose for an office romance. She wasn't the self-assured, tight young college graduate, the naive, even younger secretary, or the older, but still sexy, vice president with the failing marriage.

She may not have had the body, the age, or the power to attract lovers, but Cynthia had the voice.

And she had learned long ago that her voice was as sexual as any breast or butt or leg.

It was deep, but not too much so. Raspy, but not grating or harsh on the ear. It was a tingling, vibrating, resonant, breathy voice, reminiscent of Lauren Bacall or Kathleen Turner.

Without a doubt, it turned men on in ways her body alone never could.

It had been what had attracted her boss, what had kept him in her bed for eight months.

It couldn't, however, save her from being fired by him.

That had thrown her for a loop. Cynthia was so accustomed to maintaining the upper hand in her relationships that this single act by her boss left her feeling powerless and bereft, not knowing quite what to do with herself.

So with a couple weeks' severance, a last lunch with the girls, and a parting, bad-dog-eyed good-bye from her ex, she left, with no prospects and fewer ideas of what to do next.

Another punishing draft of hot coffee, and she flipped the newspaper open, scanned the want ads. Down the columns, through administrative assistants, receptionists, secretaries. She circled those that appealed to her; there weren't many.

Her eyes drifted down to "Topless Dancers Wanted," and she snorted, almost gagging on her coffee. She remembered fondly what Ralph in Accounting had told her on her last day.

"Well, Cynthia," he'd laughed, his voice dropping. "With your talent, I think you'd be able to find a great job in the phone sex business. You'd make a fortune. Hell, I'd call and let you talk dirty to me for two dollars a minute!"

"Ralph!" she'd protested, half-gamely, half-flattered.

Suddenly, cold and depressed and in her underwear on a Monday morning, Ralph's idea didn't seem so ridiculous. With the phone company contacts she had gained through being a receptionist with a large company, a little research, and a little money borrowed from her retirement fund, she might be able to swing this.

Then something at the back of her mind whispered to her what she was really thinking of doing.

Talking dirty to men on the phone. And not just dirty, but explicit and definitely X-rated.

Are you really going to be able to do this? the voice asked.

There was only one way to tell.

It amazed Cynthia how quickly it all came together.

She secured a business license, got a tax number, made the necessary arrangements with the phone company. Her liaisons there were more than eager to help her in getting a "900" line installed in her apartment.

While she waited, she visited the newsstand outside her building. There, under the silently amazed eyes of the old newsman, she self-consciously bought a few of the seedier men's magazines.

Back in her apartment, she sat in the little space she'd cleared for her office and flipped through the magazines, intending to go straight for the classified ads. Her curiosity, though, demanded that she scrutinize the first several carefully, until the photos all took on a surreal look, with their tangled limbs and close-ups of genitalia so tightly focused, she was sure even a gynecologist would have trouble identifying what he was seeing.

She was able to cobble together pieces of the ads she liked into a small ad for her new service. Several phone calls and overnight packages later, her little ad was scheduled to run in several of the men's magazines she'd reviewed, as well as a couple of local alternative newspapers.

Before she could sit back and wait for the phone calls, though, she needed practice.

"Hello?"

"Ralph? Hi, this is Cynthia."

"Cynthia?" he said, lowering his voice. "Cynthia Johnson?"

"Yes, Ralph," she purred into the receiver. "And do you know what? I'm sitting here totally nude . . ."

Here she paused, hitched in a deep breath as her stomach fluttered.

". . . and I'm really wet."

There was a stunned silence on the other end. Cynthia heard the tinny sound of a television somewhere on Ralph's end. She almost laughed then, imagining him standing in his living room listening to her. Here she sat in a T-shirt and jeans with no makeup.

Not nude and decidedly not wet.

"My wife is here, for chrissakes!" he whispered.

"Ralph," she moaned so low that her own phone

vibrated in her ear. "Oh, Ralph. I've been thinking about you, imagining you. Touching myself. I've been very naughty."

"Dear Lord," came a hoarse voice.

"I took your advice to start a phone sex business. You're my first customer. But don't worry," she said with a throaty giggle. "This one's on the house."

"Can I call you back?" he whined.

"No, Ralph. We've got to finish . . . right here, right now."

He did.

After that, Ralph became her first paying customer, too.

The phone rang at 3 A.M.

Cynthia didn't bother to turn the lights on as she picked her way to the chair by the phone. In the three months she'd operated the service, she'd walked the path many times in the dark, often more asleep than not.

The men who called at this hour were more lonely than horny, a bit more sincere, sweeter, and a little more desperate for simple human contact. Cynthia found that she could talk to these men about things other than sex—their jobs, hobbies, problems. Sometimes these callers even became so engrossed in their conversations that they never made it to the sex part.

Cynthia plopped into the chair near the phone, answered it without clearing her throat, knowing that these men wanted to rouse her from bed, wanted to hear her raspy, sleep-filled voice. It lent an air of intimacy to what they did, as if they had merely rolled over and awakened a lover curled in bed next to them.

"Hello, honey. This better be good."

"Hello," came the man's voice, rough and hoarse and whisper-quick.

Cynthia knew from experience that he would say nothing more, only respond to questions or ask short, wheezing queries. In this situation, very few men wanted to take the lead.

She preferred it that way.

"Does your mommy know you're waking me up? 'Cause if she doesn't, you go tell her it's two ninety-nine per minute."

"My mommy's not here," he growled.

"Good thing. Mine's not here either."

"What are you wearing?"

"Nothing, honey." Actually, she was wearing a pair of panties, but otherwise this was accurate.

"I always sleep naked," she continued. "You never know when the opportunity may . . . arise. What are you wearing?"

"I'm not wearing anything either."

"And I bet you've got quite a handful."

"You could say that," he laughed, and it raised goose bumps on her arms, for it was a disturbing laugh, confidential and low, like a rusty engine slowly turning over. She heard a sound, distant, maybe the squeaking of bedsprings, the rustle of covers.

"Tell me about yourself."

"Down to details. My kind of man. I'm five eight, a hundred twenty pounds, brown hair and eyes. Thirty-eight, twenty-six, thirty-four. Like to fuck. How about you?"

"What do you like?" he breathed, ignoring her question. "I mean specifically."

"I like it all."

"You haven't been doing this long, have you?" he

dismissed, changing his tone as if he were an actor stepping outside character. "That's the easy answer. What do you really like to do—more than anything else?"

Cynthia rolled her eyes. Obviously the guy was looking to talk with someone who liked the same things he did. But what?

"I like to be spanked," she finally said, and that was a safe answer. Kinky enough to satisfy wilder men, not so perverse as to disgust the milder ones.

"You do?" he whispered after a moment, lapsing back into his previous hushed tone.

"Yeah," she said, relaxing again. "Do you?"

"Yeah, sure," he responded, a bit distractedly. "Sure."

There was a moment of silence.

"You like pain?" he asked from its depths.

"That depends on who, what, and how much," she said, fumbling for her cigarettes and sensing that control was coming back to her.

"I like pain."

"Great," she said, inhaling. "You like to be spanked? Whipped? Bitten?"

"Cut," said the voice, quivering in anticipation. "I like to be cut."

Here, Cynthia hesitated.

"Cut?" she asked, crushing her cigarette out. "How?"

A deep, rattling sigh from the other end.

"A sharp knife. A razor. A piece of glass. It doesn't matter."

If that litany was not unsettling enough, he did something then that almost made her drop the phone in horror.

He moaned, soft as a caress.

"What are you doing?" She swallowed, hoping to change the subject.

"Stroking myself."

"Are you hard?"

"Yes. And so is it."

"Is what?"

"My knife."

"Knife? What are you doing with a knife?" she asked, covering herself with a blanket, sliding her feet up underneath her.

"Cutting myself," he said, and his voice was rapturous. "Little lines across my chest, my abdomen. Around my nipples . . . Ohhh!"

And she felt the shudder in his voice.

"Keep talking to me. I like your voice," he said.

"Are you going to keep doing that?" she asked, her stomach folding in on itself.

"Oh, yessss! OHHHH!"

"Doesn't it hurt?" she moaned, biting a finger.

"No! Yes!"

"Stop!" she screamed, leaping up, the blanket falling forgotten around her feet. "Please stop!"

"Jesus! OH! OH MY GOD!" he yelled, his wavering screams descending into a series of broken sobs.

Cynthia stood shaking, her hand cupped over her mouth.

Neither said anything for a minute.

But neither hung up.

"Are you OK?" Cynthia asked, her hand still not far from her mouth.

"I cut off my nipple."

"Oh my God," she whispered, her eyes fluttering back in her head.

"I've got to go now. I've got quite a mess here. But you were wonderful. I'll call again."

With another moan and a creaking of bedsprings, the receiver clunked into place.

The rest of the night, Cynthia sat upright in bed wrapped in her quilt and stared at the phone. It rang several times, stopping at around 4:30 A.M., but she did not answer it.

She'd heard many things over the phone in the last three months; things that were exciting and intriguing, rude and disgusting, uncomfortable and unpleasant. But this had gone far past those other calls, too far.

Into territory within herself that she found unfamiliar and frightening.

Cynthia replayed the conversation over and over in her head. Each time, the feelings surged back, as strong and vivid as they had been during the experience. Strangely, even though they never talked about sex, the call left her with an overwhelming feeling of being used.

Being out of control.

She hadn't experienced that yet. Up to now, she had always been in control on the phone.

This man, though, played her as deftly as she played other callers.

There was something else that disturbed her even more, something that clung to the borders of her conscious mind, hid in the shadows.

Cynthia caught only a glimpse of it, but that was enough.

Excitement.

She'd been excited by the conversation, by the man hurting himself.

Enjoying himself.

Unable to think of another explanation, unwilling to accept this one, Cynthia sobbed herself to sleep just as the morning sun poked through the slats of her bedroom blinds.

And the phone rang.

Two days later, Cynthia felt good enough to begin taking calls again.

Passing the jangling phone late in the afternoon, a soda in one hand, cigarettes in the other, she picked it up on impulse.

"Hello?"

"I didn't frighten you, did I?"

Cynthia stiffened, fumbled a cigarette out.

"You're still there. I can hear you . . . smoking," he said just as she exhaled.

"I'm sorry if I upset you," he went on after a minute. "I tried to call back for two days."

Cynthia exhaled another cloud of thin smoke, took a drink of soda, sat down. She was going to make sure she was in control before she answered, even though her heart was vibrating inside her chest, her mouth bone-dry.

"I really enjoyed our conversation. It was the best I've—"

"Did you really do it?"

"Good, you are there," he said, amiably.

"You really cut . . . it off?" Cynthia couldn't bear to say the word.

"It only hurt after, and then for just a little while."

"I can't believe you did that to yourself," she said, her own nipples beginning to ache with imagined, sympathetic pain. She crossed an arm over her breasts, crushed them to her as if to reassure herself that they were intact.

"Why not?"

"Is that a serious question?"

71

"Sure."

"You're not going to do it again . . . are you?"

"Who says I'm not doing it right now?"

That stopped her. Of course he was doing it now. That's why he'd called again.

"You are, aren't you?" She puffed, keeping the cigarette perched close to her lips.

"You don't even know if I really did it or not. It excited you, though, didn't it? Even if it scared you, repulsed you?"

Blood, hot and angry, flooded her cheeks.

"That's just sick. You're sick. You're a fucking weirdo!"

"Ohhh . . . ummmm . . . I love your voice. It tickles my ear."

"Stop it," she pleaded. "Whatever you're doing, stop it."

"I've got my knife again . . ."

"No! I'm hanging up!"

"I'm . . . uhhh . . . making three or four . . . uhhhhahhhh . . . little incisions along my erection. There," he breathed. "Yeah, that's great."

"Oh my God!" she shrieked. "Stop it!"

"Ohhhh!" he groaned. "Just enough to get a little blood. It's nice and warm, and it's a great lubricant. If it doesn't dry, that is. Gotta . . . uhhhnn . . . keep it fresh."

"Please stop," she whined, twisting and untwisting the phone cord.

"So hard now . . . kind of stings . . . have to make a . . . ahhhhh . . . another cut. Ohhhh. Talk to me."

"No. Stop. Just stop."

"If you don't want to . . . listen, hang up the . . . awwwww . . . phone."

"Don't do this. Please."

"But it feels so good. Stings a little, but . . . ahhh!"

An image of him appeared unbidden in her mind: a vague face grimacing, a nude body writhing upon the white sheets of a bed at the center of a Rorschach test of blood. The straining, swelling thing he held in his closed fist was a deep, dark red, the secret, warm red of the interior of a cherry pie.

Warmth spread out in waves from her pubis, even as her stomach shivered at this image.

Cynthia found, perversely, that her own disgust only seemed to heighten the arousal she was now fighting. It was illicit and forbidden, and she hadn't felt that since having sex long ago with her teenage boyfriend while her parents were away from home.

"Are you still with me?" he moaned, his voice tight and distant.

"Yes."

"Good. So good."

"Yes," and it was the tone of defeat and remorse, edged with the instinctive desperation of sex.

The caller moaned through clenched teeth, redoubled his efforts.

"Do you want me to finish?"

"Umm," she breathed in assent, plopping onto the chair near the phone, her fingertips brushing lightly down her belly, pulling her robe apart, her panties to one side, sliding through the tangle of hair.

"I'm feeling a little . . . faint. Gotta hurry. Talk to me."

"I want you to finish." And her voice was low and husky, commanding. Cynthia threw her legs over the arms of the chair, struggled out of her panties. Freed, her fingers teased her exposed sex.

"Finish now."

"Yeah. Ahhh . . ."

"Right now. Do it!" she commanded, using her shoulder to clamp the phone to her ear, freeing both hands to dance between her legs.

"Ahh! Yes! Oh God, yes!" came his reply, his mouth sounding as if it were pressed close to the phone.

Cynthia lapsed into silence as an orgasm, painful in its intensity and lightning quickness, flashed through her. One of her legs spasmed, lashed out, knocked a lamp off the table near her.

The lightbulb popped as the lamp shattered, and suddenly the afternoon room was engulfed in darkness.

"Did you come?"

"Yes," she panted dryly. It had happened so fast that beads of sweat were only now beginning to form on her forehead. Her aching arms twitched loosely.

"So did I. Are you still wet?"

Cynthia brought her fingers close to her face, rubbed them together.

"Yes."

"So am I," he laughed. "I always have a big mess to clean after I talk with you."

The image of him lying on his bed, the sheets like an ink blotter, came to her again.

In the shadows, her own wet hands were slicked with darkness.

And a smell drifted from her fingers, whose tips had dipped gently inside her.

It was a flat, acrid smell, metallic. The smell of dirty metal and copper pennies.

Blood.

Her stomach, which she had ignored, leapt uncontrollably. It was all she could do to drop the phone and lower her head before she vomited.

As she shook and gasped, the man's tiny voice chirped from the receiver on the floor.

"Hello? Are you still there? Are you all right?"

But she could not answer him, could not even pick the phone up, her hands shook so badly.

It was all she could do to stumble into the bathroom, vomit again into the open toilet, fall into the shower.

There, she checked her fingertips to see the blood.

But they were unstained.

Cynthia stayed in the shower until her skin pruned, obliterated the phantom smell with soap and water.

It was dark again when she awoke, the covers curled like a lover around her naked body. She inhaled deeply, hesitantly, expecting the blood odor, but all she smelled were the warm, clean sheets with their stolen scent of the fabric softener.

Her stomach rumbled, loud enough to hear, and she realized that she'd had nothing to eat since getting sick yesterday.

The mere thought of eating brought a rush of saliva.

Swinging her feet off the bed, she stood, wobbly and stiff.

She grabbed the robe hanging from the bedpost, thrust her arms into it, pulled it closed and knotted the tie.

The kitchen was flooded with the moon's translucent silver light until she snapped on the harsh fluorescents, whose light seemed to ooze from the fixture, creep across the countertops and the white tile.

An omelette, she thought, that really sounds good right now.

Soon she was beating eggs, pouring them into a hot skillet.

The refrigerator held any number of ingredients that would be good in her omelette, but she selected grated cheddar cheese, mushrooms, and a tomato. Her movements were as spare and unconscious as any cook working in a familiar kitchen.

Until she opened a drawer to get a knife to cut the tomato.

They gleamed from where they lay within the drawer, long and tapered like a mouthful of razor teeth.

Cynthia reached tentatively for one, as if the drawer might close around her hand like a hungry mouth.

Snatching the knife out, she slammed the drawer shut with her hip.

She'd selected a paring knife. It was slim and tapered, curving to a point like a miniature scimitar, its gentle, upward angle not unlike that of a . . .

Shaking her head, she frowned, thrust the knife into the tomato, cored it, divided it.

In her haste, though, the knife slid across her finger, whisper-soft.

She didn't even realize she had cut herself until she had dropped the cubed tomato into the bubbling center of the omelette and washed her hands.

Under the water, blood welled from the cut, hair-thin but deep. When Cynthia, grimacing even though it did not hurt, pulled its edges apart, it opened to reveal a moist, red interior.

It made her finger feel warm, her body a little faint.

Was this what her caller felt each time he did this to himself? she wondered.

Did it heighten his sexual response?

Her gaze drifted back to the cutting board, to the compact knife that rested there on the damp, red cutting board.

Her fingers curled around it, tickled the back of her other hand with its tip.

Behind her, the tomatoes melted into the mass of the omelette.

Her robe slipped open, and she pressed the flat of the cold blade against her breast, the sharp edge just circling her nipple. It became hard immediately.

She flicked the blade's tip to her other breast, traced the nipple.

Goose bumps rushed in a wave up her abdomen, across her collarbone, down her arms.

The knife's blade became warm, moved.

There was a momentary sensation of heat, which swept across her like a scouring, dry wind.

Then a sudden coldness that engorged her nipples so much, she thought they might explode.

She cried out.

Simultaneously, and quite unexpectedly, she orgasmed, her legs buckling beneath her.

Her free hand caught the counter as she fell to her knees, bent her head, and gasped for breath.

Beneath her, bright red pennies dripped unnoticed to the ground from her nipple, pooled loosely on the floor.

The omelette burned in the pan.

Cynthia was in control.

She'd cleaned the kitchen, scouring the charred egg and cheese from the pan.

She'd mopped the floor, trying not to distinguish

between the pulpy tomato drippings and the other spots that were thicker, more red.

The bandage she had applied after she had collected herself chafed the sore, raw nipple it covered. She had already changed it twice, and blood still oozed from the wound, soaked through the bandage, her T-shirt.

When she had first gone into the bathroom, she was surprised at first to see blood, dripping from her nipple like red milk, running in a rivulet down the curve of her breast, beading on her stomach like water on a finely waxed car.

With hesitant, probing fingers she discovered that the sharp little paring knife had nearly sliced off her entire nipple. It now hung from her breast by a small flap of skin. When she touched it, it moved away like an opening door, exposing bright, red tissue beneath.

She quickly closed it.

Amazingly, it had taken nearly an hour for it to begin to hurt, first in a tentative, stinging way, then in great, gasping throbs of pain that made both breasts ache in rhythm with her pulse.

Once the kitchen was clean, she poured herself a glass of soda, gathered her robe around her, and sat down in her chair near the phone.

She did not cry, and her stomach ached only in a vaguely threatening way.

Rather, she felt she understood the caller better, as if they had bonded in some secret, bloody way. For the first time, she felt she could handle him better when he called next.

Cynthia felt in control again.

And, she had to admit, for some strange reason, what she had done, and done almost unknowingly, had felt . . . good.

Or at the very least, it hadn't been merely painful.

The phone on the table next to her rang shrilly, and she set the glass down, answered it.

"Hello? Hi, Steve," she purred to one of her regular customers. "Is your wifey asleep? Great. Yes. Uh-huh. I bet you are hard, Stevie.

"I've got something with me tonight that's hard, too."

Steve stayed on the phone, angry at first, then scared, then weeping.

When she was through, he asked if he could call her again.

The phone rang, as it did more and more often these days.

So many calls, so many callers.

Many times, they didn't like what Cynthia wanted to offer them.

With most, though, it only took a phone call or two to turn them on, just as it had been with her.

Then they were easy to control.

But it was getting harder with each caller.

It took more and more of her to keep that control.

Cynthia grunted as she fought to pull herself up from her sticky, crusted bedsheets. She spent most of her time here these days, the phone now moved to her nightstand, where it was within easy reach.

Cynthia was naked, as she was all of the time now. She found that clothing of any kind, even a loose robe, chafed the many wounds on her body, some still oozing fluids, some scabbed over, some already covered with thick, ropy scars.

There were far too many to worry about Band-Aids.

It was difficult to walk now. She was weak so often,

and it was hard to maintain her balance without any toes. The neighbors had started to complain, too, first to her, then to the building manager, about the screams, the strange smells coming from her apartment.

"Cynthia?" asked the voice on the receiver, and it trembled through her.

Her ex-boss. Her ex-lover.

"Hello," she croaked, her voice hard and hoarse. It had suffered the most over the last six months or so, through all of the shouting, the shrieking, the crying. The toll of that stress was as apparent in her voice as it would have been in the lank, lusterless hair or wrinkled, saggy body of a burned-out topless dancer.

For a moment, she felt like she had when he had fired her; when the man who cut himself had called her for the first time.

Powerless. Out of control.

Pushing that aside, her hand fumbled for something on the nightstand, just out of reach.

It sparkled in the low light of the room as she brought it around, settled back in bed.

It was awkward to hold the knife these days. All the fingers on her left hand were gone, and on her right hand only a single finger and thumb remained. This, she found, was the minimum number of digits necessary to hold the knife.

"Ralph told me to call you."

"He did? What else did he say?"

"He said I'd never forget it."

"Ohh, you'll never forget it. I'll make sure of that. You'll *never* forget."

"What are you doing?"

"I'm stroking the tip of the knife over my skin . . .

ahhh . . . goose bumps are covering me *everywhere,"* she whispered.

Clumsily she moved the knife, trembling a little when the tip of the blade skipped over a scar, slid through a raw, wet patch. She sought out something she had given to no caller as of yet; some part of her body that was whole and unscarred to offer him.

To control him.

"Ahh," he groaned, a noise that sounded as if it were ripped involuntarily from somewhere deep inside him.

"Ummm. It feels nice. Doesn't it?"

"Yes," he answered shakily.

He hesitated briefly when he heard something in the background, underneath her heavy breathing; the corrugated sound of metal cutting into something soft.

The knife moved against her, into her.

"Yes."

Warmth spread within her, upon her.

Her voice cracked with pleasure.

"Good. So good."

She screamed, her hips bucking up from the bed uncontrollably, shuddering with the powerful waves that crashed through her, the warm liquid that spattered over her.

Through everything, she heard him, on the other end, gasp through the spasms of his own orgasm, his breath grating in her ear.

She smiled fiercely as her vision lurched, dimmed.

It came out with little difficulty, and she held it glistening and dripping in the blackness of the room. She was surprised by its smallness—no bigger than her fist—and the fact that it still shuddered timidly in her hand.

"Never forget," she muttered thickly as the receiver dropped to the bed, the still-beating heart squeezed slickly from the ruin of her hand.

Cynthia was in control.

BLACK AND WHITE AND BED ALL OVER

James Crawford

T hey were wild and crazy times. Hollywood was still new and stars were being born every day. You couldn't turn around without bumping into someone who had just made a film. Studios formed and disappeared. Cameras cranked nonstop and movie productions were multiplying like rabbits.

There were actors and then there were the Stars. The brightest of the stars weren't just found, they were made for the camera. An actor might be typecast, but these new players could do anything. No stunt too dangerous, no pratfall too outrageous—they were like the early gods of film.

There was jealousy, of course, but most of us were in awe of them. Many a live actor would have sold his soul to be able to do the things the Animates could. Director didn't like your looks, you changed them. Got flattened in a bad fall, reinflate yourself and do something else. They were amazing.

They made us laugh and that was a good thing, because some of them were not so comical in private. Some of them could be downright nasty. I'd heard stories about pranks Animates had pulled on Reals, stunts that put the less resilient Reals in the hospital. They were wild, and there wasn't anything anyone could do about them. I mean, how do you lock up someone who can turn into a pool of ink and pour himself down a drain?

There was also talk about what happened to Reals who had sex with the Animates. No one had any specifics, but the word was, it wasn't anything you'd ever forget. A friend of mine had heard there was a special wing at the laughing academy reserved for those Reals crazy enough to do it with an Animate. He said they were all checked into the rubber room wearing the latest in straitjacket fashions. I told him he was full of it, but I was curious.

My name is Josh Merriweather and I come from a small town in the East and made my way west by working odd jobs till I got to California. Once there I found HOLLYWOODLAND and my fate was sealed. It was magic and I wanted to be part of it.

There were jobs all over the place. No one knew what they were doing, so everyone was making it up as they went. I worked behind the scenes on a couple of pictures and even did some work as an extra.

I had heard some of the others talk about the Animates, but hadn't actually seen one. Sure I'd seen them on the screen, but I'd never met one on the street.

Then my life changed, maybe not for the better, but it changed.

The word was out that one of the newer studios was looking for help. No big deal; until I heard it was a studio that only produced Animated films. That's all I had to hear. I think I knocked a couple of guys over as I ran out the door and made a beeline for the Fletcher Studio. It wasn't far, so I ran all the way. When I got there, I was so out of breath that I couldn't even tell them why I had come.

Finally I caught my wind and told them I wanted a job. They sent me to talk to the head man. Mack didn't much look like a tycoon, but he had given a start to some of the biggest Animates in the business. I admit I was a little in awe of him when we first met.

"Well, kid, what do ya want?" Mack looked up from a viewer as I came into the room.

I knew what I wanted to say, but my tongue had gone on strike.

"You want a job?"

I took a deep breath. "Yes!"

"A man who knows what he wants. Good. Okay, you're hired. What's your name?"

"Josh, and I just want to say—"

"Enough talk; you think I've got time to interview every little schmuck that comes along? You can thank me later. Now I want you to run these pages over to that big building over there. Can you do that?" I nodded my head so hard, I could hear my brains rattling around. "Then go already."

Off I went, and that was the beginning of my time with the Fletcher Studio. Wild times and a couple of scary times. I got to work with the Animates, and for the most part they were a swell bunch of guys. Maybe "guys" is too loose a term; they were a swell bunch of clowns, dogs, creatures, and things. It was amazing.

My job description varied from day to day. One day I was a gofer, the next the light man. I never knew where Mack would send me next, but for him I would do anything. Which is what got me into the biggest trouble of my life, because one day Mack asked me to do something that again changed my life.

It started out like any other day. I was running errands and stopping to watch the filming whenever possible. Mack had three Animates he was grooming for stardom. Two had really good careers in radio and comics, and one had something that Hollywoodland had patented . . . *sex appeal.* I had seen the studio's other stars, the mumbling merchant marine and the big blue Boy Scout, but I had yet to catch a glimpse of *her.*

It was about time to do a deli run when Mack saw me and called me over. "Hey, Josh, I got a job for ya."

"Yes, sir, anything you want." Mack liked enthusiasm.

"Great, I want you to get your ass over to Stage Five. Tell the director you're to talk to Tiffany about the matter she and I discussed."

"Tiffany?" My blood started pounding. I was finally going to meet *her.*

"Yeah, Tiffany. Josh, you do this for me and I'll make sure you go far in this business." Mack clapped me on the shoulder and pushed me toward my destiny.

Tiffany had *it.* She had already done a couple of films for Fletcher Studio, and the audience loved her. There was a bit of innocence mixed with a whole lot of lust. You saw her up there in a short little skirt and garters and you had thoughts that could get you thrown in jail in most states. I'd seen her on the screen, and now I was going to see the real thing. Hooray for Hollywoodland.

I found the director, Mack's brother Morrie, and delivered the message.

"Thank God!" Morrie seemed genuinely happy to see me. "That little tootsie has been driving me nuts. I want you to go to her dressing room and help her."

"Me?" My throat closed up and my knees developed a rhythm all of their own.

"Listen, kid, Tiffany likes them young and handsome. You play your cards right and this could be the day you become a man." Then he looked around to see if anyone else was listening and said under his breath, "Just watch out for yourself, and if things get too weird, don't be afraid to run for it."

"You mean, she might . . . ?" I began to wonder if this really was a good idea.

"I mean the little honey has a libido the size of Texas. She's tired of the Animates she usually hangs around with and wants a Real to play with. Sometimes it can get a little hairy. You got a problem with that?"

"A problem?" Sex toy to an Animate? What if the stories I had heard were true? Would I ever have another chance to find out? Curiosity got the better of me and I shook my head no.

Morrie took my shoulder and guided me on my journey. "You're a great conversationalist, kid. That'll come in handy. Now, get in there and make her happy."

Tiffany had her own private dressing room, with a big star on the door. I found a shiny surface to give myself a quick brushup and then I went to tap on the door.

"What do you want, punk?" a voice snarled as I raised my hand. I looked around, but didn't see anyone. "Right in front of you, you stupid Real."

I dropped my hand and stared into the rather belligerent expression of the star on Tiffany's door.

"Are you going to tell me what ya want? Or are you

just going to stand there with your dick hanging out?" My mouth opened and I looked down quickly to check my fly, but before I could answer, the star said, "Trying to cop a peek at the Star? Hoping maybe you'll see her in the altogether?"

"No!" I blurted out. "I was sent by the director to see if . . . if . . . I could . . . I mean . . . if she needed . . ."

"I know what you think she needs!" snarled the star. "What she doesn't need is some Real hoping to get lucky."

Its little mouth twisted up to spit, but suddenly the door swung open. "What is all the noise out here?"

She was amazing. About five feet tall and with so many curves, I didn't know how they all fit. Everything about her was black and white. Her dress, what little there was of it, was jet black. Her eyes and lips just as black as the dress. The most amazing thing was her skin—there was no shading, no hint of color; it was the whitest thing I had ever seen. Put them all together and they spelled Tiffany.

Tiffany looked at me and then her attention swiveled to the door. "You! I told you it was over between us."

"But, Tiffany . . ." The voice had dropped down to a whine.

"Leave my butt out of this. I'm sick and tired of your jealousy. Now, get the fuck off my door before I call security."

If the star had a tail, it would have been between its legs. It slid down the door to the floor. Two points acted as legs and two others gestured like arms. "Honey, listen to me. I can change. I promise you."

"It's time for a change and you're not it." With one shapely little foot, in an ebony stiletto, she kicked him down the hall. "And I'm warning you, turn up on my door again and I'll nail your little glittering butt there for good."

The star gave me one more sullen look and then slunk off down the hall. Tiffany watched him for a second and then turned her attention to me. "And just who might you be, tall, dark, and fleshy?"

I was about to do a repeat of my earlier stammer, but Tiffany put her slim finger to my lips. The finger was cool and soft. My eyes crossed as I tried to get a good look at it. Tiffany smiled with her sweet, kissable, Cupids'-bow sable lips and took ahold of my lapels. Then she pulled me into her dressing room.

The room was like Tiffany. It was all in black and white and there wasn't a straight line anywhere. Every wall, piece of furniture, and accessory seemed to flow gently into whatever was next to it. That and the fact there didn't seem to be any shadows made the whole thing fairly disorienting.

"What'sa matter, honey, the room too much for your Real mind?" She reached up and patted me on the cheek. "Let Tiffany fix."

Abruptly everything seemed to run together. One moment I was looking at curves, and the next, the room looked like any other. I staggered to a chair, hoping it wouldn't talk to me, and grabbed hold of it.

"First time?" Tiffany purred as she moved over to me and rested her hand on my chest.

"Yeah, what happened to the room?" Reality didn't seem to be playing by the usual rules, and I was trying to figure out the new ones before the next game.

"Ooh, a virgin!" Tiffany pushed me down onto a couch that might not have been there a moment before. "Let me try to explain, sweet pants."

Tiffany straddled my lap. My first thought was that

she didn't weigh as much as I had expected. My next thought went into a whole new area as she moved around to make herself comfortable. I opened my mouth to ask a question that had become very important.

"Excuse me, Miss . . . "

"Call me Tiffany. And I'll call you sugar pants."

"Excuse me, Tiffany, but I wondered if you had . . . I mean . . . can you . . . do you have . . .?" How to ask this question tactfully?

"Oh, aren't you just the cutest little Real. You want to know if I have a pussy?"

"Well, it's just that when I've seen Animates in the movies, they don't seem to have any privates. I mean most of them don't even wear pants or anything."

"Baby, does it feel like there's nothing down there?"

I had to admit that right then there was absolutely no question in my mind at all that she was all woman. In fact, I got the strangest sensation that she could unzip my trousers without using her hands. She ground down on me with her hips, and I thought it was going to be all over before it even started.

"There, I like that. Now, what was I saying?" I might have been able to help her out with the question, but she did a little move and my train of thought got completely derailed. "Oh yes, I remember now. What happened to the room and do Animates have goodies?

"I'm an Animate and that means I can pretty much do what I want."

"Well, yeah, you're a star." I had to say something or this session was going to be over real quick.

"Yes I am. That's good. Move a little more like that. But that's not what I mean. I mean I can control the way things look around me, and when the need arises, I can have enough goodies for everyone."

The mind can only handle so much information at once, and my brain was slightly south of my belt buckle. Tiffany saw I wasn't paying attention to what she was saying, so she did something to refocus my thoughts.

She leaned forward and her chest began to inflate. She had a nice little set on her before, but now! They kept growing until I was engulfed in the biggest tits I have ever seen. Soft, white, and so light, you almost expected them to float her off the couch like a couple of helium balloons.

"Begin to understand, lover? I can change how I look, what I'm wearing, and the room around me, just by thinking." The tits resumed their normal dimensions.

What followed was amazing. I know I've said that a lot, but there isn't any other way to describe it. Tiffany went through a barrage of changes. She was taller, slimmer, blonder, more curves, less curves, better curves. The outfit changed from a minidress to a formal gown, to a period piece out of some swashbuckler, to a swimsuit, and for a couple of glorious seconds . . . it was gone altogether.

All the time she was doing this, she was rocking up and down on my lap till I began to change shape too—I was getting harder and stiffer. She grinned at me, and the couch was suddenly a very big bed.

"Now, honey, why are you here?"

"Morrie sent me over to see if there was anything you needed." I was very proud that I could still put two words together.

"Morrie is such a nice man." Tiffany reached down and the buttons of my shirt got all of her attention.

I needed something to think about and I didn't like baseball. "What's the story with the little guy on the door?"

She stopped undoing buttons (by that time she had worked down to the pants) and looked at me with big black eyes. "Jealous already?"

"No, I was just wondering if you two . . . ?"

"You don't know much about us Animates, do you?"

"I've been around." I hadn't, but I wasn't going to admit it.

"Then you should know that there is nothing like sex between two of us. We can be anything and do anything, and we never get tired."

"But he was such a little guy."

"Didn't anyone ever tell you size doesn't matter?"

"Once, but I think he just felt inadequate in the shower."

"Well, to an Animate it doesn't matter at all. Twink can do more with his five little points than you can with your one." With that she reached between her legs and gave my "one" a friendly little squeeze. "Now, let's see what you can do."

The bed gave a small shudder and I noticed, barely, that it was changing again. It now was a bit more severe and I saw what looked to be handcuffs hanging off one post. Tiffany smiled down at me and once more her chest expanded. This time the dress didn't and her breasts exploded out of confinement, so very white, though the nipples were black and tasted a little like ink. I bit down and she moaned. "Come on, lover, you can play rougher than that." I reached up and grabbed her other tit and squeezed hard.

She retaliated by grinding down with her hips. I shifted my grip and caught hold of her hips. Still wearing some of my clothes, I thrust up at her. Tiffany yelled and her dress shifted to a bra with nipple cutouts and garter belt and stockings. I could feel the heat between her legs. All I wanted now was to get out of my shorts and slip into something more comfortable—*her*.

I reached down to tug off the last article of clothing that kept me from entering paradise. Tiffany caught my hands, and with surprising strength forced them back to the bed. The cute little face shifted and the new one was a bit slimmer and definitely sexier.

"Not so fast." She bounced up and down a couple of times and a groan escaped my lips. "You're not an Animate. Once you explode, you're no good to little Tiffany."

I tried to grab her shoulders and roll her under me, but she wasn't having any of it. Her strength was all out of proportion to her size, and I was easily outclassed.

"Oh, you want to try another position?" Her features flowed around her face and suddenly I was looking at a face that looked very doglike. She had a little snout and her hairstyle was now dog ears, but you could still see Tiffany's features. My mouth dropped open and she bent down and licked my nose with a tongue like sandpaper.

"How about . . . doggy style?" Tiffany threw her head back and did a sort of barking laugh. The features shifted into a caricature of an African native. "Or maybe . . . missionary?"

The changes were playing havoc with my lust, and part of me began to wilt. It was not a pleasant look that crossed the face above me. "You better not be going soft on me, or I'll try something you might not like."

My imagination stalled at the threat, but it didn't help the little pointer. Tiffany saw the problem and the next change was much more human; in fact, it was the best look yet. Her raven black hair grew longer till it covered her face and tits. Once more I had lead in the pencil and she was a happy Animate.

"Look who's back." She slid down my legs, and the shorts went south for the winter. I, or at least part of me, sprang to attention. She peered through all the black hair and began little nibbling kisses at my toes and moved upward toward my exclamation mark.

I was thrashing like mad and trying to get ahold of her. I didn't want to wait another second. All I wanted was to be inside her and ride off into the sunset. Trouble was, I just couldn't get ahold of anything. She'd shake me off, or what I grabbed flowed between my fingers and left me empty-handed.

"Please," I said in a very strained voice, "Tiffany, hurry up or I'm going to die."

"Relax, you can't die from blue balls." She stopped torturing me for a minute and looked at me quizzically. "Do you think we Animates will ever come in colors like you Reals?"

I screamed and grabbed her. This time she stayed solid and I thrust her down on the mattress. Her legs flew open and my arrow went right into the bull's-eye. I don't know if she was fooling with reality or if it was just me, but rockets went off, there were fireworks, and for some reason, I could picture a train hurtling into a dark tunnel. It was earthshaking and over in an eternity; at least it felt like that to me.

The earth spun for a while, and when it stopped I was lying on my back gasping for air. Tiffany ran a hand over my chest and I shivered happily. I reached over to her and noticed that while I was covered in sweat, she was still dry as a bone. Inky black eyes gazed down at me and I drifted toward sleep. She shook me.

"Don't doze off on me, boobsie. That was great, but not nearly enough." She slid her hand between my legs and fondled the victim of hit-and-run sex.

"You're too much, Tiffany. Let me rest a little bit and I'll spring back for you." I started to flop down on the bed, but I hit my head on a hard surface. I turned around and saw the mattress was gone, and we were now on a wooden table.

"I said, I'm still horny. I'm horny now, and I don't feel like waiting for some limp-dicked Real to recover." Her edges looked harder and her face was becoming more severe.

"I want to, but I can't work miracles." I started to slide off the table, but she pinned me down. The handcuffs were back and ready to be used. Down at the end of the table was another pair. I figured this had to be the weirdness that Mack had warned me about. But I was wrong—this was a walk in the park compared to what was about to happen.

"Please, I have to go now." I tried to shake loose again, but no luck.

"Too late, sweetie, you've already come . . . too early to go. If you can't satisfy one way, then I guess you'll just have to be flexible."

Struggling wasn't doing me any good. She had a tight grip on my wrists and a leg over my waist to hold me down. Sex had retreated a long way from my mind, and fear was banging on the door to get in. Then she started to change again.

Her face stayed the same, but her body was flowing into new formations. The shoulders got broader, arms thickened, and there seemed to be more than two. I could feel her legs changing, and not for the better. It felt like she had coarse fur, and something like a claw scratched me.

It was then that I felt it—between her legs it was still hot, but now there was a bunch of writhing things growing down there.

I struggled upright to see what I already knew. The face was still the Kewpie doll I had just had sex with, but the body wasn't even remotely human anymore. My eyes popped open, and if I'd been an Animate, they would have rolled out onto the floor. Tiffany had parts I'd never seen anywhere before, and they were growing larger by the second.

"Like I said, if you can't get me off one way . . . I'll have do something else to get my kicks."

She let go of one wrist to reach for a set of handcuffs. I screamed and thrashed with all my might and bucked her/it off of me. I hit the floor running toward the door. The room whirled and the exit now looked about a mile away.

"Give it up, sweetie. You're not going anywhere. Just relax. Hell, you might even enjoy it more than the last one did." A chair stuck a leg out to trip me, and a lamp cord slithered across the floor like a snake.

I just kept running and eventually got to the door. Out of breath and too terrified to look back at what might be gaining on me, I grabbed for the doorknob, but it slid across the surface of the door and out of my grasp.

"Knobby, don't you dare let him out of here till I'm through with him." The Tiffany creature was up and the room reverted to normal dimensions. It started toward me and its appendages almost reached to its chest. They were very white, very thick, and very, very frightening.

"Please," I said to the doorknob, "let me out."

It made a face and slid to the other side of the door. "No way, buddy. I want to watch this."

"Pervert!" I clutched at it again and missed. Behind me I heard Tiffany moving slowly and deliberately toward me. There was a weighty thump at each step and a sound like something heavy dragging behind it. My mind raced and an idea came to me.

I looked up at the door and cried, "What a set of knockers!"

Knobby, the doorknob, stopped sliding all over the place and tried to look up to see what door knockers I was talking about. While he was distracted, I grabbed the knob and wrenched the door open. Then I ran like a thief into the hallway.

Behind me I heard a scream of pain from Knobby and one of rage and frustration from Tiffany. Both were music to my ears.

I ran onto the lot buck naked and didn't stop till I reached my apartment, where I threw my things in a bag and caught the next train out of Hollywoodland. Didn't care where I was going, just so long as it was far away from anyplace that had Animates.

That was years ago. I settled back East in a boring, but safe and sane job. I married a nice girl who doesn't change shape when we make love, at least not any more than anyone else does.

We've been married for years and we have three great kids. I'm lucky; the three boys think I'm just about the best dad in the whole world. We do everything together; well . . . almost everything.

Even though it's been more years than I can count, there are just some things I'm never going to be able to do with them. I'm never going to take them to an Animated movie and I'm never going to be able to explain to them why I get the shakes every Saturday morning when they turn on the television.

And now there is a new horror—cable. All those channels, all those choices. And hidden somewhere among them, lurking, waiting for me . . . I know she's out there.

Maybe I can get my kids interested in reading.

HANDYMAN

Jeff Gelb

*R*ob Parvis overheard snippets of their conversation from three barstools down, and decided to move closer. As he edged past the other men and women seated around the bar, he was thankful for its no-smoking rule. It kept the bar from becoming too noisy or crowded, and seemed to bring in a better clientele. His kind of clientele: attractive, single, horny women.

He placed his Cabernet on the glass countertop, which was lit from beneath by neon, giving nearby patrons unusual flesh hues. The women he was spying on were both attractive. The shorter one was a dirty blonde with a tomato face, a cute smile, and small breasts, dressed in a conservative white silk blouse and drawstring pants. The taller one next to her was a brunette with a strong chinline, thin eyebrows, which he disliked, and who also, he noted, had small breasts, concealed under a leotard top tucked into blue jeans. He dubbed them the Itty Bitty Tittie Committee as he leaned closer to hear more.

"I haven't been laid in years," the blonde complained. "But it's so scary out there these days, I just can't see picking up just any guy. I'm going crazy!"

"What do you mean, 'going'?" Her friend laughed.

The blonde ignored her. "You're better off married, Vickie, even if you're not getting along with Jack right now."

Her friend answered, something Rob couldn't hear, and then they both laughed. Rob waited till the laughter died down before handing the blonde his business card.

"What's this?" she asked, straining as she read it aloud by the room's dim light. "'The Handyman—Your Sexual Stand-In. No money, no diseases, no questions. One hundred percent satisfaction.'" She looked at the card for a moment and burst out laughing.

"You're kidding, right?" she managed between chuckles. "Sounds too good to be true."

"What an opening line!" the brunette said, clucking her tongue in obvious disapproval.

But the blonde extended her hand to him, noticing his perfectly polished nails. "Christine Kent," she announced. "You must have heard me complaining. I guess I should be embarrassed, but fuck it, it's just so depressing these days, you know?"

"Chris!" Vickie was surprised by her friend's candor with this stranger. "Either you two know each other, or you have had too much to drink, girl!"

"Neither," Rob said, making sure they had to lean in closer to him to catch his words. Baiting the hook, he thought, using his best radio voice to snag their attention. "I couldn't help overhearing Christine's complaint, and I decided to offer her my services."

Vickie shook her head. "Sorry, Charlie, we're not looking for a gigolo. Nice try, though."

Chris placed a hand on her friend's shoulder. "Speak for yourself," she said. "Your card says no money." She checked the card again and smiled as she spoke his name: "Rob, Is that false advertising?"

He smiled. "Not at all. You might just say I'm a good samaritan, offering my unique services to a select group of people like yourself."

Vickie interrupted. "Chris, you don't know anything about this guy."

"And he doesn't know anything about me."

"But he's not even your type," Vickie argued, in obvious disregard of Rob's presence. "You can do better."

Chris looked over the man who'd given her his business card. It was true he was no GQ model. His silk shirt was wrinkled, he wore his hair in an out-of-date ponytail (and it didn't look particularly clean, either), and there was some sort of stain on his jacket collar. Still, she'd slept with worse—an awfully long time ago, she reminded herself. Finally she answered her friend, "That's where you're wrong, Vickie. I think he's just my type."

Vickie grabbed Chris by the arm. "Will you excuse us a moment, Mr. Studley Do-Right?" Without awaiting his response, she grabbed her girlfriend brusquely and walked out of Jay's earshot. He watched them argue back and forth, straining in vain to hear their words. He smiled as Chris turned to him at one point and winked. Finally they returned to his side.

"So what's the catch, Rob?" Chris asked, exaggerating his name as if he were famous. "Do you have six months to live, a girlfriend you want to piss off, or are you a porn film producer?"

He shrugged. "None of the above. I just take the stress and games out of finding a partner for the night." He took a sip of his wine. "You'd be surprised how many women welcome my offer with relief. It's sex with no strings attached. Tomorrow morning, we've both gotten something we want and we say good-bye, satisfied and with no regrets."

"As easy as that?" she said as she reached for her glass of cranberry juice and vodka.

"As easy as that." He placed a hand over hers as she grabbed the tall glass like a cock. He squeezed her hand softly and she gasped. The physical contact was electric.

"I'm going to powder my nose," she said. "You get the car and I'll meet you outside."

As they entered his apartment, he turned on a light switch that controlled not only the lighting but his CD player, which immediately fired up a Yanni CD at a comfortable background level.

"Ooh—you do know the way to a woman's heart, don't you?" Christine cooed as she allowed herself to be led to his living room. Privately she winced; actually, she hated this sort of music. She glanced around at his apartment. It was drab, dark, and messy. It didn't look to her as if Rob Parvis had thought he was going to get lucky tonight.

"Remember the rules." She spoke to his back as he retrieved a bottle of white wine from his refrigerator. "You show me the doctor's note you claim to have. I want to know the person I'm climbing into the sack with isn't dangerous."

"Me too," he laughed as he showed her a computer printout of negative HIV blood test results that was indeed dated that day.

"Fair enough," she breathed as she allowed herself to stroke the front of his trousers.

"And you?" he asked.

She shrugged. "You'll have to take your chances. You heard me—I haven't been laid in years. It would be pretty hard to catch anything . . ." Her voice trailed off.

"Why no action?" he asked, massaging her shoulders and allowing his hands to drop lightly to her small breasts, where he traced her nipples through the silk blouse.

She whispered, "You said no questions, right? Let's just fuck."

He raised his hands in submission. "Right you are." He popped the cork out of the bottle. "It's a Vouvray—a sweet French wine. I find it tastes especially good when licked off nipples."

She shuddered at the statement. It had been so long . . .

He unbuttoned her blouse, tugged it out of her pants, and tossed it on the floor. He gently guided her backwards to his couch, where she sat back against a cushion and allowed him to dribble the golden liquid on her tiny areolas. Then he lowered his head and slowly licked at the dark bumps of flesh, encircling one with his mouth and then sucking at it until it had grown twice its normal size. Chris sighed with pleasure and grabbed at his crotch, where she felt a medium-sized bulge. She was momentarily disappointed he wasn't even bigger, but she enjoyed the feel of a man's dick in her hands nonetheless.

He continued to lick at her nipples, gently biting them and then sucking, kneading her breasts like bread dough beneath his strong fingers.

By this time she'd slipped his pants down to his knees and was pleased to find he was wearing no underwear. She pushed him off her and made him sit down so she could pay attention to his erection. She smiled as she noticed the precoital fluid dribbling down his throbbing dick; it looked as if he hadn't gotten any in a while either.

She decided to see if she could still throat; it was a talent she'd honed over the years, and she hoped she could still control her gag reflex. She took the head of his dick into her mouth and he squirmed in obvious pleasure. She kept going and was thrilled to discover that throating was almost like riding a bicycle. Once learned . . .

He bucked like a bronco as she tickled his balls with one hand while tweaking his nipples with the other, throating him at the same time. He was already gasping for air like a fish out of water, and before she knew it, she felt his hot come spurting down her throat. She sucked him bone-dry, disconnected her face from his genitals, and smiled at him, a thin line of come dribbling down her chin.

"Boy, you were eager for some beaver!" she chided playfully. But he turned away from her. "Hey, what's wrong?" she asked.

"I . . . didn't expect to come so fast. Sorry."

"I thought you said you got sex all the time. Maybe your card trick doesn't work so well after all."

He turned back to face her and she noticed his face was red. Studley Do-Right was embarrassed, she thought with amusement.

"It's not that, it's just . . . well, I didn't get to—you know—get you off."

"So who's stopping you?" She pulled the drawstring and her pants slid noiselessly to the floor. She stepped out of them and glared at him defiantly, allowing him to notice that she too had neglected to wear underwear that evening.

He gasped at her bare beauty and at his first-ever view of shaved pussy. He approached her slowly, trembling slightly, and finally allowed his hand to caress the soft mound of skin directly above her vagina, rubbing his hand up and down, exploring her innermost secrets with his eager fingers, slipping one, then two deep inside her. She stood as still as a statue as he finger-fucked her and he kissed her breasts while pushing his fingers in and out of her vagina. Then he replaced them with his again engorged dick.

She moaned as he pushed into her and they started a love dance, still standing while moving slowly around the small living room, their every movement ecstasy to her supersensitive pussy. Despite her own preferences, she felt herself on the verge of coming. All too soon she was forced to allow herself to experience a thunderous orgasm while still standing and locked in his sexual embrace. The climax was better than she remembered, and a thousand times better than the orgasms she'd given herself over the years as she waited for the chance to fuck a man again.

Finally her orgasm ended and she disengaged from him and fell back on the couch, catching her breath. He lay down next to her. She looked around lazily until her eyes spotted an ashtray.

"Oh God, you smoke! I'd *kill* for a cigarette right now."

"No problem," Rob said, reaching to open a drawer of an end table next to the couch. He sifted through it and brought out a pack of Winstons, displacing a book from the drawer. They both watched it fall to the floor.

"Oh shit." Rob blanched as Chris read the title aloud.

"'How to Seduce Women: A Failsafe Guide for

Bachelors.'" She reached down for the book, but Rob caught her arm.

"Please," he said, obvious strain in his voice. "Don't."

"Is it yours? Let me see it." She shrugged his hand off her arm with surprising strength and flipped through the book's pages.

"Oh, this is great," she said sarcastically. "This is priceless." She held the book up for him to see the page featuring the "Handyman" business card. "I don't fucking believe it! You got all this from a fucking book!" She laughed at him. "Where's the page that tells you what wine to use on nipples? Or how to do it standing up?" She threw the book down in disgust.

"I've been had," she said as she stood up and gathered her clothing. "Well, it serves me right, I guess, for being so anxious myself. I mean, I just got out today, so you can imagine how horny I was after eight years in the asylum."

Rob was quickly putting on his pants to hide an erection that had faded with embarrassment down to a dick that was smaller than he could remember having since he was in grade school. "What . . . what did you say? What do you mean?"

She took a deep breath of smoke into her lungs, held it for a second, and exhaled in his face. "Eight years—that's a long time to waste away. But they were convinced I was crazy for killing my boyfriend Rob." She blinked twice. "What did you say your name was?"

"R . . . Rob."

"Rob. Well. Of course." She thought about that for a moment, chuckled to herself, and then continued: "My Rob, he was a liar too. Told me he wasn't having an affair when he was actually fucking his secretary.

Are you fucking your secretary too, Rob? Did you use the book on her too, Rob? I can't stand liars, Rob."

Slowly she placed the pack of cigarettes in her purse. "Thanks for these, Rob. You remember what I said before?"

Stunned that she'd found him out, stunned by everything she'd said, he could barely concentrate on her words, as she repeated softly, "I said I'd kill for a cigarette."

As she removed the long, razor-sharp knife from her purse, she stepped menacingly toward Rob Parvis, once a lonely, desperate bachelor, soon to be deceased.

Christine Kent and Vickie Wayne sat at the bar, sipping cranberry juice and vodkas. Chris spoke first: "First round's on me because you won the bet. How'd you know I'd kill him?"

Vickie shrugged. "It doesn't take a brain surgeon. As soon as you said his name, I knew he was a goner. I just hope you cleaned up after yourself."

"The place is spotless, I promise."

Vickie shook her head. "You really are crazy, Chris."

"That's what they said at the asylum, till I convinced them otherwise. Took eight years, though. Needless to say, I'm still horny."

As if on cue, a short, overweight, sweaty man with thick glasses in a dirty Grateful Dead T-shirt walked up to them, glass of beer in one hand, business card in the other. He handed the card to Chris.

"Oh shit," Vickie said as her friend read aloud: " 'The Handyman.' "

The man nodded eagerly. "That's me. I couldn't help hearing you mention how horny you are."

Christine put up a hand to silence him. "Well . . . Matt," she said, exaggerating his name, "I'm sorry, but I've already read that book."

She laughed as she dropped the card into his glass of beer and turned away from the man. A look of disappointment spread across his face.

"Shit," he cursed. "I just can't get lucky."

Vickie eyed him for several seconds before responding, "Mister, you don't know just how lucky you are."

AIRHEAD

Michael Newton

*T*ar baby don't say nothin'.

Where the hell did that *come from?*

It took a minute, Larry Gaskins thinking hard, before he got it. Uncle Rastus. No, that wasn't right, but it was close.

Forget it. He had work to do.

The thing that made him think of Uncle What's-his-name just then was Sucky Suzee. Not that she was black or anything. To hell with *that* noise. But you couldn't beat her when it came to keeping secrets. She was Larry's favorite kind of woman when it came to noise, in fact. Bitch never said a word.

Of course, she couldn't, really, since she had no tongue, no vocal cords, no lungs.

At that, she was a bargain. Fifty-seven ninety-five, plus tax, and Larry never had to feed her, never had to buy her drinks or clothes or gifts or any other fucking thing.

Because the lady was inflatable.

She wasn't absolutely lifelike, granted, but the industry had come a long way since the fifties, when you paid your ten or fifteen dollars for a blow-up doll that looked like Howdy Doody, with the tits and features simply painted on, no hair and precious little satisfaction for your money.

Sucky Suzee measured five foot six when Larry stood her up, and she had blond hair cut to shoulder length. He favored blondes, and if the hair was artificial, what the hell could anyone expect?

She had a nose, eyelashes, curly pubic hair, and perky little tits with half-inch nipples. Anything beyond a mouthful's wasted, as the old man used to say, and Larry liked them slim, young, blond.

For dress rehearsals, he decked Suzee out in sexy underwear he bought from catalogs. The size had been a problem, to begin with, but it helped that he had samples, pilfered over time on visits to the Laundromat. The blouse and skirt were strictly K Mart, chosen for economy instead of style.

The only reason that he dressed her up at all, in fact, was so that he could practice for the main event, when clothes got in the way.

He used a rubber knife for their rehearsals, to avoid the risk of damaging his silent partner. Hold the floppy blade against her throat with one hand, while he cranked the left arm up between her shoulder blades. She had no joints per se, and you could twist the limbs at crazy angles, but he tried to keep it reasonable. Nothing that would knock her out or cripple her right off, if she were flesh and blood.

It got a little awkward sometimes, since he only had two hands and liked to grab her from behind. The knife helped, though, and Larry practiced speaking with authority.

"Don't fight me, bitch! You scream or try to get away, I'll cut you!"

Make believe she whispers *No, please don't,* all panicky and teary-eyed, the way he likes it.

Larry didn't fuck around with buttons. Rip the blouse and feel around a little bit, enjoying silk against her skin before he yanked the fancy bra up to expose her tits and pinch the nipples. Foreplay. Use the knees to force her legs apart and ruck the skirt up on her ass. No panties on a trial run, since he doesn't like to shred the good stuff, but he still goes through the motions. Snatch and grab. An awkward moment with his zipper, but he always manages to get it with a little fumbling, bring the one-eyed monster out to play.

The rest of the scenario is flexible. Sometimes he nails her in the ass, bent double, with her head down on the floor. He rolls her over sometimes, so that he can watch her face while he is fucking her. Sometimes he forces Suzee to her knees and lets her live up to her name. The blade beneath her chin reminds her not to bite.

The only drawback with a mute is that she can't provide the sound effects that Larry craves: the sobbing, pleading, whimpering, that go with fear and pain. No matter. He makes up for the deficiency by talking to her while he works.

"You love it, don't you, bitch? I know you love it. Let me hear you say it. *Say it!*"

Stiffening, Larry shoots his load in Suzee's ass, cunt, throat, whatever. Sweating with his eyes closed. Winding down. Sometimes he takes her through the paces more than once, imagining that he has time to change positions. You can never really tell, before the Main Event.

When he is done, each time, he has to practice killing her, a slash across the throat.

No witness means no case.

Their sessions always leave him slumped across his conquest, whipped and sucking wind. It takes a while for the sensations raging through his mind and body to recede, like murky water swirling down a drain. It still needs work, the bounce-back, just in case he has to flee in haste.

No problem. He has time.

The Main Event would only fly when Larry felt that he was ready. In the meantime, there was Sucky Suzee. They would whip each other into shape.

Relaxing as he helps his playmate back onto the bed.

"You know you love it."

Watching Karen is his second favorite pastime. Five weeks into the surveillance, he can spot her from a distance, on a crowded sidewalk, by the way she squares her shoulders, flicks her hair back, swings her hips with each long-legged stride. If struck blind on the spot, he reckons he could track her by her scent.

Obsession. The perfume, that is.

Her hair is different from the style she wore in court, more casual, a bit provocative. She doesn't have the haunted look that he remembers from the trial. More self-assurance these days, thinking she's invincible.

But Larry means to wipe that smug look off her face, and soon.

She had been lucky number seven, and the first to offer serious resistance. Screaming. Kicking. Scratching. Putting him to flight. The pigs came out of nowhere, cruising on routine patrol. He was about to ditch the ski mask when they pinned him with a spotlight, ordered him to freeze.

And Larry froze, all right. It didn't stop the older of the two pigs wading into him with fists and boots, a macho cowboy, landing half a dozen solid blows before his partner pulled him off.

It was enough.

The DA talked about an airtight case, but that was for the cameras. Karen never saw his face, and in the darkness, the excitement, she could not describe his clothes. It was a winter night, and cold: the ski mask easily explained. The beating muddled any references to scratches on his face. On top of everything, the pigs forgot to read him his Miranda rights.

Case closed, but not forgotten. Larry learned from his mistakes. Stay clear of parking lots. Immobilize the bitch, first thing. No witness means no case.

Sweet Karen is the one who got away . . . but not this time.

No fucking way.

She works on Wilshire, at a travel agency, concocting getaways and dream vacations for a clientele that is predominantly forty-plus and upper middle class. Nine-hour days, with lunch from noon to one o'clock. Two days a week, on average, Karen skips the meal to use her free time window-shopping, anywhere within a half-mile radius of work.

Today, a Friday afternoon, is one of those. He spots her coming out. The clinging slacks and frilly blouse are businesslike, yet somehow still provocative. The scary part, for Gaskins, comes when Karen looks straight at him, blue eyes burning into his from less than thirty feet away.

She made me, Jesus!

No. She breaks the contact, heading south, without

a backward glance. It was a fluke. No recognition in her eyes . . . or was there?

Larry gives her half a block before he falls in step behind her. Karen never seems to hit the same shop twice, and that suits Larry fine. He treats it as an education, concentrating on his quarry, working hard to shake the sense that she has spotted him.

The witchy shop is a surprise, no place that he has seen her go before. Two blocks off Wilshire, tucked between a tattoo parlor and a pawnshop, with assorted books and jewelry in the window. Larry watches from across the street, as best he can, with sun glare on the window. Glimpses Karen talking to an aging hippie type behind the counter, plain-Jane in a tie-dyed peasant blouse. He can't hear what they're saying, natch, but Karen makes a purchase, giving up a few dead presidents. Receives some object in return and tucks it in her purse.

Emerging from the shop, she hesitates once more and turns to look across the chrome-bright traffic flow, direct at Larry. Blue eyes fixed upon him like the laser sighting mechanism of a Hellfire missile.

Shit!

He turns away, the sudden panic burning in his chest like Texas chili with an extra shot of jalapeño. Twice, that is, in half an hour, and he has to watch his ass from this point on. If Karen doesn't know he's dogging her by now, a third time will erase all doubt.

Goldfinger speaks: "We have a saying in Chicago, Mr. Bond. The first time is coincidence; the second time is happenstance; the third time, it's enemy action."

Fucking-A.

Cheeks flaming, Larry walks due east, away from Wilshire and the travel agency. Too risky, trailing

Karen back to work. She doesn't have a thing to tell the pigs, so far, but he cannot afford to have her on alert.

Surprise is half the battle. Half the fun.

Anxiety propels him toward his car, the long way round. Frustration broods beside him, in the shotgun seat.

No sweat.

He has the Little Lady waiting for him, back at home.

"You love it, don't you, bitch? I know you love it. Let me hear you say it. *Say it!*"

Pumping into Suzee's rubber rectum like some kind of robot, piston-powered. Feeling Karen. Listening to Karen cry for mercy. Shooting deep inside her, just because she begged him not to.

Later, he can always make her lick him clean.

The handcuffs are a new refinement, $16.95 at The Survival Store, on Sunset. They are loose on Suzee's wrists until he clamps them down, and cold against his belly as he reams her ass. It adds a little something extra to the dress rehearsal, this time.

Better.

He can start to work on new positions, for the main event. With both hands free, all kinds of new refinements come to mind.

The very thought of Karen, helpless, stiffens Larry's cock. Say no to *this,* you snotty cunt. Just try.

He rolls her over, stubby nipples pointed at the ceiling. Blue eyes staring up at him. A captive audience.

"You love it, don't you, bitch?" He smiles. "Cat got your tongue? Okay. We got all night."

* * *

The old apartment house stands one block south of Pico, sturdy willows ranked outside the six-foot wall of cinder blocks that rings the parking lot. A nod to privacy. No sweat for Larry, scrambling up the middle tree of five with leather gloves on, cheap binoculars around his neck. The now familiar perch is waiting for him, on a level with the second floor.

The drapes are open wide, as usual. No sign of Karen on the first sweep, but the lights are on, and Larry knows the bitch is home. He cannot see inside her bedroom, but the broad glass sliding doors provide a clear view of her living room and tiny kitchen. The binoculars put Larry right inside there, like a cockroach on the wall. With any luck, he may catch Karen in her bra and panties, like the last time, wandering around the flat, oblivious to prying eyes.

A private show.

He spends a moment checking out the empty rooms and taking inventory. On his right, directly opposite the couch, a Sony Trinitron, the twenty-six-inch console model. Copper knickknacks hanging on the kitchen walls. Above the couch, a reproduction of a painting Larry knows he ought to recognize by name, but doesn't.

Something different, on the glass-topped coffee table, wrapped in plain brown paper, resting on a saucer flanked by stubby candles. Are they black or navy blue? No telling, from a distance, and he doesn't really give a shit. The knife seems out of place, though. Something from the kitchen, maybe, six or seven inches long.

He is considering the items, frowning to himself, when Karen makes her entrance from the hallway on his left. She wears a plain white terry robe, hair tumbling loose around her shoulders. Getting ready for the shower, maybe, since her hair is dry, feet bare of slippers.

Larry curses when she kills the kitchen light and blacks out the apartment. Wasted time and effort, if she turns in now, without a single glimpse of flesh.

But no.

He tracks her silhouette as Karen moves into the living room and kneels before the coffee table, with her back to the TV. The bright flare of a match as she leans forward, lights the candles. Soft light on her profile, like a trick shot from the movies.

Larry feels his Jockey shorts begin to shrink as Karen slips the robe off, dropping it behind her. Candlelight and shadow on her perfect body, breasts defying gravity, strong muscles rippling on her flank and thigh each time she moves.

He finds it difficult to focus on her hands as Karen reaches for the parcel on the coffee table, peels the wrapping back, distributing the contents. Nothing he can recognize, offhand: some kind of gnarly root thing; reddish powder in a tiny glassine envelope; a six-inch strip of something that resembles jerky. Karen sprinkles powder in the saucer, spreads it with her fingertips, then slices little flakes of root and jerky into it. The knife looks sharp.

She proves it with a move that startles Larry, opening her left palm with the blade. She splays her hand above the saucer, dribbling crimson. Stirs it with her index finger.

What the hell?

Her lips are moving, Larry wishing there were some way he could figure out what she is saying. Screw it. Focus on the tits and ass, his boner hot and cramped inside his jeans.

She makes it easy for him, standing up and turning

toward the balcony. He nearly creams, the glasses zooming on her nipples, dropping to her pubic thatch. An honest blonde.

Reluctantly he pans back up to Karen's face and freezes when he finds her staring back at him.

Impossible.

He's covered by the darkness and the drooping willow boughs. No way the bitch can see him from her living room. And yet . . .

He feels his stomach churning as she brings the left hand up and aims her index finger, pointing at him like a pistol. One long stride to reach the window, and she presses her open palm against the glass. A smear of blood obscures her face, but not before he sees the lips turn upward in a mocking smile.

It's easy, climbing down, when you let gravity take over. Touchdown is a problem, but it doesn't feel like anything is broken, as he scrambles to his feet. Disoriented for a second, Larry gets his bearings, takes off running in the dark.

A half mile south of the apartment complex, he remembers that he has to go back for his car.

Humiliation rarely makes it as an aphrodisiac, but rage gets Larry off just fine. He's steaming by the time he makes it home, drags Sucky Suzee from the closet. Fractured images of Karen standing naked in her living room, his own embarrassing retreat, are jumbled in his brain, a grim kaleidoscope.

He takes it out on Suzee, slapping her a few times, dragging her behind him, toward the bed. She offers no resistance as he drops her facedown on the mattress, reaching for the handcuffs on his nightstand. Kneeling on the rumpled, unwashed sheets, he makes a grab to bring the left arm up behind her back.

And Larry's mind could never really grasp what happened next. Some kind of a delayed reaction to the fall, the way his bedroom seemed to tilt and blur, his balance going. For a second there, it felt like Suzee rolled away from him and grabbed *his* wrist, for Christ's sake, using leverage like some kind of fucking judo expert, so that Larry hurtled forward and his skull collided with the headboard.

Coming out of it, he feels like puking up the two Big Macs he scarfed for supper, but he swallows hard to keep them down. Another moment, riding out the nausea and recognizing where he is. Same shitty bedroom, lumpy pillow underneath his head, the nightstand inches from his nose. Dull pain throbs from its epicenter, at the crown of Larry's head.

The worst of it comes home when Larry tries to rise. His arms are pinned behind him, somehow, and it takes another moment for his fuzzy brain to register the bite of metal at his wrists.

The fucking handcuffs.

There is someone in the room, behind him. He can hear the prowler moving, whisper-steps like corduroy, or chunky thighs in pantyhose.

"Who's that?"

No answer, but the prowler hesitates a moment, somewhere near the foot of Larry's bed. More whisper-steps, in the direction of the bathroom, coming back for Larry just when the suspense is getting to him.

"We can work this out," he says. "You want the stereo, it's yours. Hell, take the TV and the fucking VCR. No problem."

Whisper-steps around the bedside, coming closer.

"Hey, I got my eyes closed." Conscious of the tremor in his voice, and hating it. "I don't know who you are, and I don't *wanna* know, okay? Just take the shit and go."

A tapping on the nightstand makes him crack one eyelid, coming into focus on a wooden stick. Some kind of *handle*. Is it . . . ? Sure, the fucking toilet plunger from his bathroom. Fingers wrapped around it, near the suction cup.

The fingers look familiar.

Both eyes now. He tracks the wrist, arm, shoulder. Curve of naked breast and hip. Blond pubic hair. Smooth rubber thighs.

"What *is* this shit?"

It comes to Larry that the prowler is manipulating Suzee like a puppet, using her to taunt him. Crazy fucker. When he cranks his head around, though, looking for the stranger's hands, he can't find any. Suzee standing on her own, for Christ's sake, no visible means of support.

Concussion, Larry tells himself. *I'm losing it.*

The whisper-steps resume as Suzee backs away from him and takes the plunger with her. Gentle pressure as she crawls up on the bed, beside him.

No.

Some kind of fucking nightmare, as the rubber hands slide underneath him, fumbling at his belt and zipper. Cool air on his buttocks, as the jeans and shorts inch down his thighs. Somehow, impossibly, her touch is warm against his ass.

"You love it, don't you, Larry?" Sounding breathless, like a dream voice in his head. "I know you love it. Let me hear you say it."

Right. So this is what it feels like when you lose your mind.

The plunger handle brings him back, a cautious

probe at first, then piercing, burning, filling him. He strains against it, wriggling like an earthworm on a fishhook, feels the scream exploding from his throat before the pillow smothers it.

Same whisper in his ear: "Cat got your tongue? Okay. We got all night."

FIVE SECONDS

J. L. Comeau

J ane Hodges sits knitting furiously behind the wheel of her parked rental sedan while a tedious patter of autumn rain pummels the slick gray streets of downtown Washington, D.C. Intermittently she looks up from the flashing aluminum needles to dart a glance toward the dripping Spector Building, a ten-story Gothic monstrosity where her current lover is employed.

Lover. A sweet tingle spreads through her chest, making her vaguely sick with its intensity. *Dorian.*

Jane's fingers tremble at the thought of him, and she has to put her knitting down before she botches the intricate cable pattern of the sweater she is making for her sister's child, Patricia. Jane is childless, and knows that a niece is as close as she will ever come to maternity. She adores children, and tries her best not to be jealous and bitter; truly, she does try.

Jane turns her thoughts back to her lover, her beautiful Dorian, and wonders what kind of child they might have produced together. A son, she imagines. A tall, rugged boy with wavy dark hair and a strong jawline, like his father. Blue velvet eyes, quick smile. Dorian's features, not hers. Never hers.

Jane would not want a child like herself, no. Not a child who would be teased and ridiculed, shunned by other children. No, no, no. She knows what that's like. In her bones, she knows what that's like.

She squints through the lenses of her thick trifocal glasses at the large black numerals of her Timex wristwatch. Almost noon. Almost time for her tryst, her assignation, her *affaire.* Within minutes Dorian will emerge from the revolving doors across the street and she will be with him. In just a little while, she will become his entire world.

Jane picks up her knitting and sets the needles chattering again, letting the pale beige wool skein out across her nimble fingers, wondering why it is that doomed romances are the most sublime. Her relationship with Dorian has been like a piecrust from the beginning: made to be broken. Dorian has a wife and three small children. Married. Jane lets the word surge and ebb through her mind and wonders at the complexities besetting a secretly passionate nature such as her own. To date, all of Jane's romances have involved married men exclusively.

She sighs, working a complicated turn of stitches that will form a cabled buttonhole when the next row is finished. Why married men? Is there some malfunction of her spirit, some wicked anomaly in her make-up, that draws her toward forbidden delights?

Her colorless cheeks twitch with sudden mirth. Wouldn't the rest of the female faculty at Dearborne Elementary School gasp with shock and disbelief if they knew how dowdy little Jane Hodges spends her lunch hours? Plain Jane. That's what they call her behind her back. That's what everyone has always called her for as long as she can remember. Plain Jane. Poor plain Jane, can't get a man, poor old spinster plain Jane, ha, ha. Wouldn't bed her, wouldn't wed her, plain old Jane.

How Jane burns to tell them, all those smugly symmetrical faces painted up like common whores, high-heeled sluts who think their wedding bands give them license to feel superior, to pity poor little Jane Hodges. Click-clack, click-clack, strolling the school hallways, their conversations muting to whispers as they pass Jane's classroom. Flitting glances inside and looking quickly away, never inviting Jane to join them in the teachers' lounge, never offering to include her in their impromptu faculty planning meetings.

If only they could imagine what passions stir in Jane's soul, what elaborate hungers beset her, drive her. If only they could know what illicit acts she is capable of performing to experience those blissful five seconds she craves so much.

One, two, three, four, five.

Jane's heart hammers against the delicate bulwark of her breastbone just thinking about it. It's been too long, too long, and now her desire has become a raging hunger that demands satisfaction. Now.

The slender shafts of Jane's knitting needles become a blur of motion and her breasts rise and fall, rise and fall, her breath quickening with the increasing tempo of her heartbeats. Again she twists her head toward the Spector Building. Men and women dressed in suits and coats have begun to stream out through the twin revolving doors and into the ebbing rainfall, popping open umbrellas or sheltering under newspapers as they take to the wet city sidewalks.

Where is Dorian? Jane squints through the misty

window glass, blinking. He's usually one of the first to exit, dark head bobbing as he strides along, chest forward, chin aloft.

Jane's thighs tremble as memories of their first meeting drift past her mind's eye. It was just three weeks ago that Dorian Webster came to Jane's classroom for a routine parent-teacher conference about his son, Erik. The moment Dorian entered the room and sat down in the chair opposite her desk, Jane knew they were going to be lovers, that Dorian would be the next married man to slake her forbidden thirsts. Her entire being had vibrated like a high-tension wire during their initial meeting; she hardly remembers what was discussed. By the time their conference ended, Jane was already in love with Dorian. She'd seen it in his blue velvet eyes: Soon, very soon, she would become his entire world.

It always happens like that, just like that. A word, a look, and she knows.

And now Dorian is her lover. How many others have there been? Thirty? Forty? The numbers blur with time, their faces growing indistinct once the trysts have been consummated and the affairs are over.

Jane giggles. How mischievous I've been, she thinks, both frightened and amused by her wholesale promiscuity. What would Daddy have thought?

Whore.

The word stabs into her consciousness, hurting, making her flinch. The voice that says the word is not her own. The voice adds: *The ones that like it are whores.*

Jane's knitting needles click in precision machine-gun bursts. I am not a whore, Daddy! I'm not, I'm not!

The ones that like it are whores.

I don't like it! I don't! Stop, Daddy, please stop! You're hurting me!

Jane fights to push out the images crowding into her mind, but her efforts are useless, always useless when Daddy decides to batter his way into her head the way he used to batter his way into her body.

Jane drops her knitting into her lap. "Stop!" she shouts, ripping a handful of hair from her scalp. "Go away, don't touch me!"

But Daddy won't go away. Daddy won't ever go away completely. He always comes back. Even from his grave, he is still able to violate her mind whenever he pleases.

Jane begins to cry. "No, no, no," she burbles wetly.

Jane knows it is useless to beg. It never stops him. The scenes unwind, unstoppable:

Jane is fourteen years old, asleep in her bed. She is awakened by the weight of a hot, heavy body crushing her down into the mattress. It's Daddy. He's been drinking again. He always comes to her when he's been drinking. He fumbles with her nightgown, pulling it up over her face. He kisses her mouth through the thin shroud of cotton fabric.

"You're my whole world now," he mumbles drunkenly, sobbing. "Now that your mama's run off, you're my whole world."

"No, Daddy. Please," Jane begs, knowing it's useless to beg. "It hurts, Daddy. I don't like it."

"The ones that like it are whores," he grunts.

Jane clamps her eyes shut and bites down on her tongue, trying to bear the pain. She swore she wouldn't let it happen again. She made herself a promise to make it stop. But now she is afraid to act.

Jane forces the fear back, making her hand slide beneath the mattress where she's hidden a long, slender

Phillips screwdriver. Her fingers close around its cool plastic handle.

She hesitates, terrified by what she's about to do.

"You're my whole world, my whole world, my whole world," Daddy grunts, hurting her, hurting her.

A black tower of rage rises up in Jane, taking control of her, directing her actions. Her hand rises, dreamlike, silvery gleam of moonlight on the screwdriver's metal shaft gauzy through the fabric of her nightgown. And then—

Jane's head falls forward against the steering wheel as the vision releases her. It always ends at the same moment. She has never been able to recall the rest of it, although the therapists forced her to say she remembered before they allowed her to leave the hospital and go to live with her aunt Ellen. All she has ever been able to recall is the anger and the shame. And counting:

One, two, three, four, five.

Jane rests against the wheel for several moments, gasping for breath, trembling.

Suddenly she remembers where she is and why: *Dorian.*

She jerks her back straight and sits up in the passenger seat, rubbing a clear circle into the misty glass with her quaking fingers. It has stopped raining and the sidewalk outside the Spector Building throngs with lunchtime office workers.

A rattling moan rasps in Jane's parched throat. What if she's missed him? What if he's already gone?

"No," she groans, gathering up her knitting and stuffing it into her handbag. She can't bear the idea of missing this meeting with Dorian. Jane needs him too much. She needs to be Dorian's whole world, if only for a few stolen moments.

Shaking with mingled desire and terror, Jane steps out of her car, her sensible lace-up shoes touching wet pavement just as she catches sight of Dorian pushing through the revolving door.

Jane's breath snags in her throat at the sight of him, so tall and strong and handsome. Quickly she works her way through halted rush-hour traffic jamming the street, never letting her lover out of sight. Breathless and shivery as a schoolgirl, Jane watches Dorian's figure as it moves through the crowd. She angles recklessly between the stream of cars and trucks to place herself on the sidewalk just ahead of him as he heads down K Street. He will be so surprised to see her. She is going to be his whole world.

She centers herself on the sidewalk, waiting, just able to see the crown of Dorian's dark head bobbing up and down as he walks in her direction. Soon, soon.

Jane stands still, letting oncoming pedestrians stream around her, knowing they won't notice the mousy little woman in their midst. Nobody will notice her but Dorian, and that is just as she wishes it.

The moment has arrived. As Dorian surges toward her, Jane shifts to her left and positions herself directly in his path.

He stops, looking down at her with blue velvet eyes.

"Hello," Jane says breathlessly, smiling.

"Hi there," Dorian returns, studying her with a quizzical smile as if straining to remember something. His smile deepens, a flicker of recognition. "You're Erik's teacher, aren't you?"

"I'm your whole world," Jane whispers.

He leans toward Jane. "I beg your par—"

Jane does not give Dorian time to finish the thought. With a quicksilver movement, she plunges a glistening knitting needle deep into the tender tissue of Dorian's brain with one deft thrust into his right nostril. Just as quickly, she withdraws the instrument and replaces it in her handbag.

Dorian sways slightly on the pavement before her, still standing, a thin trickle of blood coursing down his chin, blue velvet eyes wide in a silent shriek that consumes Jane entirely, body and soul.

Jane has become Dorian's whole world.

Dorian staggers forward a step, placing a hand on Jane's shoulder to steady his failing legs. And then he falls, crumpling down onto the sidewalk, his eyes never leaving hers.

As she watches Dorian's final spasms, a volcanic orgasm wracks Jane's body, coming in a shock wave that roots her to the pavement, paralyzing her for the full count.

One, two, three, four, five.

And then it's over.

Jane turns away from her lover's lifeless body and passes through the gathering crowd of spectators like a ghost, transparent and unnoticed. As she wends her way across the street toward her rented car, she hears the first shouts of comprehension. A shrill scream. Someone is calling for an ambulance.

Jane eases the car out into traffic and drives away. She glances at her watch and smiles, realizing she'll have time to stop at the bakery for cupcakes on her way back to school.

Won't the children be surprised?

SYMPATHY CALL

Michael Garrett

The impoverished appearance of his hometown came as no surprise to Mark Morgan. It had been years since his last visit, and hell, the whole fuckin' world was going down the toilet, so why should his boyhood stomping grounds be spared? Scanning the streets he'd roamed as a child, he found even long-standing landmarks barely recognizable. The neighborhood school looked like an abandoned prison, deserted and vandalized, scarred by broken windows and graffiti. Several houses along the encircling block had been condemned. But just ahead, with bright curtained windows, unretrieved mail spilling from the mailbox, and unopened newspapers scattered across the porch, was *her* house, or at least the house where she'd lived as a kid. An inhabitable house seemed oddly out of place despite its own deteriorated condition. The roof needed patching, the shutters were rotten, and the lawn and shrubbery were ragged and neglected. It was the same place, though, he was sure.

Mark sighed. Tracking Beth over the years hadn't

been easy. She'd married, changed her name, divorced, then remarried, changed her name again. Though he and Beth had been apart for almost twenty-five years, Mark had constantly monitored her from a distance, watching the latest developments in her life from afar in hope that still another divorce might create an opportunity for reunion between the two of them. That's why he'd checked the new telephone directory year after year to make sure her parents were still listed. Through them, he'd be able to locate Beth if her name changed again, or if she moved away without his knowledge.

Mark exhaled and slowly shook his head, surprised that her folks had never moved to the suburbs. Couldn't Beth have offered them financial help? Of course, she would have—if she hadn't married an asshole.

Make that *two* assholes.

Mark, I'm so happy. I've never gone steady before.

Mark sat in silence, her voice drifting through his mind. He cut the ignition of his Jeep Cherokee, the engine ticking as it cooled, while he stared blankly at the house. A youthful image of Beth's face was branded in his memory, and Mark sat in frozen silence until the wind swept a wave of dead leaves across the pavement.

A feverish tingle seared his veins. Having repeatedly parked in this exact spot so long ago, Mark envisioned sitting behind the wheel of his '66 Mustang, his fingers tapping to the rhythm of the Beatles on the AM radio, his high school graduation tassel dangling from the rearview mirror. In his mind he saw her seated in the worn bucket seat beside him, her lips protruding in a playful pout in an attempt to have her way.

A nearby police siren jarred him back to reality.

Glancing around, Mark noted a rusted Chevy parked in the driveway against a ragged row of shrubbery that lined the side of the house. Despite the unretrieved mail and newspapers, there was still a chance that Beth's parents were at home.

As he exited the Jeep, Mark noted the sound of speeding automobiles on a nearby freeway that hadn't even existed when he and Beth dated. A squirrel scampered along the power lines overhead; a dog howled down the street. Mark shook his head, his stomach quivering as he tracked mud up the cracked walkway to the front porch. Anxiety grew with every step.

At the door he hesitated. He'd endured almost a quarter of a century of pain and loneliness since he'd last stood in this very spot and held her in his arms. He rubbed his eyes, recalling the soft texture of her lips, how thick and creamy they felt, and the smell of her freshly shampooed hair. He could almost feel the fur collar of her coat tickle his neck as they kissed good night, the memories so intense, it was as if it had been only yesterday. Though they'd lived separate lives, she had always been with him in spirit.

Always.

Not tonight, Mark. It's . . . my time of the month.

Mark finally punched the doorbell, imagining the scent of her perfume as he scrubbed his shoes across the welcome mat. He shifted nervously on his feet and swallowed hard as the glass panes of the front door vibrated from movement inside. What if her parents didn't understand? What if they sent him away?

Two dusty white blades of the venetian blinds separated and an elderly bloodshot eye peeked through, rolling from side to side in a cautious examination of the surroundings. When the blinds were finally released, the door creaked open a couple of inches and the wrinkled face of Beth's mother peered out over a dime-store security chain.

"Yes?" she said, her voice weak and suspicious.

Mark cleared his throat. "Mrs. Arvin, you may not remember me, but I'm Mark Morgan. I was one of Beth's first boyfriends."

The old woman stared at him questioningly until her grim expression finally softened. "Mark? Hmmm. I'm sorry, but it's been a long time." She glanced over her shoulder and called out into the darkened recesses of the house, "Ralph, come in here. One of Beth's friends stopped by." She unlatched the chain and swung the door open. "Come on in," she invited Mark.

We can't do it if you don't wear protection.

The living room was gloomy and not at all as he remembered. But then, he and Beth had spent as little time here as possible, preferring the privacy of his parents' home when they were away or the seclusion of a remote lovers' lane for their many lovemaking sessions.

"Please sit down," Mrs. Arvin offered, motioning toward the sofa. Mark hesitated, then finally sat. Floral arrangements decorated the mantel, clashing with the drab atmosphere of the otherwise dismal room. Unopened envelopes lay scattered on the coffee table before him.

Mr. Arvin hobbled into the room, impaired by a bad limp, and made no effort to shake hands or acknowledge Mark's presence. A faraway look controlled the elderly man's eyes.

Mark examined the saddened faces of Beth's parents as they stared back at him from a rocker and a straight-back chair near the fireplace. "I was at the funeral," he said softly. "I wanted to talk to you then, but it wasn't the right place. I wanted to see the house again, and remember the way she was." Mrs. Arvin sniffled; her husband hawked a hoarse cough.

I need to date other guys. You're the only boyfriend I've ever had.

"It's all been . . . such a shock," she muttered.

Mark shifted on the sofa and exhaled deeply. "You lost her a couple of weeks ago, but for me it's been a lifetime," he said. "I've never hurt so badly in all my life as the day we broke up." Tears leaked from his eyes.

Mr. Arvin mumbled something incoherently as Mark continued. "She's never been far from my thoughts, though." He stopped to sniffle and clear his throat. "That's why I'm here. I want to know what I missed in her life after we broke up. She never confided in me. She didn't understand how much she meant to me." He paused for a deep breath. "If you don't mind, I'd like to see some photos, and swap stories about her with you. It could be sort of like a private memorial service, just between the three of us. One last tribute to her. I owe her at least that much."

Mrs. Arvin sniffled again. "Well . . ." she began, "it's only been a week since . . . *the funeral . . .*"

"I understand," he whispered, a lingering moment of tension electrifying the atmosphere, "but I've got to pay homage to her in some way. After all we've been through, I think she'd expect it." Mr. Arvin finally stood and ambled feebly to his wife's side.

"We've got to face up to it, Evelyn," he said. "It don't do no good to hide our feelings." He reached toward a nearby bookcase and removed a photo album, then laid it to rest atop the unopened envelopes on the coffee table in front of Mark. "She was our baby," he mumbled in a gruff voice. "Always will be."

Mark leaned over and flipped open the cover. Mrs. Arvin sat stiffly in her chair, finally muttering, "I can't look at the pictures yet. I'm just not ready."

But already selfishly engrossed in the photographs, Mark didn't hear her as he scanned the pages, observing the maturation of a woman with whom he'd always been so desperately in love. Yet these photos spanned a period of her life that began as many as ten or fifteen years after their breakup. "Do you have any photos when she was younger?" he asked.

Without a response Mr. Arvin returned to the bookcase and searched for an older, more worn photo album. Mark tried not to show his excitement.

In the opening pages Beth was younger than when he'd first known her. In one faded photo she stood arm in arm with a friend at the beach, her bust not yet fully developed, but the features of her face becoming more like those of a young woman. He flipped ahead a couple of pages and stared face-to-face with the girl who had dominated his life from afar, whose memory had haunted him endlessly. He felt himself shiver, his reaction so intense.

Please don't call me anymore. I want you to leave me alone.

"She's in high school there," Mr. Arvin said, pointing to a picture at the top of the page. "That's the day she was tapped for the National Honor Society."

But Mark paid no attention, his eyes fixed instead on a photograph mounted at the lower corner of the adjacent page, a snapshot that actually included an image of himself as a teenager. It was a group picture at a family reunion he had long since forgotten. But there he was, in clear view, holding hands with Beth in the forefront, her brother and sister also accompanied by dates, with a stream of her relatives in the background.

"She was so beautiful," Mark mumbled with a hint of a sob, perspiration beading across his forehead, "but she never had a mind of her own. She let her friends affect her too much." Page by page he watched her mature, beyond high school and college graduation, through marriage and her childbearing years. "Her daughter is beautiful," Mark exclaimed as he examined a photo of a cute four-year-old in curls. "She has a lot of Beth's features."

Mr. Arvin cleared his throat. "Angie's in college now. She was the Homecoming Queen at Auburn last year."

A tinge of jealousy gripped Mark at the sight of a photo of Beth hugging her husband. "Angie doesn't resemble her father at all," he remarked as if he didn't know.

"Oh, that's not Angie's father." Mrs. Arvin finally spoke up from across the room. "Beth divorced Angie's dad. When she remarried, she wanted all the pictures of Charlie taken out."

Mark nodded, his hatred for the man in the photograph rekindled. A snarl registered in his expression as he scolded, "He should have known how dangerous it would be for Beth to drive those dark roads at night. He should've taken better care of her."

You've got to leave me alone! You need to get on with your life!

Mr. Arvin cleared his throat. "Well, now," he said,

"we shouldn't be blaming Tom. He's suffered enough already."

"He didn't deserve her," Mark interrupted. "She could've done much better than him." A nervous tic twitched at his eyebrow.

Mark returned his attention to the family album, watching the love of his life age before his eyes like a flower blossoming in a timed-exposure nature film. Her brown hair showed signs of gray in the more recent shots, but her figure remained trim as she aged. He witnessed a changing culture through variations of her hair length and clothing styles, and in some photos he imagined indications of stress in her face. "I never got over her," he sighed, more to himself than to her parents. "I got married, even had a kid, but I could never get Beth out of my system." Tears seeped more freely from his eyes. "I met her for lunch once, years ago, even followed her sometimes just to watch her shop at the mall. After my divorce I tried to see her again, but she wouldn't even talk to me. This son of a bitch changed her. He fuckin' *ruined* her."

"Oh, my," Mrs. Arvin said in reaction to Mark's vulgar language.

He flipped back to the earlier photographs, to the way Beth looked when they were involved. Scanning the years was riveting, the hold she'd had on him throughout his life intensified now by the sight of her in the photographs. Mark's skin began to itch and burn; his pulse quickened. He focused on a torn Polaroid snapshot that had been repaired with transparent tape, a close-up of Beth and her dog. Feeling as if he might burst with emotion, he swallowed hard. He felt hot; he swallowed again and tasted bile in his throat.

Please, Mark. When will this end? Don't you have a life of your own?

"I ran over her dog, you know," Mark confessed without a hint of remorse.

Mr. Arvin scratched his head. "Well, don't worry yourself about that now, son. It was a long time ago, and accidents like that happen all the time."

Mark looked up at Mrs. Arvin, a glazed expression on his face. "No, I mean intentionally. She never knew. It was a couple of weeks after we broke up. I wanted her to see how it feels to lose something you love, so I waited till the mutt ran out into the street and I flattened him."

Mark! Is that you? Help me—please!

The elderly couple sat in stunned silence. Mark's grip on the photo album tightened until pages began to tear loose from the binder's metal rings. Mrs. Arvin rose from her rocker and eased to her husband's side, a look of fear and anger scarring her already stressed face. Her hands shook noticeably.

His mouth dry, his forehead beaded with sweat, Mark saw Beth's ghostly image appear in a vacant chair across the room. She was wearing a miniskirt and crossing her legs, her luminous form teasing him, daring him to say more. "I was the first to fuck her, too," Mark blurted, watching for a reaction from a woman who wasn't even there. "She wasn't my first, but I was hers. And she loved to fuck. Once she wanted to fuck while we were parked outside the airport and I wouldn't do it, just to show her who was in control, and she begged me—"

"Please," Mrs. Arvin interrupted. "This is uncalled for. I think you should leave now."

Mark raised his head, a blank expression on his

face, veins bulging from his neck. "But these are things you never knew about her, don't you see?"

"Son, we've heard enough already." Mr. Arvin finally spoke up more forcefully, but his voice still wavered. "You'd better go."

Mark didn't budge. "Can I have a couple of these pictures?" he asked.

"Of course not!" Mrs. Arvin interjected with a bitter tone. "Now, leave. *Please.*"

No, Mark, don't. I'm hurt.

Mark stood, his temples pulsing like the throat of a frog. He reached deep into a pocket and pulled out a tear-shaped gold pendant, clusters of dried dirt spilling onto the floor from the movement. "I'll give you this," he pleaded. "I'll trade this for one picture."

Mrs. Arvin's eyes widened in horror. "Oh, my God!" she gasped. "Ralph—*it's the pendant Beth wore when she was buried!*" Visibly shaken, she grabbed for the gold chain, but Mark thoughtlessly snatched it away.

"You don't understand," he growled as he wiped his forehead. "She's lost her looks. I need to remember her like she was."

Mr. Arvin nudged him toward the door, but Mark stood his ground. "Get away from here, you maniac!" Mr. Arvin raved. "You've robbed my daughter's grave!" Then he turned to his wife and stuttered, "C-c-call the p-p-police."

Mark's nostrils flared. "Sure! Go ahead!" he yelled. "You probably made her dump me in the first place. You never liked me anyway." Again he stopped for a deep breath. "Call the fuckin' cops!" he howled. "You don't give a shit about me." He stomped maddeningly around the room mumbling to himself, banging a knee hard against the coffee table without even reacting to the pain.

Mr. Arvin backed away, his eyes reflecting horror. Hyperventilating, Mark ripped several pages from the open photo album, rolled them up, and stuffed them into his dirty pocket, the photo of Beth and her husband slipping free and falling to the floor. Mark leaned over to pick it up. "I hate this son of a bitch," he growled through gritted teeth. "She wouldn't leave him, so I took her the only way I knew how."

Mrs. Arvin squeezed against her husband's side. *Stop it, Mark. That hurts!*

"It was no accident, you know," he admitted, the fear in their faces spurring him on. "I ran her off the road. There wasn't any traffic. Not a single car came by." His eyes widened; his cheeks tightened. "The son of a bitch shouldn't have built a house so far out in the woods."

"Oh, my God," Mr. Arvin moaned, a shudder in his voice. He clutched his chest and dropped to his knees as his wife cried hysterically at his side. The fear and revulsion in their faces reminded Mark of Beth's expression as she died, encouraging him to continue. *Don't, Mark. I'm hurt. I'm bleeding.*

"Even after her car hit the tree, she was still alive," he boasted. "I fucked her right there. For old times' sake, just like I used to do when she was bleeding for different reasons." His eyes were as big as walnuts, and he hardly blinked. "She was hurting too bad to resist. Hell, what did it matter?"

Despite increasingly trembling hands, Mark managed to light a cigarette. Mesmerized by the glow of the lighter's flame, he took a deep draw, then exhaled a plume of smoke. "I used a rubber, though. She always made me use a rubber. When we were through, she wouldn't stop screaming. She wasn't hurt bad enough to die, so I smashed her face into the steering wheel as hard as I could." He stopped for another draw that filtered through his teeth. "I had to save her from that asshole husband of hers. I had to spare her from any more misery." He stopped suddenly, cocking his head to one side as if straining to hear a voice.

Mr. Arvin fell forward, bracing himself against the floor with his hands and knees. Mrs. Arvin trembled.

Mark flashed a sickening grin. "It took years, but I finally got her back," he said. "We're together again." He dropped his cigarette butt and ground it into the carpet. "She's waiting in the car. Would you like to see her before we leave?"

Mrs. Arvin bolted for the kitchen, where a telephone hung on the wall. "Go ahead. Call the fuckin' cops," Mark yelled at her. Then he turned his attention to Mr. Arvin on the floor, smiling as the grieving man gasped for air. "That expression on your face. It looks so painful. Beth looked just like that before she died."

Finally Mark stood and stretched, gazing out a window at a shovel visible in the back of his Jeep. With the brilliance of lightning Beth's face reappeared and he imagined her sizzling touch. "I know you're waiting for me," he said to her. "I'll be right there." With a deep breath and a high-pitched maniacal whine he dug into his soiled pocket in search of his keys. "I enjoyed our visit. It's been a blast."

At the sound of movement from behind, Mark turned to stare down the wavering barrel of a shotgun.

Michael Garrett

The wrinkled, tear-streaked face of Mrs. Arvin stared from the other end of the unsteady barrel, her finger poised at the trigger. "We're still having a blast," she mumbled.

With an explosive roar and a blinding flash, memories of Beth, as well as half of Mark's brain, were gone.

OVEREATERS OMINOUS

Stephen R. George

*A*gatha's mouth watered as the waitress wheeled up the dessert tray. A slice of Black Forest torte in the center of the spread caught her eye. Dark chocolate, rich cream, ripe cherries. She licked her lips.

"Get it out of your head," Nick said.

Agatha glared at him and blushed. Nick grinned up at the waitress, a slim, dark-haired girl, whose narrow face was made-up too heavily, just the way he liked it. He looked like he wanted to make love to her.

Agatha looked quickly away. Make love? Nick didn't make love anymore. At least, not to her. Sex between them had degenerated into a biweekly suck 'n' fuck. That's what Nick called it. *Hey, Aggie, time for some suck 'n' fuck!* They hadn't made love, real love, in years. They'd been married six, and the love had ended after two. After the miscarriage, after the depression, after the eating, after the weight. Love had turned into *suck 'n' fuck.*

"I'll have that one," Nick said, pointing to the torte.

The waitress picked up the plate with fingers tipped in long, pink, press-on nails, and slid it in front of Nick, then turned to Agatha with a questioning look.

"Does she look like she needs anything?" Nick said. "I don't think so."

The waitress smiled nervously. Agatha could not speak. She couldn't even breathe. Her flush intensified. She felt as if her face were on fire.

"You give her something off that tray, she'll never get out of her chair, right, Aggie?"

Agatha shook her head slowly, mortified, trying to avoid the waitress's eyes. What was the girl waiting for? Why didn't she leave? Agatha turned away and saw in horror that diners at neighboring tables had turned to look. Nick's voice was loud and carried well. A middle-aged woman to Agatha's left smiled at her and shook her head, then leaned toward the man beside her and whispered something. The man, who looked so much like Agatha's father it hurt, smiled, nodded. Nearby, two slim, attractive women, both spooning luxurious-looking desserts into their mouths, looked over at Agatha with frowns.

"Are you sure?" the waitress said to Agatha.

"Doesn't she look sure?" Nick said. "She eats anything else, she won't even fit in the damned car."

Now the waitress chuckled. Agatha found her voice.

"I'll just have coffee, please."

"And make it black," Nick said. "She's sweet enough as it is. Isn't that right, honey?"

"Black is fine."

Nick forked a piece of torte into his mouth. Cream and cherry sauce caught at the corners of his lips. The tip of his tongue darted out to catch the stray cream. Agatha's mouth watered.

"What's wrong with you?" he said, swallowing.

"You humiliated me."

"Look at you. I can't humiliate you any more than you humiliate yourself."

"I want to go home."

"I'm not finished with my dessert, or my coffee."

"Everybody is staring at me. I want to go. Please, Nick."

"Staring at you?" He raised his voice, as if astonished, and looked around. "What the hell would anybody stare at? You're not all that much bigger than a bus."

Agatha lowered her face, fighting back tears. Nick sighed. He pushed away the remains of the torte. Half of it was still on the plate. He nudged it towards her.

"Go on, eat it."

"I don't want it."

"One more pound isn't going to make a difference, is it?"

Agatha lifted her face and glared at the torte. She could not help herself. Don't touch it, she said to herself. Don't demean yourself. Please, God, don't humiliate yourself further.

"I know you want it. What's stopping you?"

"Nick, don't."

"Jesus Christ. Take it!"

Heads turned again. Agatha's world shrank to the size of the plate in front of her.

"I hate you," she said softly, and did not know if she meant Nick or the torte.

"How many calories does hate burn?" Nick sneered.

"Don't, Nick."

"There should be a law. A guy should get to see what his wife is going to look like after six years. Save a lot of grief that way. I have to whiz. I'll be back in a minute. If you're going to eat that thing, do it while I'm gone. Watching you shovel it down would make me sick."

Nick stood and walked away. Agatha lowered her head, stared at the table, blushing so hard, it felt as if her skin were peeling. Everybody in the restaurant was staring at her. She could feel it.

"How are you doing?"

Agatha looked up, startled. One of the two slim, beautiful women who had been looking at her earlier was standing by the table. Her long blond hair was impeccably styled, hanging to her shoulders like a waterfall of gold. Her makeup, too, was perfect. Full lips, wide eyes, high cheekbones. Agatha felt gigantic, slothful.

"Pardon me?"

"Your husband was a bit of a brute."

Agatha blushed, tried to smile as if it had meant nothing.

"May I sit for a moment?"

Agatha wanted to say no, to make the woman leave, but something about her manner, the tone of her voice, breached her defenses and she nodded.

"Your name is Agatha? My name is Helen. Agatha, I'd like to give you something."

From her purse she removed an envelope and handed it to Agatha. Agatha took the envelope, looked up at Helen's eyes.

"What is it?"

"Open it."

Frowning, Agatha slipped her finger under the lip of the envelope and pulled it open. Inside she found a photograph. She took it out and looked at it. It was of a very large woman, larger even than Agatha herself, sitting on a sofa, smoking, arms bulging like gigantic sausages, neck a pale roll of fat, cheeks hanging in jowls. Something about the eyes was familiar.

"That's you," Agatha said in a small voice.

"Yes."

Agatha looked up at Helen. There could be no doubt that the person in the photograph was the person beside her. The eyes were identical. And yet, it *couldn't* be the same person.

"That was six months ago."

"No."

"Yes, Agatha."

Agatha's heart pounded. When Helen put her long-nailed hand on her arm, Agatha jumped, looked up into her eyes.

"The same thing can happen for you, if you want."

"How?"

Helen handed her a business card. On it was an address on Fourth Street South. One word. OVEREATERS.

"Diets don't work for me."

"This one will. Guaranteed, permanent results. *Permanent.* No cost to you unless it does."

Agatha shook her head.

"You want to lose the weight, don't you, Agatha?"

"Yes."

"Think of how you'll look. Think of how your husband will react. Think of what other men will think."

Other men.

"Tomorrow evening, seven o'clock. We can help you."

Agatha could only nod, mouth locked shut.

Helen stood. "See you tomorrow, then."

As she walked away she winked at Agatha and smiled warmly. Agatha felt a flutter in her stomach and looked down at her hands.

Nick came back, adjusting his belt.

"Guess you didn't want this," he said, pulling the torte towards him. "Too bad. It's delicious."

There were six women in the meeting room on the third floor, sitting in a circle around a glass table. On the table was a lump of what looked like fat. The women were staring at it, concentrating. Positive thinking, Agatha thought. They're making themselves hate the fat. The women, each and every one, were strikingly slim and beautiful. Agatha's legs felt weak as she came through the door. A mistake, she thought. A big, big mistake.

Worse than the women in the room were the pictures on the walls. Huge pictures, poster-sized, of gigantic, obese women. Bulges and rippling flesh filled every open space, eyes squeezed to slits by pockets of fat, ankles flowing like melted butter over sensible, ugly shoes, chins falling in cascades like fleshy necklaces.

Helen left the circle and came to the door. She took Agatha's hand.

"I'm so glad you could come," Helen said.

"I feel so . . . out of place."

"You won't for long. I promise you that."

Helen led Agatha down a narrow hallway to a small office. In the office, Helen sat behind the desk. Agatha took the seat by the door. Helen put her hands under her chin and studied Agatha speculatively.

"This is always the hardest part," she said.

Agatha smiled nervously.

"How badly do you want to lose weight?"

"I *do* want to, but I haven't had much luck."

"We don't depend on luck here, Agatha. Our program works. It has never failed."

Agatha stared at her. "Those pictures on the walls in the other room . . ."

"Us. Yes. Before the program."

Agatha shook her head.

"Do you want the same thing, Agatha?"

"Yes."

"What will you give for it?"

"Give?"

"Everything has a price, Agatha."

"What do you want?"

"Nick."

"Nick?"

"He's not much of a husband, is he?"

"He's *my* husband."

"When was the last time the two of you made love?"

Agatha started to answer, then closed her mouth. Their last suck 'n' fuck had been two weeks ago. They were due for another tonight. Nick had a biological clock that never failed. Two weeks, suck 'n' fuck. Two weeks, suck 'n' fuck. Exceptions made for his birthday, and their anniversary. Suck 'n' fuck bonuses, he called them. Two weeks . . .

"You deserve better," Helen said, as if Agatha's thoughts were obvious.

"You want him?"

"We need him. So do you."

"I don't understand."

"I'm asking you to give up Nick. That's all."

"What if Nick doesn't want to be given up?"

"I'm not asking Nick. I'm asking you."

Agatha thought of the pictures in the other room.

She thought of the women sitting in the circle. God, to be one of them.

"Last night, you said you hated him," Helen said. "I heard you, Agatha. Did you mean it?"

Hate him? Her husband? Suck 'n' fuck Nick Galas? The man who humiliated her every chance he got? The man whose eyes judged and condemned her every night, every morning, every hour? The man who made her wish that she had never been born?

"Yes," she said softly.

"All right. Will you give him up?"

"Yes."

"I'm glad. I knew we could help you."

"What do I have to do?"

"Something very easy. Something you like to do. Just eat."

"Eat?"

"Whatever you want. In whatever quantity you want. No restrictions. There's only one requirement. One mandatory meal. Something for you and Nick to share."

Helen opened her desk and pulled out a sheet of paper. On it was a photocopied recipe. Two additional ingredients had been penciled in.

"Oh, God," Agatha said as she read the recipe.

"Our program works, Agatha. Guaranteed."

Agatha could not speak. She crumpled the recipe and shoved it into her purse.

"We have another meeting next week. Will you be here?"

Agatha could not find her voice. Her stomach rolled and contracted. With a hand over her mouth she stood and fled the office.

* * *

Agatha was in the kitchen with a glass of wine when Nick got home. It was after 9:00 P.M. Late at the office, he said, but he stank of cigarette smoke and perfume. Agatha's stomach knotted. She tried to smile.

Nick went to the liquor cabinet and poured himself three fingers of Johnny Walker Red Label. He drank half of it in one swallow, and eyed her contemptuously. He took a deep breath.

"Suck 'n' fuck night," he said, as if he found the thought distasteful.

"I'm having my period."

"So what? Use your mouth." He finished his scotch. "I'll be in the bedroom."

He left her alone in the kitchen. She could hear him in the bedroom, whistling as he undressed. Tonight she'd do all the sucking. He avoided her vagina when she was having her period. He said the smell made him sick. Still, he wouldn't let that interrupt his schedule. Two weeks, suck 'n' fuck. Clockwork, baby.

She finished her wine. The alcohol made her throat contract. Her tongue felt thick. She wiped her mouth.

Standing at the mirror in the hallway, she applied lipstick. A lot of it. Ripe Plum, the label said. Dark and rich, the way Suck 'n' Fuck Nick Galas liked it.

He was lying on the bed, naked. His penis lay across his left thigh, a soft, thick rolling pin. He was the only man she had ever had, but she knew from pictures in magazines that he was well endowed.

She sat on the end of the bed and leaned over him. His eyes were closed. He never looked at her when they had sex, and she had long ago stopped wondering whom he was thinking about.

"Ease it in, baby," he said hoarsely. "Let me feel that tongue. Now, tighter. Yeah."

She worked him the way he liked it, the way he had taught her. His flesh thickened in her mouth, flattening her tongue. He slid to the back of her throat, crushing her uvula. She did not gag. He had taught her how to control the reflex. She made the motions of swallowing and his legs kicked beneath her.

"Yeah," he said. "Slowly, baby."

He tasted funny tonight. It took her a minute to figure out what it was. His skin had the sour, salty taste of vaginal secretion. He'd been with another woman.

She closed her eyes, fought back tears. It hurt. It still hurt. She made the tears stay inside. She'd given him up. He wasn't hers anymore.

When he climaxed, he withdrew so that only the smooth, throbbing head of his penis was in her mouth. His semen exploded across her tongue, around her teeth. She pushed it to the pockets of her cheeks, sucked until he was finished.

He groaned, pulled away, laughed softly.

"Better not swallow, baby," he said without looking at her. "Old Nicky's come is loaded with calories."

Before she was off the bed, he had rolled over and was settling himself comfortably. She went back to the kitchen, took a bowl from the cupboard, and spat his semen into it. The viscous expulsion, mixed with her saliva, pooled at the center of the bowl. She stared at it and shook her head.

Her mouth still tasted of another woman's sex. Even through Nick's semen.

He's not yours, she told herself. You gave him up. And the longer she waited, the harder this was going to get.

She squatted and pulled down her panties. The panty liner was thick with menstrual blood, some of it coagulated into strings of glistening mucous, so dark it was almost black. She unfastened the liner and put it on the counter by the bowl.

"I hate you, Nick," she said.

With a spoon, she wiped off some of her blood and dipped it into the bowl. Blood and semen coiled in a whirlpool of white and red. The smell was acrid enough to make her nose wrinkle.

From her purse she retrieved the recipe Helen had given her. Blueberry muffins. The kind of thing that Nick liked for breakfast. The blueberries would cover the taste of the two extra ingredients. And finding small, gelatinous lumps in blueberry muffins was natural.

Nick would never know.

Two days later, Agatha woke before the alarm buzzed. She inhaled deeply, feeling rested, energized. Nick slept on beside her, breathing deeply. He had come home late again last night, smelling of the same cigarettes, the same perfume.

He's not yours. It doesn't matter.

She got out of bed and went to the bathroom. After she washed her face, she stepped onto the scale. She stared down at the numbers and rubbed her eyes. She stepped off and stepped back on again. The pointer rested at 190 pounds.

No, that can't be, she thought. Not yet.

Yesterday morning she'd topped out at 210 pounds.

She stepped off and checked to make sure the pointer rested at zero. It did. She stepped back on: 190. Her heart raced.

She laughed softly and went back through to the bedroom. Nick was up, sitting on the edge of the bed.

"What are you smiling at?"

"I went down. I lost weight."

He looked at her, eyed her from head to foot, snorted. "Not so's you'd notice," he said.

He started to get dressed. When he pulled up his jeans, he swore. Agatha, sitting at the dresser, watched him. He pulled hard to get the top closed. His belly bulged over his belt.

"Fucking jeans have shrunk," he said, turning to her. "Look at this."

He kicked off the jeans and took another pair of pants from the closet. These, too, would not close properly.

"Shit," he said, and would not look at her.

His belly bulged like a white balloon full of water. He held it in both hands and looked down at it. It jiggled.

"Son of a bitch," he said. "I feel bloated. Do I look bloated to you?"

Agatha stared at his reflection in the mirror. She did not dare speak. She felt cold.

"Better stop making those damned muffins," he said. "I'm going to end up looking like you."

"All right," she said.

When, at last, he left the room, she looked at herself.

He's not yours, she told herself. It doesn't matter.

Slowly she began to put on some makeup.

"You are Nicholas's wife?" Dr. Binder eyed her with appreciative astonishment.

"Yes," Agatha said.

She caught a glimpse of her reflection in the glass door. She still had not grown accustomed to her new appearance. It all seemed like a dream. She had never looked this good in her life. Had never dreamed she could look this good.

"I'm afraid it's very bad news," he said.

He was young, slim, healthy. He was standing much closer to her than he should have been. She held his arm for support. Even her hand, long fingers tipped with red nails, did not look like her own. He guided her to a chair and sat her down. His office walls were bare but for his diplomas.

"Nicholas is suffering from an acute buildup of fatty deposits. It's an uncommon condition, but not unheard-of. It happens only to men, usually in their late thirties. I've done a little research. There have been only a couple of thousand recorded cases like Nicholas in the past twenty years."

"Is he going to get better?"

"At this stage, I can't say. This is not a well-known condition. It *can* be fatal. I'm not saying it will be in your husband's case, but I wanted to let you know."

"He was fine three weeks ago."

"What do you mean by fine?"

"Normal. He weighed about one eighty, I think. He always said that. That's what he weighed when we got married."

Dr. Binder almost laughed. "I think he was pulling your leg. He can't have weighed only a hundred eighty pounds just three weeks ago. That would mean he gained nearly two hundred pounds since then, and that's just not possible. His heart couldn't take a catastrophic change like that."

Agatha frowned but said nothing. She looked down at her hands.

"Can I see him?"

Binder frowned. "I should warn you. We performed

emergency liposuction on his throat last night because he was having trouble breathing. He may look a bit . . . well, I just wanted to warn you."

Binder led her down the hallway to Nick's room, then left her there. Nick lay on his back in the bed, covered by a blue sheet. His throat was swaddled in white bandages. His arms were on top of the sheet. The skin of his arms was shiny, taut, bulging. He seemed to have turned yellow in the past day or two. His breathing was slow, labored.

She went to the side of the bed. His nose wrinkled. He opened his eyes.

"Aggie."

She touched his hand. He felt hot and slippery. When she took her fingers away, they left an indentation in his skin that slowly filled again.

"The doctor says you're going to be okay."

"You're lying. He already told me."

"I'm sorry, Nick."

"No you're not. You did this to me."

"Don't be silly."

"How much weight have you lost? A hundred pounds? In three weeks? For every pound you lost, I put on two. Bitch."

He lifted his hand, as if to reach for her, and she stepped back. His hand hit the rail at the side of the bed. The impact split his skin, a thin fissure from between his pinky and ring finger to his wrist. He cried out as if he'd been burned, and yellow fluid spurted out of the cut, thick and sluggish. It slid down the side of the bed in lumps.

When Aggie turned around, Dr. Binder was there. She leaned into him.

"It's awful!"

Two nurses came in behind the doctor and went

immediately to Nick. Binder led Aggie out of the room.

"I'm sorry," he said, holding her close, supporting her. "If there's anything I can do, you'll let me know?"

His face was close to hers. The look in his eyes was not just sympathetic. There was something else there, barely hidden below the surface. My God, was that desire? He wanted to kiss her! Wanted to do more than kiss her. A lot more.

"I'll try to come by later to see Nick."

"Have a nurse call me when you're here. We'll see to it that Nick's kept comfortable."

"Thank you for your help."

"It's the least I can do," he said.

His hand lingered on her arm. She did not look back at him as she walked away.

"Everything has a price," Helen said carefully, looking at Agatha across the desk.

"He's going to die," Agatha said. "He's gained over two hundred pounds in three weeks. His heart can't take it. He can't breathe."

"You gave him up willingly, Agatha. You gave him to us."

"I didn't know what you were going to do to him."

"We helped you, that's all. Haven't we been successful?"

"But Nick . . . I know you're responsible."

"So you know. Are you happy?"

Agatha hesitated only a moment before answering. "Yes."

"I promised you that you would be. Now, take a month or two to enjoy yourself. Enjoy your new body. Take three months. You won't have to provide a man until September."

Agatha felt suddenly cold. "I don't understand, Helen."

"Everything balances, Agatha. What you lose, somebody else must gain."

Agatha stared at the other woman. "I won't bring anybody else."

"That's your choice. I felt the same way. Let me show you something."

Helen reached into the desk and pulled out a photograph. She handed it to Agatha. Agatha held it gingerly, studying it with dismay. It was Helen. Helen corpulent, bulging.

"I've seen this already."

"No, you haven't. This is the *after* shot. After I learned how I lost the weight the first time. Four months after, to be exact. I'd been married a month. My new love. I couldn't give him up."

Agatha stared at the photograph, horrified more by Helen's words than by the image. "It all came back," she said.

"And more. Pretty soon he didn't want me. In the end, I gave him up. What choice did I have?"

"Oh, God."

"Everything has a price, Agatha. We all pay it. Twice a year. It isn't much to ask. One man does the group for nearly a month. That gives you at least six months between. Sometimes even as long as a year. It can seem like a long time. A lifetime."

Agatha covered her face with a hand. "It's horrible."

"What's horrible is the way Nick treated you. That wasn't so long ago. Do you want to go back to that?"

"No."

"We all pay the price," Helen said, leaning close. "Look at yourself, Agatha. You're a new person."

Agatha left the office with Helen, followed her outside. A car was waiting.

"There's only one other thing we ask," Helen said. "That you bring us some interesting recipes. Something simple, something that will camouflage the required ingredients. All right?"

Agatha nodded, numb.

"You won't have trouble finding men, will you?" Helen said.

Agatha didn't answer.

Helen slid into the car. The man driving was named David. Helen had met him only a week ago, she'd said. Sweat glistened on his forehead. His fingers were plump worms. She kissed his cheek. David looked up at Agatha, smiled weakly. As the car pulled away, Helen waved.

Agatha thought of Dr. Binder. The way he had looked at her.

No, she wouldn't have trouble finding men.

GRUB-GIRL

Edward Lee

*L*emme guess. Head, right? Ten bucks a pop is what I charge. Cheap.

That your car there, the blue Metro?

Huh? You wanna *talk* a little first? Oh, okay, I get it. You don't know the full scoop about things. Okay, fine.

But . . . shit, look, see that fat guy in the red Escort right there by the Exxon station? He's one of my regulars. Hang here for ten, okay?

I'll be right back.

Okay, the full scoop on me? Sure. Shit, I got time. You've heard about the grubs, you must've. Probably just haven't heard that some of us are hookers. Not the kind of thing the state legislature wants getting around. Bad for tourism, you know?

Average john, all he wants is head. No mess, no fuss, just a quick suck in the car, parked in some dark cranny off West Street at three in the morning. Look, I'm just your average garden-variety alley pross, not some fancy streetwalker or stuck-up call girl. Standard price on the street is twenty for head, thirty for a straight lay, and forty for an ass-fuck, but I can charge half that and pull twice as many tricks 'cos, well . . .

'Cos I'm what you might call special.

They call us "grubs." Nice, huh? Well . . . I guess we *are* a little on the pasty side. But, look, don't get freaked out. I heard somewhere there are over ten thousand of us total. It all started with that ramjet thing, I don't know, a couple of years ago. Christ, I'm sure you heard about *that*. NASA and the air force were testing some new kinda plane, remotely piloted, they called it, flying it a hundred miles off the coast over the Atlantic. It was a nuclear ramjet or some shit, could fly indefinitely without fuel, no pilots, ran by computers. The idea was to have these things flying around all the time real high up. Cheap way to defend the nation. "The ultimate deterrent," the president said when they announced that they were gonna spend billions developing this thing. What they *didn't* announce was that plane kicked out a trail of some off-the-wall kinda radiation wherever it flew. The government wasn't worried about it 'cos it flew so high, the shit would go right out of the atmosphere. Well, something fucked up during one of the test flights, and one of these things wound up flying up and down the East Coast at treetop level on something they called an "emergency urban alert bomb mode" for something like five days before they could veer it off course over the sea and shoot it down. Thing was flying over *cities*, for shit's sake. And I was one of the ones lucky enough to get pissed on by it.

I'd just come up from the docks down there, you know, by the Market Square, and I was walking up toward Clay Street. 'Rome, my man, he usually picked me and his other two girls up at about four A.M. Best time for us alley girls to turn tricks is after two, after the bars are closed, 'cos then the cops stop buzzing the street to bust our chops. Fuckin' cops, nine times outa ten when they catch you, all they do is make you give 'em a quick blow job, then let you go. Anyway, here I am, hoofing it up to Clay after turning about five tricks, and then there's this rumble way down deep in my belly and this sound like slow thunder, and I look up and see this ugly thing flying about hundred feet over my head. Didn't know what to make of it. It looked like a big black kite in the sky, and when it passed, I could see this weird blue-green glow coming out of the back of the thing, its engines, I guess. I died a couple hours later, and the next day I woke up a grub.

There was a big whupdeedo for a little while. All of a sudden there were ten thousand dead people walking around and not knowing what the fuck hit them. President called an emergency meeting or some shit. Oh, you should've heard all the fancy talk they were spouting. At first they were gonna "euthanize" us "to safeguard the societal whole from potential contraindications," until some egghead at CDC verified that we weren't psychotic or contagious or radioactive or anything. Then some asshole Republican senator made a big pitch about how we should be "socially impounded." "Protean symtomologies," see, that's what they were worried about. These shitheads wanted to round us all up and put us on an island somewhere! It all blew over, though, after the activists started gearing up, and they let us be.

After all, grubs are people too.

* * *

It didn't hurt really. Just felt sick for a few minutes, got a headache, and died. Woke up the next day feeling pretty much the same as I always did. Woke up a grub. We call live people "pink" or "pinkies," and they call us grubs. Only fair, they got names for us, we got names for them. 'Rome didn't get it, the prick, he stayed pink, and so did his other two hookers. The shit from the plane wouldn't get you if you were in a car or under a roof. About a dozen other hookers got it, though, 'cos they were out on the street just like me when that fucked-up plane flew by, and now every pink hooker in the city hates us. See, johns want grubs more than pink girls 'cos we're cheaper and we ain't got diseases. AIDS, herpes, and all that shit, I had it all when I was pink, but not no more, and a john knows that if he buys himself a nut with a grub, he ain't gonna catch nothing.

Here's why I killed 'Rome, though. After I got grubbed, he got this brainstorm that he could really cop a bundle off me with the kinks. He'd work me right out of his crib, hitting johns up for a couple hundred bucks an hour! These sick fucks'd come in and do anything they wanted, and I mean *anything*. Bondage, S & M, scat, that sort of shit. 'Rome's only rule was that they weren't allowed to break any bones or cut off any parts. These kinks were a trip, let me tell you. You'd be surprised how many really sick motherfuckers there are in the world. They'd tie me up, jack me out, stick needles in my tits, shit in my mouth, you fuckin' name it. Grubs don't feel pain, so 'Rome figured it didn't matter. Anything goes, you know? Then he gets this bright idea about how he's gonna start his own video line called "Grub Paradise" and how I'm gonna be the star. The fucker wanted to film me while these kinks were working me over! Well,

I started to get sick of this shit real fast. Grubs don't gotta sleep, so 'Rome figures he can turn me into a twenty-four-hour-a-day enterprise. Here's this scumbag making cash hand over fist offa my ass, and I don't get shit out of it. So I . . .

Well, if you wanna know the details, I busted a toilet tank cover over his head one night, cut his belly open, and ate his guts.

Hell. Sometimes a girl's gotta do what she's gotta do.

See, grubs can only eat raw stuff. You eat regular food like the pinkies and the shit don't come out, you bloat up. There was this one gal named Sue who got grubbed just like me—blond, kinda heavyset, *really* big tits—and she just goes on eating the regular shit that the pinkies eat, and one day I saw her walking past the hotel and, I swear, she's big as Jabba the Hut, and before she could make it to the bus stop, she, like, *exploded* right there in the street, made one holy hell of a mess.

And this shithead Republican senator I was telling you about, you should've heard the guy, like because we can only eat raw stuff, that means we're gonna go on some zombie rampage eating people in the streets like some horror movie, so that was his case for "socially impounding" us. Glad that asshole's shit didn't fly. Of course, it probably sounds pretty hypocritical of me, since I just got done telling you I chowed down on 'Rome's insides. I just figured it was the thing to do, that's all. I got tired of being used by this scumbag, so I did the job on him. It wasn't like his guts tasted any better than anything else—grubs don't have a sense of taste.

One good thing about being a grub hooker, though,

you start to stick up for yourself. You get a case of the ass and you don't take shit anymore. The rule had always been no girl works solo. You wanna work the street, you gotta have a pimp. Ask any hooker in any city in the world. You try to work solo, you get your face beat to mush or wind up in some Dumpster with your throat cut. We'd always be too afraid to fight back, stand up for ourselves, you know? Shit, most girls are strung out anyway. I was. Back when I was pink, I was firing up scag four times a day, had to shoot up into my foot 'cos the veins on my arms all collapsed and turned black. I'd turn over my take to 'Rome every night like clockwork, and he'd keep me in junk, and that was all I cared about. When you're strung out, you really don't have a soul anymore. Yeah, turning my tricks, keeping 'Rome happy, and getting my fix—that's all there was for me. It was hell, let me tell you. But after I got grubbed, I didn't need the scag anymore, and it finally dawned on me that I didn't need 'Rome, either. All the other grubs working the street got the same gist, and all of a sudden a lot of pimps were winding up in body bags. The pink girls, sure, they're all still in their stables, but their pimps don't fuck with us grubs 'cos they know that if they do, they'll wind up just like 'Rome.

Fuck 'em.

Shit, man. I can't hardly tell the difference. Sometimes I'm not sure if there *is* a difference. Pussy's pussy, and cock is cock. And when I'm sucking a nut outa some john in his car, it don't make no difference if my mouth is alive or dead, and it's better in a way 'cos I don't taste his jizz when he comes, and if he's a stinker, I can't smell him. And best of all, cash is green whether you're a grub or a pinkie, you know?

I go shopping, I buy clothes, I watch TV, I got myself a decent little apartment. Shit, I'm just like anyone else out there trying to make it.

All right, I can tell you're new in town, and you're probably thinking, shit, this chick's fuckin' *dead,* but those girls across the street are alive. Well, let me tell you something, man. That little blondie there with the glasses, the one by the MOST machine—she'll rip you off. And those two black chicks at the corner of Calvert, both of 'em got AIDS. And how do you know any one of 'em won't take you to some alley where they got their pimp waiting to bust your head, take your cash, jack your car, maybe even kill you?

You wanna take a chance like that?

So come on, man. Let's party. Shit, I'll give you the cock-suck of your life, and you can take all the time you want to come. And I won't fuck you over like those pinkie bitches across the street. Straight up, man—ten bucks for a blow job so good, I guarantee you'll be comin' back for more, and I'll swallow it, too, no bullshit. Whaddaya say?

All right!

Hey, nice car. Just keep going, and I'll tell you wh—okay, turn here, pull into this little alley right here. Yeah, good, now turn off your lights.

And pull your pants down, partner.

Hmm, let's see what we got here, yeah. Hard already, that's what I like. Lotta times at this hour most guys are on their way home from the bars and they're shitfaced. Takes 'em forever to get it up, you know?

All right, time for me to do my thing. Just lay back in the seat and relax . . .

Wait a minute, what the f—

Hey, look, buddy, I'm sorry, but . . .

I didn't do anything wrong, shit! It ain't my fault the skin came off your dick! I was just—

What gives here, man? What the hell's wrong with you?

You—you're a . . . *what?*

Oh, man! What a trip! You're a grub too! Just like me!

Calm down, will ya? Lemme fix ya up here, the skin only came off at the base. Don't worry, I'll get it back on, no sweat.

There, see? Still works.

Okay, okay, just lay back and relax. A grub, huh? That's really cool.

I'll give you this one for free.

HUNGER

Kathryn Ptacek

Sex is power.

Or is it the reverse: Power is sex?

Whichever is true, I ought to be—by that definition—a powerful woman. I've had a lot of commerce, shall we say, with the opposite sex. A lot.

And wanting too much of some thing, we're told by heads thought much wiser than ourselves, points to a little something called addiction.

There are many varieties of addictions, those guys with the string of fancy degrees inform us. And I guess they're right. I don't have much education—I finished high school with average grades and no particular distinction, took a few courses at a local community college, but I know about some things that just aren't learned from textbooks. There's addiction to nicotine and your thirty-one flavors of mind-bending chemicals and exercise and sugar and mental abuse and alcohol and power and sleep and food and danger and flattery and—

Sex, too.

No kidding.

It's a real addiction. Believe me.

Do you know what it's like to be hooked on sex?

I didn't think so.

It pierces and stings, throbs and aches.

Among other things.

You know that old-time song by Peggy Lee? "Fever?" That's pretty damned close to an accurate description of what I go through. It's a fever that has to be reduced, a hunger that has to be fed, a thirst that has to be quenched.

Sometimes I'm just sitting in my office, staring at boring grocery accounts, my mind filled with numbers that need sorting, and suddenly that one particular sensation comes over me. It's halfway between a cramp and an itch, and it's more than a little painful, and it's all inside where I can't reach. I can't scratch; I can't relieve it except one way. And I sure can't ignore it.

Usually I have to wait until my lunch hour, sitting there at my desk with my legs squeezed together, trying not to gasp aloud. I squirm, try to concentrate, fail. My face is flushed, my breath rapid, and ripples of pain and pleasure roll through me as the gnawing inside increases. I watch the sweep hand on the huge white face of the clock, watch it going around and around all too slowly, the minute and hour hands inching upward. Finally, when the hands get straight up, I grab my purse and leave the office. I half run, half walk down the street to a bar I pass every morning on my way to work.

It's not a great lounge; that is, you probably won't find many yuppies hanging out there with their white wine-drinking pals, but it suits me fine. You can get a tolerable sandwich or two, some draft, and something more than that. A lot of guys hang out there. A lot of guys who are just as hot as I am.

I've been here before. They know me, I suppose, but I don't care.

I stroll into the cool darkness; my heart still seems to be fluttering inside my rib cage, and I wonder if any of the men seated along the bar can hear that or see my flushed skin. Apparently not. I lick my dry lips and nod casually to the bartender, a fellow some years older than myself and fairly stocky; he has a nose that looks like it was broken a long time ago, over and over. I find a booth toward the back of the room. I look down at the scarred wooden surface of the plank table, at the wet rings left by someone's glass. I'm wet, too.

I have an old-fashioned figure—large breasts, nipped-in waist, and curving hips—and blond hair halfway down my back and a face that, while not glamorous, is attractive. They've served me well.

I wait.

Not long, though.

Someone slides into the booth across from me.

"Hey," he says.

"Hey."

I look up.

He's got hairy forearms, not like an ape's, but nice; the type you could run your fingers through. The sleeves of his blue work shirt are rolled up to mid-biceps, and those are fairly large. So he must work with his arms, his hands; I like that. His shirt is open a little, and I can see the chest hair, dark with one or two strands of silver. Not a kid. That's okay too. They're usually too anxious; they tend to pop before I get filled. Then I've gotta have two or three of them to make it worth my while.

His face is slightly scarred, maybe from acne when he was a teenager. It's a pleasant face, though it won't win any awards. His hairline is receding slightly. I put him in his mid to late thirties.

He smiles. His teeth are white, fairly even. At least it's not all fake enamel, I realize.

I put my leg out under the table and massage his calf with my bare foot.

I see him jerk slightly. He wasn't prepared for that. It amuses me that they never are, no matter how strong they come on to me.

"Want another beer?"

"Sure." I have barely touched the one in front of me, have barely nibbled the sandwich on the paper plate. It's not what I want to eat.

He waves to the bartender, who nods and within a few minutes comes by with our new drinks. He takes away my half-filled glass and uneaten sandwich.

"What's your name?" I ask after a moment.

"Barry. You?"

"Eleanor."

"Nice name."

A prim name, I think, for someone who definitely isn't. "Thanks."

Now, I didn't claim that I was some kind of brilliant conversationalist. Oscar Wilde I'm not, I know that. On the other hand, that's not the reason I came to the bar, remember.

I find out within minutes that Barry works on a road crew and is hoping to get promoted to the office. He is close to having a bachelor's degree and wants to go someplace other than the outside with unbearable heat in the summer and unbearable cold in the winter. I always like ambition in my bed partner.

I tell him I work in Accounts Payable at a grocery wholesale warehouse.

"Not precisely exciting, but it pays some of the bills," I remark.

He laughs, just as if I'd said something witty. Barry's not here for my conversation, either.

We polish off another beer. Talk about the weather, which is hotter than usual and more than a little humid. The long hot summers of the Northeast. Sweltering. Simmering. Moist.

I'm very humid as I sit across from him. My other shoe is off now and both feet are rubbing his legs. I breathe faster. His hand has crept up under cover of the table, and he's brushed his fingertips against the inside of my lower thigh. I almost wet myself.

"Kind of warm in here," he says.

I nod, hardly trusting myself to speak.

"Want to go someplace?"

Never thought he'd ask. "Sure." I smile and lean forward, and he looks down my front at the shadow between my breasts.

I get up, pay for the drinks—I always make it a point of doing that, even though it's generally the guy who makes the first move—and he follows me outside.

We find a somewhat seedy-looking motel on the outskirts of town. I've been there before. The desk clerk, a pale, nervous-looking boy of nineteen or twenty, knows me; we've done it a few times as well; he hasn't been quite the same since. I rent a room— my usual, a small corner facing the back—and Barry and I go in. I kick the door closed. As many times as I've been here, I still don't think I could say what color the walls are.

Barry's arms snake around me almost instantly. I am pressed solidly against him and I can feel his hardness. I want his hardness. I want to eat him alive. Figuratively speaking, of course.

While I kiss him, forcing my tongue into his mouth, I start to unbutton his shirt, unzip his pants. He tumbles out of his jeans, and boy, is he ever ready. I pull my clothes off quickly; lots of practice— maximum effect with minimum effort; I don't wear underwear any longer. His lips are burning, delicious, sucking at mine, and he fondles and pinches my full breasts. The nipples are erect.

When I cup him in my hand, he throbs. I squeeze, and he moans.

We fall back on the queen-sized bed, and fuck like frenzied ferrets.

It's very good with Barry. Very, very good. Not the best, perhaps, but closer than the last few times. I savor every last mouthful of him.

When I leave the motel room, Barry is asleep.

He'll sleep for a long time now.

A long time.

And I bet he'll want that transfer to the office even sooner than before.

I wave to the clerk, give him a thumbs-up signal. He appears a little paler than before, and I know his palms are sweating. As I drive, I whistle; and I return to the thrilling world of lost cases of Vienna sausages, shipping and handling, and freight charges.

Even as I'm sitting down behind my desk and

sorting through the papers in the wire basket, I can feel that hunger consuming me all over.

And I know I've got to do it again. Soon.

I wasn't always like this.

Like everyone else, I started out a virgin. Only, from an early age I realized something was wrong . . . that I was a little different from my girlfriends. Certainly they were interested in boys just about the same time I was, but I realized my fascination was a bit more serious than theirs.

They just wanted to date and hold hands; I wanted to fuck.

I managed to hang on until I was fourteen; then I just had to do it.

I had to have it.

It was either that or explode. Better to relieve the pressure first, I thought. I didn't know what would happen if I didn't, and I suspected it wouldn't be good for me. No sir.

Now, we run into a problem with the language here. A guy would boast that he had his first pussy. I can't say that; I mean I'm not a guy, and that's not what I got. I guess, then, I had my first cock.

I liked cock a lot.

I did it with another kid—my next-door neighbor's son; he was fifteen—on a Monday, then the next day, and the day after that. I devoured him. It was incredibly fun—after all, it was uncharted territory for us. The ultimate adventure, I thought. Finally on the fourth day he burst into tears and begged me to leave him alone or he'd tell his parents.

I was surprised. I thought he enjoyed the sex just as much as I did. He'd made just as much noise as I had, thrashed around like he was having a good time. I guessed I was wrong. I guessed he'd just chewed off more than he could swallow.

After that, he took the long way around to school so that he wouldn't have to pass our house, and whenever he was outside and I came out of the house, he'd go back inside. I laughed. What a wimp. But I shrugged. Didn't bother me. There were more cocks out there.

I waited, biding my time.

The next occasion, only two weeks later, was with the guy delivering my parents' dry cleaning. He came in with these suits and dresses all in their plastic wraps. My parents weren't home, so I said I would take them. I took him by the hand—he was about ten years older than me, with a ragged haircut and green eyes—closed the door, and pushed him down onto the pink and beige plaid couch. My mother never suspected. This time made me think of that old well-thumbed paperback I found in my mother's lingerie drawer. *Candy,* it was called. Pretty weird. This girl makes it with a hunchback one time. I don't know about that sort of thing; I mean she humps his hump, if you can believe that. I read the book in snatches, while my folks were at work or at the store. Pretty tame by today's standards. Trust me.

The third occasion was with another boy from school, a guy I'd known all my life. We were good friends, had never dated, but we also had a healthy interest. So we met every day after school at his house; his parents worked and weren't due home until well after six. We would sit down in the living room for an hour or so and dutifully do our homework, and then after a while the tension would get so great that I would put my hand on his crotch, and he'd slip his hand into my sweater, up under my bra—I still wore underwear then—and I would squeeze, and then he would squeeze, and next thing you know, we'd fall right onto the floor, on his bed, on the kitchen table—I saw it once in this film called *The Postman Always Rings Twice*—or on his parents' bed. We even tried it standing up in the shower. We were too slick and giggled, and he kept slipping out, until finally we gave up and I just went down on him. That was nice, although not as nice as when he went down on me. It was like he swallowed every bit of me.

Our arrangement worked well until his mom arrived home early a few months later and found us fucking our brains out on her fine and fancy Oriental carpet with its knotted-by-hand threads. Sometimes I think where we were upset her far more than what we were actually doing. Anyway, that was the last I saw of him. My parents screamed at me, lectured me about being irresponsible—I wasn't; I'd taken the proper precautions; I wasn't about to get pregnant at my tender age—shouted that I was incorrigible, that I was a hellion and a tramp and a number of other adjectives, that I was headed for the D-home. Mostly my father yelled, while my mother cried and wrung her hands, and kept wondering aloud what they had done wrong. This from a woman who was pregnant at her wedding. I was what you would call an eight-pound preemie. Right.

I worked very diligently for the rest of the school year to be a pleasing, docile, oh-so-obedient daughter, someone my parents could trust.

Of course, I didn't stop screwing around. I just took more care, that's all.

The doctors lecture about guys having wet dreams. Women have them, too, only they're slightly different.

My wet dreams started right after my first encounter. I would wake up just drenched in sweat, my breath rapid, my heart fluttering, my body tingling, and the sheets very moist under me. I knew what was happening. Inside would be that gnawing hunger, that appetite that I had to satisfy. I would get up, no matter the time of night, dress, and go run two or three miles out on the high school track. Then I'd let myself back into the house—all without waking my folks, who would probably have slept through the Resurrection—take a cold shower, and still none of that would relieve that fiery craving.

Nothing would until the next time.

I went through a lot of boys in high school.

Now, men sharing the same desires that I have are called satyrs after those Greek half-horse, half-human things that pranced around in olden times and fucked, plucked, and sucked anything that moved. Woodland deities, the dictionary says. Right. Deities, my foot.

Women like me are labeled nymphomaniacs. A rather cold and impersonal term, if you ask me, and one that has more than a little disapproval attached to it. I tell you, we got screwed with the terms, too. How come it's not satyrmania? Anyway, most of the time that long term for the women gets shortened to nymphs, which doesn't sound too bad when coupled with satyrs, as it were. Of course, sometimes guys think women who want it more than once a year are nymphs. I'm afraid quite a few females get tarred unfairly with that brush.

Still, both conditions, as my onetime therapist explained, are characterized by an excessive desire for sex. A frenzy for coitus. What a way to put it.

Takes some of the pleasure out of it, don't you think?

If you have to do something, it's no fun, right? It's a duty, God forbid. A burden. A *chore*.

And where's the adventure in that? Where's the enjoyment?

My pattern, after a number of years of fine-tuning, is fairly predictable.

I work, I leave at lunch, I find some guy to fuck. We screw our brains out. I leave him sleeping.

I go back to work. I get that feeling again. After work, I cruise by another bar, see what's being offered, get a good lay or two in. Go home and fix myself something to eat that's not human.

I get that urge again by bedtime. Sometimes I try to ignore it. Mostly I'm unsuccessful. Mostly I have to go back out one more time.

There's always room for one more, right?

I don't get much sleep, but hey, I don't seem to need it much anymore. I think my partners sleep enough for me. I like to lie next to them as they doze, snoring most times, and just watch them. I like to watch the rise and fall of their chests, like to trace the sweat across the mat of chest hair, like to lick the saltiness on their skin. Like to listen to them moan from some dream. I like to feast on them, sexually and visually.

I like it all, and I don't take weekends or holidays off.

I've slept with tall guys, little guys, skinny ones, chubby ones, bookish ones, and muscle men; even tried it with a woman once. Drew the line at a German shepherd, though. Just joking. About contemplating it with a dog, that is. I'm not *that* screwed up, believe me. The names, the bodies, the methods, have blurred after all this time. All I remember is the sex and the wonderful relief that it brought for me, even for such a short time.

Honey, I've tried it so many damned ways—I could probably add a page or two to the *Kama Sutra*. It's a wonder I don't walk bow-legged.

So what did I get out of all these hot and cold fucks, you wonder?

A lot of good sex. A lot of so-so sex. And a helluva lot of bad lays. But I think I had more first-rate times than bad. At least I remember the good more often than not. Selective memory, maybe, huh?

Maybe that was my hobby, after all. Finding the ultimate lay, the primo prick. The *crème de la cream*. Maybe.

After a while, after the years went by, after a decade or two passed, I decided that wasn't enough. I had to have the sex more frequently, with more partners, in many more variations.

I have to confess that, by then, my rather unbridled sex drive was frankly driving me up the wall. I wasn't having fun any longer. I didn't do anything but fuck. I was having a hard time paying my bills, going to work, even getting up in the morning and doing simple chores like brushing my teeth or getting dressed. My thoughts all centered on one activity. Sex, sex, sex. Too much of a good thing, as they say, sucks.

Something had to be done.

So I went into therapy.

What a mistake. Got nothing out of that except some exorbitant bills, and a clear understanding that those guys with the elaborate diplomas can pitch a first-class *theoretical* argument but don't know shit when it comes to real life. Plus they're not so hot in bed. Trust me on that.

So all the doctors I've ever visited have claimed this addiction, this craving, exists solely in my head. Not precisely. I know what they're saying, or rather what they're trying to express. It's fine for them to suggest one mode of therapy or another; it's fine for them, because they're not the one who experiences this *hunger*. I am. And believe me, it's inside me—not my head—and nothing they've ever recommended has helped.

Some termed it a fugue, but it's not that because I recall my acts afterward. Boy, do I ever. And some suggest a mania. "Excessive enthusiasm," says my dictionary about that word. Maybe that's the closest definition, because I am *very* enthusiastic.

The problem is, though, it's only gotten worse over the years. It's all I think about during the day. All I dream about at night. The only thing I crave.

I don't eat food much now, don't sleep much. Don't have any hobbies, or go out, except to pick up men. All I do is fuck.

I'm real tired—tired of fucking and being fucked. Who's being devoured now?

I've given it a great deal of thought, and I think I know what I have to do to help myself, help get rid of that itching hunger inside.

I've made my preparations carefully, decided I've got to do something; can't wait any longer. I've gone to the store and bought what was necessary. I had the plastic bottle already, left over from one of the kits I bought some time ago. And I've mixed the proper amount—had to guess here, though, what with no recipe—of vinegar and water with the crystals.

These crystals are pretty potent, making my eyes water, and I have to glance away and take a deep breath.

It's all set up now. I sit down on the toilet, spread my legs, and reach for the filled bag.

Nothing like douching with Drano. A little dab'll do you.

THE WATCHER

Rex Miller and Jeff Gelb

*F*or many years George Winters had fantasized about the same basic scene: two women, one of them his wife, making love, with himself as coach, director, onlooker, and commentator. "Pull the hair away from her face," he would say, having seen his share of hard core.

His wife, Karen, was a statuesque natural redhead, heavily freckled over her upper torso, with a long, slim neck, a chest that other women envied, and a little hint of tummy. Karen had kept most of her figure. At forty-one she still looked like a woman in her early thirties, and was just beginning to fight the battle of the middle-aged bulge. Her long legs were as fine as they'd been when George had first seen her, in the lobby of First Financial, where he was the junior lending officer in the mortgage department. That had been nearly twenty years before, and the sizzle had long since died between them. They still had sex, but it had become infrequent and routine. He thought that intercourse with Karen had become like masturbation with legs and a vagina. He could admire her aesthetically, still, but for the last few years he did not eye his wife with lust in his heart . . . unless he thought of her with another woman. Then—BOING! That was all it took. His fantasies, the way he looked at it, were saving their marriage.

When the spark had sputtered, George began spending more time reading the out-of-town newspapers he collected, much to Karen's chagrin. She claimed to be allergic to newsprint and paper pulp, but these days it seemed she was allergic to almost everything. He felt maybe she was really just allergic to him.

To ease the frustration of a marriage that seemed directionless, and over which he appeared to have lost complete control. George started writing. He plowed the darkest depths of his mind to come up with a pseudonymous self-help revenge book called *How to F—Somebody Over.* No one was more surprised than George when the book was actually picked up by a small company called Landfill Press, which sold it both in-store and by direct mail. One of the big chains picked it up. It became a publishing freak, a word-of-mouth success, even reaching the *New York Times* best-seller list. George made a ton of money.

When the sequel, *How to F—Somebody Up,* went into its second hardcover printing literally before the Landfill sales department finished the initial solicitation, he quit his mortgage-lending gig and started writing full-time. He'd been tremendously successful, and could indulge himself. That meant outcall ladies. Scenes.

One of these scenes had brought him Gayle, a lovely, smiling, bimboesque girl of twenty-two who was obviously selling her body as much for the taboo kick as for the dough. She was slim, small-boobed, with a great face, super ass, and a hot way about her that instantly turned him on. He made her model sexy lingerie for him while he beat off, and then she sucked him while he thought about how crazy it would get him to watch her go down on Karen.

That night he popped the question—for maybe the fiftieth time—to his bride of nineteen and a half years.

"I've found somebody for us. I know you'll go nuts when you see her," he told his wife, describing Gayle, the beaming bimbo, in minute detail while leaving out the precise details of their money-for-sex encounter. Karen's response floored him.

"She sounds quite fuckable, actually," she said in her soft, cultured tones. For the first time she agreed to participate in a three-way. A two-way, technically, as his thing was watching from the sidelines, as it were.

George asked why she was willing this time; what had finally made the difference? She said she was tired of fighting him, and besides, she said she'd been doing some fantasizing herself lately, and his constant harping about another woman had started her thinking along those lines.

"Most of all," she'd said, "I'm afraid of getting too old to try something new."

The big scene was arranged. Gayle lived some twenty miles away, so there would be an extra hundred to cover the "travel" both ways, which would, with her basic fee, buy her for the entire night. Camcorder loaded, wife primed and waiting nervously in the next room, he sat—vodka collins in hand— ready for company.

The doorbell went through him like a direct current of electricity. He couldn't recall being so up for a scene, both literally and figuratively, and he opened the door on Gayle's big, sexy smile. She had one of those MTM mouths with about a thousand white Chiclet teeth in it, full lips that were so youthfully pretty she didn't bother with lipstick, and a tongue she couldn't keep out of sight. She was always smiling, or holding her mouth open as she listened, or licking those thick lips, or pouting, or laughing or chewing on a finger—something. Very busy, that ripe mouth of hers. He couldn't wait to see her with Karen.

Drinks. Introductions. He was about to explode in his blue bikini briefs, which is all he wore under the black and red silk kimono. The women took to each other immediately. It was all he could do not to touch himself, he was already so hot with the anticipation of the event. They put their partially finished libations down and headed for the master bedroom.

George triggered the camera, surreptitiously, and took a seat near the bed, preparing to begin instructions and suggestions, but they were miles ahead of him. Karen pulled Gayle on top of her and they jumped into the sack like two schoolgirls, kissing with a kind of heat he found totally alien to Karen. This wasn't Karen at all—this was some sex-mad twat fiend who'd been released from dormancy. His wife ran every change imaginable on the more than willing Gayle, and it was unlike any scene to which he had ever been a voyeur. It was so exciting, he forgot to jack off!

They kissed as if they were writing a book on the art. Karen would open her mouth and sort of begin eating Gayle's lips, and then Gayle would imitate the same type of kiss, then Karen would try a face-sucking corner gobble, and Gayle would duplicate that, and then they each began innovating, working their way up and down and over and around. Karen was on those little breasts with a mad devouring passion that was amazing to behold, and then down on the shaved patch of snatch in the heart of Gayle's unsuntanned love triangle, going at it lickety-split. Then it was Gayle on Karen, then each of them after the other's asshole, just fucking incredible. The videocassette ran out. He went to the bathroom. He got tired of watching.

After Gayle's first visit, everything between Karen and George improved. Sex, naturally, warmed up; they lived off the event for weeks, but their attitude toward one another changed. Karen no longer treated him like a necessary evil in her life, she seemed to suddenly care about him again. There were other changes as well. She became a better housekeeper almost overnight. Now she was cooking the meals he liked again, and her constant criticizing had abated. In turn, he treated her with more respect, not being so critical of her every decision, allowing her more freedom. She loved to take hours and hours shopping, and now he let her shop till she dropped, and never threw it up to her when she came home. He even made sure she had plenty of extra money in her checking account, something he'd never bothered to do in the past.

George was so pleased with the way things had changed for them, he was stunned when he suggested a possible ménage à trois with Gayle, whom they hadn't seen in some weeks, and she nearly jumped down his throat.

"Just leave Gayle the fuck out of our fucking lives, all right?" she'd shouted.

"Sorry," he said, meekly.

Karen became instantly contrite, and that night she made his favorite meal and served it to him as if it were going to be the last food she'd ever cook for him. The next morning he found out why. The phone rang. He happened to pick it up just a beat after Karen did.

"Hm-um," he heard his wife whisper into the phone, "can't right now."

"Ten OK?" Gayle's voice, he was certain.

"Yeah, gotta go."

"Love you," Gayle said.

"Me too," he heard Karen whisper. The two words ice-picked him in the heart. He fucking knew it all in that instant.

The next few weeks played themselves out in slow motion. He owed Karen something, and he was a man who paid his debts, always. With interest. He owed her nineteen and a half good years; she'd done a million things for him, held his head while he puked —back in his heavy-boozing days—loved his family as if they'd been hers, a zillion things he owed her for. He would pay her back with loyalty and friendship, he decided. Kill her with kindness, so to speak. It was the only decent thing to do.

He said nothing, never let on, just made his plans. Each day was one day closer to divorce—there was never a question in his mind. He knew Karen well, and he knew he was watching someone in love. Jesus, it was really pretty funny. The thing he wanted most finally happens, but it's so good, it destroys him. Very fucking funny. If he'd written it, no one would have believed him. Life was a certifiable bitch. And in this case, he'd brought the bitch home. He couldn't complain.

Karen? In love with another bitching *woman?* Nah . . . Yeah. Might as well face it, stud, he told himself, it would be bad enough to lose her to another man, but you lost your wife to a fucking *cunt,* you no-dick loser piece of shit. Then he was able to look at his twisted goofiness, immaturity, sexist pigitude, and the whole nine yards of torn cloth that let him fuck his own nice marriage into the ground, and he stepped back, laughed at himself, and took a vow of reasonableness. George would be a mensch and let this play itself out.

It did soon enough. Karen was just back from the grocery store, and he'd helped her put groceries away, and had asked her to help him wash and wax the Regal. She had on short shorts and a halter top and looked so suddenly sexy to him, he was irritated with his weirdness. Here he was rubbing the same spot with a chamois cloth, trying to look down his old lady's top at those nice, hard nipples he'd become so bored with. What was sex, and in fact marriage, but a nutty head game? The car shiny, chrome agleam, they emptied their buckets, wrung out their sponges, and went inside to cool off with some drinks.

She brought him a special treat, Hires in a frosty mug that had been icing down in the freezer. He took a sip of root beer and she told him, matter-of-factly, that she was leaving.

"You know this is over. I still care about you, but I can't go on like this anymore. I've found someone else. I'm moving in the morning." She began an itemized list of what she was taking and what she was leaving. He tried to keep an even keel, but it was difficult.

"I've withdrawn half the money—exactly to the dime," she said, with almost a hint of pride in her voice, "and I'll take the car. You can always buy another set of wheels, but I like the Buick and feel safe in it. You can keep the house," she said. That was big of her.

"You and Gayle setting up housekeeping?" he asked, keeping his face and tone neutral. She looked at him sharply.

"Yes." No *how did you know?* No hint of surprise. Letting him know with her equally flat gaze and tone that she didn't care what he knew or for how long. "Neither of us meant this to happen, you know."

They discussed the affair at some length, but Karen was not willing to divulge much. He could tell she'd slammed a door on any intimacy between them. He played to that, saying that he hoped they'd be very happy together. She relaxed a bit.

"I guess I owe you," she said, "since we'd never have gotten together if you hadn't insisted I meet her."

"That's true," George said with a chuckle. "Maybe I should become a matchmaker. You two are obviously in love. I could tell from watching you together how good it was for you."

"We're pretty *gushy,* I guess," his wife said, in that self-deprecatory way she had that drove him up the wall. They discussed the details of her move and he decided to follow through on his plan to be a real friend.

"I'm going to help you move," he said.

"No, I don't want you to do that."

"I insist," he said, and began producing suitable boxes, helping her call an appropriate moving company, and busying himself with the details of her immediate exit.

They worked most of the night packing boxes, and when the moving men arrived he was still in a sleepy fog, but somehow he got through the day, and by evening she came to kiss him good-bye.

"I'm just a few miles away," she said, gently, "and we'll still see each other a lot. I always want to be your friend."

"I'll always be here for you, Karen." They kissed and she left for the apartment where her new wife was waiting. Or was it husband? It didn't matter to him at the moment. He was crushed. Demolished. The house was screamingly empty without her. Nearly twenty years had just been flushed down the tubes. It was like a death. Worse, because the loved one was still around. Terrible. Devastating. All the clichés rang true. He was alone. Fucked.

Many tears later, many curses and prayers later, but only a month on the calendar, things were beginning to sort themselves out. It was true, those hackneyed phrases, like "one door closes but another opens." It was the beginning of a new life. And George was prosperous and healthy—being alone wasn't such a sentence after all. He would be able to rationalize his way back to some semblance of what passed for normalcy inside his head, in time. He'd work at it. He was strong.

Oddly, for a man who—for decades—had thought of nothing but another woman balling his old lady, he never thought of Gayle and Karen making it together. He didn't try to picture them, and he never asked Karen how they were getting along. What he did was try to help her so that she could be free from the details of life, free from the daily pressures, as much as possible.

He helped her with her investment program, even added money to the half she'd taken in order to buy her a mutual fund he thought had great promise; he paid for the $204 extra each month on her car insurance, "so you won't have to dig into your principle so much," he'd said. He suggested courses where she might sign up to learn a possible career, if she found herself, at forty-one, immersed in the strange waters of the workplace again. Housewife work was tough, he was learning, but it didn't prepare a person for becoming an independent breadwinner. He deposited money in their joint money market account, and would pay her taxes at least for another year, he promised.

At every turn he acted as her friend, confidant, and adviser. He even took her car in for servicing, their car but *hers* now. He referred to it as "my wife's Regal" when he left it at the shop. He kept up his insurance premiums so that if anything happened to him, Karen would still be beneficiary of a fairly tidy sum.

"I have to tell you," she said on a visit, "you've really surprised me. I never thought you'd be so good about everything. It's made something that would be difficult at best so much easier and more pleasant for all of us involved. Gayle is bowled over about the way you've behaved. She never thought you were such a good guy, even though I told her you were."

He fought to hold his temper. "Well, you've had nearly twenty years to know me. Gayle and I don't really know each other." He kept his voice modulated and calm, but inside he was picturing the blond bimbo bitch with her boyish tits and shaved pussy; he could imagine her talking her baby-talk bullshit to his ex-wife.

The day after the papers came from the lawyer, announcing it was an uncontested divorce and that they were no longer man and wife, Karen began to have problems. The first thing was the car. She was driving down Main and tapped the brakes at a stoplight, went right through and smacked a produce truck hard on the bumper, crushing the Buick's front grille.

"I don't know what happened!" she told the investigating officer. "I didn't have any brakes at all. My God, if a child or somebody had been crossing the street, I would have hit them!"

A couple of weeks later the insurance company informed a startled Karen that she hadn't been covered with comprehensive when the mishap had occurred.

"According to our records, you let your car insurance lapse two months ago." Karen phoned her ex-husband, who was shocked and chagrined.

"Jesus, honey, I'm sorry. I don't know how it happened." He checked their stubs and the master file under Auto Insurance. Sure enough—somehow—a few weeks ago he'd managed to make out the check and all, but he'd apparently misplaced the envelope. Yes, sad to say, it seems he had let their insurance run out.

Then there was the Turkish rug. George had bought it for Gayle and Karen at a local flea market, saying he hoped it would brighten up their apartment, which was still sparsely furnished. The women were thrilled by his kindness, but within hours of setting it up in their living room, Karen's eyes started watering profusely and her breathing became labored.

"Jesus, Karen, what's wrong?" Gayle had asked, rushing to her lover's side. By that time, Karen was gasping for air and pointing at the rug. "Allergic . . . reaction . . . something in the rug."

Gayle called 911 and the ambulance workers fed Karen oxygen as they rushed her to the hospital, where she was diagnosed with an acute allergic reaction to chemicals in the rug. Somehow, at some point, someone had dumped a shitload of cleaning solvent on the rug, and Karen's allergies had kicked in mightily, nearly fatally.

George removed the rug and later told the women he had cut it into small pieces and burned them in his backyard barbecue. Again he apologized profusely, and again his former wife forgave him. After all, she said, it was hardly his fault if some jerk had done that to a beautiful rug. How, she asked, was he to know?

After Karen was released from the hospital, George encouraged her and Gayle to stay at his house until the last of the rug's smell had dissipated. Besides, he reminded them, he was going out of town for a few days for a regional book-signing tour. They accepted his offer gratefully, which appeared to make him extremely relieved after his rug faux pas.

But tragedy struck again. Later they recounted to George how, during the second night they were house-sitting, they had thrown popcorn into the air popper and had let it warm up, while they warmed up each other with a double-headed dildo—a part of the story with which they delighted in torturing George. They explained how the smell and sound of popping corn had fueled their passions so that they had initially failed to notice the cord to the air popper sparking, then starting a kitchen fire that quickly raged out of control among the piles of George's old newspapers. Worse still, the windows were all stuck shut because George had painted the exterior of the house days before, and was none too fussy about where the paint stopped and the windows began. The house went up like a matchstick in a volcano, and by the time the women were aware of the blaze, their path to the front door was already blocked by hellish flames. Karen doubled over in cough spasms while Gayle, just short of panicking, picked up George's favorite lamp and threw it through a side window, then pushed Karen through and followed, tumbling to the ground outside just as the house blew itself up, a noise that shattered windows for blocks around.

Both women ended up back in the hospital, suffering second-degree burns along with multitudes of cuts from flying glass and wooden shards.

George soon arrived, in near hysteria, at the hospital, where he kept vigil in the waiting room to the Burn Unit. When she could talk, Karen apologized for the loss of his—once their—house.

"I just don't understand it," George said. "I just bought that air popper less than a month ago." He clucked his tongue and shook his head. "You just can't buy quality anymore." He smiled at her bandaged face. "I'm just glad you're alive." As an afterthought, he added, "Oh, and Gayle too, of course."

He relocated to a tiny condo on the other side of town, and saw less of Karen and Gayle while they healed. One day he noticed he was more glum than usual, and realized it was because it was the anniversary of their divorce. One year ago, she'd left him for that brainless bimbo bitch, God knows why. What he'd ever seen in Gayle, he could no longer recall.

Just then the phone rang. "George?" It was *her,* he realized, his stomach turning. "Karen and I were just talking about how it's a special day for all of us—you know what I mean. And we wondered whether you might want to spend it together."

Before he could spit the word "no" down the phone line, Karen got on the phone. In the same cultured tone she'd used when she'd first agreed to meet Gayle, she said, "George, Gayle and I have been thinking. It's been a strange year for us all and, well, we were wondering if it's not too late to take you up on your offer."

"What offer?"

"Well, we were just reminiscing, and I remembered how mad I got that time you wanted to do a ménage à trois with me and Gayle. And, well, I know you haven't been seeing anyone, and, oh, George, I feel so bad about the house, and the divorce, and everything. How'd you like to . . . have us both for dinner tonight?"

She laughed at her own joke when George considered the offer. No fucking way would he—but wait a minute. Yes. This could work nicely after all. "Sure," he answered, putting as big a smile in his voice as he could fake. "Come on over at seven. I'll make your favorite meal: blackened redfish."

As he marinated the fish with poison, he reflected on what a lousy year it had been. All of his acts of revenge had failed to achieve their common goal: to pay back Karen for her betrayal of their marriage. Slitting the brake lines, adding the chemicals to the rug, even fraying all the wiring around the house in hopes they would start a fatal fire in his absence. It was a bit desperate, he admitted, but no less than both of them deserved. The sluts.

Well, tonight's plan was foolproof. True, he'd probably have to leave town before their bodies were discovered, but with Karen out of his life, there was nothing for him here anyway. He'd take the royalties he'd made off his books and live well in Mexico, or

South America, or one of those places he never tired of reading about in the travel sections of the newspapers he loved.

Yes, he nodded to the empty room, he'd teach these twats a final lesson and then skip town. He was ready for a big change.

He answered the doorbell and was momentarily stunned by Karen and Gayle, who were dressed to thrill, Karen in a skintight minidress that showed off her lean legs to best advantage, and Gayle in even less than Karen. She wore jeans that were cut off so that the bottom of her rump was displayed, and a sleeveless T-shirt that showed much more of her breasts than it concealed. George felt his dick stiffen involuntarily as they both kissed him on opposite cheeks, giggling as they let themselves in.

"This will be fun," Karen whispered as she brushed her hand against the bulge in his pants.

"I have wine," Gayle said cheerily. "Want some now?"

"Sure." He shrugged. No reason he had to rush things. He had to admit, he'd had no initial desire to touch either one of them. But their scars had healed nicely—the visible ones, anyway—and he was undeniably horny after a year without sex. After his experience with Gayle, the idea of paying for sex had been abhorrent to him.

Karen handed him a glass of Cabernet and asked, "Honey, where's that video you shot of me and Gayle? Let's all watch it. It'll put us in the mood." To accentuate her point, she grabbed at his crotch, giving it a healthy squeeze. "I can see you're in the mood already!"

He laughed and downed the wine. He was touched that Karen remembered that Cabernet was his favorite choice. He pulled the tape out of a bookshelf case and popped it into the VCR. He hadn't watched this tape in over a year; it pained him too much to view it.

In moments he was riveted. He'd forgotten how erotic it was to watch the two of them together, especially through his own eyes, as seen through his camcorder angles. He was especially fond of close-up shots of the most private parts of their bodies, he noted with mild embarrassment.

"You like to watch, don't you?" Karen said as she poured him more wine. He shrugged and guzzled it down, waving the real-life Karen aside so he could better see her image on the twenty-seven-inch monitor. But the picture seemed out-of-focus, fuzzy around the edges. Cursing, he stood up to fiddle with the TV controls and fell flat on his face on the condo's threadbare carpeting.

He grunted, tried to raise himself up and failed, hitting his cheek on something sharp. It was the metal toe of Gayle's cowboy boot, resting next to his face. He was momentarily angry at Gayle and then at himself for his failure to hold his liquor.

Karen crouched next to him, lifting one of his eyelids. "You won't be able to watch much longer, I'm afraid." He tried to speak and spittle drooled out the corner of his mouth.

"No, don't bother talking. Just watch and listen." Karen poured the rest of the wine over his body. "It's poison, of course. Hopefully it won't hurt too much; I understand it deadens the nerves as it destroys them." She turned to Gayle. "Better get the videotape."

George blinked; even through the drugged haze, he was beginning to comprehend what was happening.

"I know you think I'm a bimbo," Gayle addressed his prostrate form. "Karen told me so. But it doesn't take a rocket scientist to see that you were trying to kill us. Although why you would burn down your own house to do it, I can't understand. You are one sick piece of shit, George. And by the way, all those times you paid me to sleep with you? I never thought you were sexy in the slightest, you fat fucking pig." She used her metal heel to kick him in the balls, but he merely blinked faster for a moment, feeling no pain any longer. Feeling not much of anything, for that matter.

Karen moved in closer to see whether George was still conscious, since his loud breathing was becoming noticeably slower. "Can you hear me, George? After the house burned down, Gayle had her suspicions—I must admit I still thought you were innocent, gullible me—so we hired a private eye."

Gayle chimed in: "From money you'd paid me to fuck you."

Karen ignored the interruption. "He found out you hadn't gone out of town the night the house burned down. You weren't on any book-signing tour, George. You were at the same hotel you used to meet Gayle at, until you heard the TV newscast about the fire." She shuddered. "Gayle's right, you are a sick fuck, George. And we're not going to let you try to ruin our lives anymore—or anyone else's, with those sick books of yours."

She bent lower still and whispered in his ear. "No one saw us come in, George. We made certain of that. After you die, we'll wipe off all our fingerprints. Your death is going to make all the papers, George." She laughed. "Finally, George makes the headlines and he won't be around to read them!"

On impulse, she rose, reached for a newspaper, crumpled the front page, and stuffed it in his mouth.

"Read that, George." She got up, looked around. "We'd better clean up and get out of here."

Gayle shook her head. "That wouldn't be polite. Eating and running, that is. Speaking of eating . . ." She glanced over at the oven, opened the door, and sniffed inside. "Mmm. Your husband is—was—quite a good cook." She looked at the food, then at Karen. "Shall we?"

Karen hesitated. George was definitely having trouble breathing now, between the poison and the newspaper stuffed down his throat. She shuddered and turned away. Gayle came to her side. "Don't pity him. He deserves all this and more. Just think of how many times he tried to kill us."

Karen shook a bit in her lover's arms. "You're right," she said, her voice low. She turned away from George and toward the kitchen. "Oh hell, why not? I always loved George's blackened redfish."

George's vision focused one last time as he watched them take their first bites of fish. He smiled as best he could, shuddered, and expired.

"Did you see that?" Gayle asked as she stuffed more of the fish into her mouth. "It almost looked like he smiled for a second there." She shrugged. "This is delicious."

"Mmm," Karen agreed. "Pass the water, will you? This is very good, but it's even spicier than usual."

LULLABY & GOODNIGHT

Wayne Allen Sallee

Chicago is a political town, and that was why Patrolman Nicholas Raymond Rexer was confined to the T. D. Slatton Psychiatric Unit, pending the review of his actions by Internal Affairs and other lawsuits against him, the force, and the city. A political town where a man can be wrongly convicted and the DA's office in Cook County gets by with the adage "He might not've been guilty, but he probably done something just as bad."

And so it was that the events of April fell into August like lace over a corpse, and Nick Rexer sat in what could have passed for an efficiency apartment down in the South Loop, clutching exercise balls in his right hand, keeping his trigger-grip in good condition (because he knew he'd be back on the force; this was Chicago, after all). He was confined to the seventh-floor wing of the CPD's unofficial Disneyland North on West Belle Plaine Avenue.

The expatriate patrolman spent his days watching out the window for rodents to be run down by rush-hour motorists on Damen Avenue, exercising his trigger-grip, and reliving his vision of what had occurred down that alleyway off that near north side street four months previous.

He remembered it all so clearly, even to the very end:

A dull, beet-colored light in the alley behind Mohawk Street washed over the two cops' faces like blood clots bathing the brain. An April wind came off the lake, but all they smelled was oil and garbage. Stelfreeze and Rexer had been standing there five minutes, watching one of their own go through the back door of a house of prostitution. They had gone to make sure that Bill Valent wasn't accepting payoffs.

It was much worse than that.

They moved forward towards the second-floor landing. Both were out of uniform. The harsh glow from behind slatted blinds was brighter than a softer light from a third-story window. A blue light wavered, and Rexer realized it was most likely a television.

With the muted sounds of evening around them, Stelfreeze said to the darkness, "Well, here we are." The way he announced it, Rexer thought of a car pulled over into a lovers' lane, and that the two were on a first date, the lights of the city laid out below them. This is how it is with cops partnered for fifteen years.

Stelfreeze stared at the darkness that loomed above them, his lips bloodless, cleft chin thrust out in acceptance of what they were about to do. He knew stories about this place, tales he had not shared with Rexer until later. Only because he had never expected to be looking for, or *after,* one of their own here.

His partner was absently running his long fingers

through his Grouchoesque mustache as he also looked at the sky. Only, Stelfreeze was not staring at the April darkness, bruised black and purple, the light from the nearest stars barely making it through the pollution. The abyss Stelfreeze was aware of was a call girl with a unique angle, a whore who used the name Lullaby & Goodnight. The usage of dual names being the darkest sky of all.

She was a woman with a young girl's mind, who never spoke yet mewled at all the proper moments. Her real name was Celandine Tomei, and her mama charged upwards of fifteen yards for the ultimate in one-night stands. The highest-salaried men allegedly descended on this dilapidated two-flat on North Mohawk, the turks of the town come to kill or mutilate the prostitute as she orgasmed in her abnormal and childlike way.

And then to return the following month to repeat the act. Mama Tomei took Visa, MasterCard, Amex, and Diner's Club for the act itself. Other than living expenses, the funds received went towards plastic surgery and bone reconstruction. There were certainly no advertising costs, hence Rexer's ignorance of what the two cops would encounter here.

Stelfreeze knew too many people in the television industry, thanks to his sister marrying a sportscaster for the station that considered its biggest competitor to be MTV, not CNN. And sometimes Stelfreeze heard stories they kept off the air and held close to their disgusting hearts.

Stories about the ultimate one-night stand.

He thought long and hard on that; much of it coming out somewhat abstractly in his later Internal Affairs deposition. He realized that suicide came in a weak second to what was allegedly experienced here.

The porch was enclosed on two sides; Stelfreeze saw a swing near the north end of the landing, a strip of curled flypaper matted to the wire mesh behind it. Magazines were strewn across the well-swept flooring, the wooden boards the typical Polish gray on gray with whitened sawdust in the cracks. He wondered if they were skin magazines or, from what he had heard of the expected clientele, recent copies of *U.S. News & World Report*.

And if their cop friend was really here accepting payoffs, Stelfreeze envisioned Valent walking up these steps with his pockets stuffed with racing forms. In for a penny and all.

Rexer's thoughts were more metaphorical as they walked up to the wooden frame door. Yellowed venetian blinds were askew behind the dirty glass, yet he thought that they should be encountering some kind of a steel door, the kind that might be found at the Haddon Cobras' crack house on Leavitt.

But there was no eye-slit drawn back, no click of a revolver behind the walls, as the door opened ever so slowly. The woman who stood in the doorway was so frail that she made any skell under a heat vent on Lower Wacker Drive look like a television wrestler. She was framed in the kitchen light, not caring that her sagging breasts were outlined beneath her flowered beige nightdress.

Both cops were reminded uncomfortably of their respective mothers.

The light on the ceiling was one of those overhead jobs that consisted of two concentric rings of harsh milky white glow. The north side's version of the tesla coil, Stelfreeze always thought. Which was often, as there were three such lights in his flat on Aberdeen. The woman, Mama Tomei, was five feet two. Add another inch if the wind caught her off balance. Her eyebrows were penciled in and angled upwards the way a lunatic playing "she loves me, she loves me not" with the limbs of a dead rodent might arch his own quivering brows.

"You must be Mr. Stelfreeze." A withered hand reached out towards the larger cop. "Mr. Fassl told me you would be coming by. I do so love watching the way he talks about our Cubs . . ." She mentioned the network affiliate Stelfreeze's brother-in-law worked for.

She extended her hand to Rexer, continuing her talk of baseball. "That Mark Grace is just the cutest thing!" Rexer smiled, wondering why there wasn't more expensive furniture in their immediate surroundings. Perhaps it was upstairs, and the money they were making here furnished a lakefront home in Winnetka.

They still clutched hands, their calluses touching. "I am Mama Tomei. Please to call me Mama."

"The pleasure is mine," Rexer said. He smelled meat on her breath. Stelfreeze also nodded back in greeting.

Mama Tomei swung her arms in a bid for them to enter Castle Frankenstein, and they walked across cracked linoleum the shade of pea soup that had been puked up into a shadowed gutter. A black-and-white Emerson TV, antennae angled towards two o'clock, sat on a beige counter. Barney Miller was telling Wojo and Deitrich to handle a burglary over on Bleecker.

"Please," the woman said, sliding into a chair. "You sit now. Celly, she is with someone now."

Bill Valent, both cops thought. Hell, they could smell the Eternity cologne he splashed on every Friday night.

"Soon," she repeated, busying herself with fluffing napkins into a wooden holder cut into the shape of a blue duck. Her nails had been painted coral, but the color was chipping away on each finger. "Would either of you gentlemen like some coffee? Mountain-grown, the best kind."

She said this with a smile as Stelfreeze glanced towards the hallway, pushing herself away from the subject of her daughter's man friends. Mama Tomei busied herself at the counter.

Rexer looked at the tablecloth of fractal images, discovering several profiles of what could be construed as silver men smoking corncob pipes.

"I thought times like these were made for Taster's Choice," he said to himself. On the television, the ending bass strings for Barney Miller, the shot of the Manhattan skyline. The WGN announcer then related how Davenport recalls the first time she met Furillo, in the next devastating episode of *Hill Street Blues*. Late-night reruns.

Rexer suddenly wanted the evening to fast-forward. "I have to use your bathroom, ma'am . . . Mama." He cleared his throat.

She told him, "First door on left, down hallway."

There was a mirror above the kitchen sink; passing it, Rexer looked at his reflection, seeing gray hairs like cobwebs in his mustache for the first time.

Let Stelfreeze sweat it out of her, he thought as he moved down the hallway, the walls bare on either side of him. Yet he still tried not to focus on any single direction for fear of whatever hellish scenes the darkness held. She thought his partner was of high recommendation and maybe Stel could be casual about it.

But Rexer was downright claustrophobic.

The hall floor was carpeted a sickly orange and magenta, and as his eyes adjusted to the darkness, the slim cop saw shadows of branches dancing against living room bay windows. Again, as is expected in north side apartments, the bathroom light was a metal chain dangling to the right of the medicine cabinet. The pull chains always reminded him of the dog tags he wore around his neck, as a member of the air force reserves. Rexer always felt a sense of security when he touched those tags.

He turned in to the bathroom, reaching for the right spot. The white bulb flickered on, and he looked at himself in the mirror briefly. The toilet seat was broken, yellowed tape wrapped around the connected pieces.

He urinated in silence.

But he also noticed the muted amber light, a hazy cone above the stairwell landing. Then he heard a soft moan from upstairs. A female moan.

It took him less than a second to decide. Turning the bathroom light back on, he gently closed the door with hopes that Mama Tomei might think he was simply having a slow bowel movement.

Assumably looking forward to the excitement.

Rexer counted twelve steps and turned right at the top of the landing, finding himself facing several of those infamous velvet dog paintings where they all stared at you with their mournful eyes, lost dogs who gazed upon Rexer in a way that made him think of old Polish women praying at the stations of the cross at Saint Mary of Naz.

The upstairs hallway was L-shaped, and the slice of the room visible to Rexer put the nude woman on the bed in profile from the knees up. Mama Tomei's daughter lay on her back, her thin arms propped against the headboard, hands hanging limp. The handcuffs that held her that way were police-issued. With arms raised, her breasts swelled up, dark nipples pointing in a cross-eyed fashion. Rexer could smell sweat, cologne, and even a fresh aroma, like Ivory soap.

He moved to the side, looking in at a better angle, and had to bite on his palm until he drew blood. Growing out of the left side of the woman's rib cage was a small head, its eyes wide and unblinking. *A vestigial twin;* he recalled the phrase from growing up downstate; cows sometimes gave birth to such monstrosities. The head was much smaller than Celandine's, its hair like a discarded Kewpie doll's, a sharp chin curving down a long, rubbery neck.

Rexer jumped when it moved, falling back against whitened ribs so that he thought of a plaything lying atop a painted street gutter. He couldn't tell if it moved because of Mama Tomei's daughter shifting her weight, or because it was alive in some way.

Her body was so pale that he wondered if she had ever seen daylight, felt the direct sun on her stupefied body.

Celandine Tomei's face was not pretty. High cheekbones and thick hair in a widow's peak, a crooked nose and mouth that resembled a paper clip twisted by someone with caffeine nerves.

A sound came from deep within her grimaced mouth, and he would always remember what he saw next. A hand coming into view, a man's hand, fingers splayed so that it grabbed onto the vestigial head like it was a bowling ball, lifting it and letting it fall, the woman moaning louder . . .

The hand was a familiar one; he recognized a pale ring that Bill Valent had received during an altercation with a perp on PCP in the Hermitage Avenue corridor the previous summer.

But he couldn't step into the room farther, he could only stare at the head in the middle of Celandine's torso. The head had sparse black hair and was almost a pinhead, as if part of the connective skull plates were missing. It rested against Celandine's breasts as though they were deflated pillows. He could smell Valent's cologne, dammit!

The head turned towards Rexer, not of its own volition. It simply fell into the crook of the girl's arm. Orange drool formed around the mouth's gum line. Then everything started happening fast, the worst of it being the sound of a man's slacks being zipped up just beyond sight in the room. That sound would keep Rexer awake at nights for weeks to come.

He backed up, his palm striking against a small display case. The movement disturbed the doily dangling over the edge. Looking down, Rexer dry-gagged as he saw rows of gelatin eyes displayed in a cheap jewelry case. Some of the pupils had gold flecks, others were solid blue or hazel, and he knew he had to get out of there.

He backed away, towards the stairwell, knowing his hand was on his holster. He had been blinking away red spots in his mind, wanting to grab his shirt collar and start chewing on it, uncertain . . .

The next thing he remembered was moving down the stairs as quietly as he could, and Rexer almost shrieking when he saw Stelfreeze standing in the hallway.

"Let's go," Stelfreeze said, not even bothering to nod at Mama Tomei as they moved past her to the door. Rexer thought she looked ashamed.

* * *

"What is it, partner?" Rexer said to Stelfreeze as they walked out of the alley onto Eugenie Street. "If she didn't say, I can tell you Valent was up there."

Stelfreeze told him about the stories he had heard from his brother-in-law, the ones he now knew were true. Rexer confirmed what he had seen upstairs.

The thing was: Valent wasn't getting payoffs. He was going there to do what everybody else did, only at cheaper rates. Because he was a cop and could close it up anytime he wanted.

It was like eating your cake and having it too. Have sex with Celandine and strangle the head, tear at the skin, ravage the face. All without killing anything, because Celandine Tomei's decency was long buried.

Rexer thought of the jewel case of eyeballs. The cops passed a row of two-flats that displayed either plastic palm trees, plastic crucifixes, or promo photos of Richard M. Daley in the front windows.

Thunder rolled in the distance.

"The money mostly goes for reconstructive surgery," Stelfreeze said. Both wondered what they would say to Valent. The heavens suddenly opened and the April rain came down.

Jack Stelfreeze had met Rexer in the hallway, all right. He had taken the smoking gun from his partner's shaking hands. Rexer had been disgusted by what he had seen in that room, what he had watched his own friend and sometimes partner *doing* with that deformed freak.

This was the part he tried to deny, even though Internal Affairs had all the facts:

Rexer had waited all of three heartbeats before pulling his privately owned .38 from his waistband and shooting at Valent. For what he was *doing*. For what he had been *enjoying*. The younger cop was taken by surprise, falling from the bed half-erect, his face smeared with the freak's lipstick. It made him look like a clown.

Two steps in then, before the freak could scream. Didn't matter, though, with the iron thunder of the gunshots. Rexer grabbed the deformed head, pulled it from its stalk of a neck, laying it over the freak's face like a pillow so he wouldn't have to see her pleading eyes as he blew her brains out. Because he felt *pity* for her.

The freak's body going limp, spasming once, scaring him. Stumbling down the stairs, meeting Stelfreeze, Mama Tomei already dialing 911 out of rote.

Nicholas Raymond Rexer smiling, happy, victorious.

Back on Belle Plaine, Rexer smiling from his window, a beautiful vantage point for watching a rabbit blown to bits by a Gran Torino with missing plates. Rexer smiling at the smear, waiting for the knock on the door, the gentle sound his fellow officers would make as they took him into custody, out of the crazy room and off to Stateville. The big and burly coppers making a polite taptaptap, like he was considered a damn psycho.

Keeping his trigger-grip at the ready, rolling the exercise balls in his palms. His own special kind of exercise balls, better than the ones at the Academy, the ones you had to buy at the shop on Racine where you bought your winter shirts and plastic coverings for caps when you're slated for traffic control in winter.

The exercise balls Rexer had in his hands, practicing to fire a gun he'd never hold again, were two small glassine eyeballs. They were gold-flecked and, of course, unstaring.

This story is for Lee Seymour.

I AM JOE'S PENIS

Scott H. Urban

Sure, I'm curled up behind stone-washed jeans and briefs so old they're barely attached to the waistband, but I have ways of finding things out. For instance, I know Joe's chin is about twelve inches closer to the bar than it was about an hour ago, thanks to three whiskey sours.

It's almost Zero Hour at The Wall-Eyed. The beautiful people have already paired off and headed out for the Jacuzzis. The remainder—Joe included—are trying to decide just how desperate they are. *Scan the options. Christ, what are we still doing here? Catch the bartender's eye. Things'll look better through another highball.* Is it worth the night's warmth to wake up with someone you'd cross the street to avoid in daylight?

No, she's never gonna grace the cover of *Cosmopolitan,* Joe thinks, but when was the last time you were out with a model, huh? I try to tell him don't bother, it won't work, but does he listen? Of course not, he never does.

Back at her place, they clink glasses, dim the lights, and pull back the bedspread. She steps out of her slacks. Revealed are thick pasty-white thighs that would look better in front of a Greek temple. I don't want any part of this. As a matter of fact, I try to crawl back up inside.

"It's okay. We've both had a few. Let me see what I can do," she offers.

She starts working me with her hand. I suppose it's good enough for the moment, because I stand up at attention. But it takes too long, and when she pulls away I begin to wilt like an hours-cut blossom on a hot afternoon. She stretches back against the stacked pillows. Joe positions himself between her knees. Both of them move with the exaggerated care of a lush trying to walk a straight line under the trooper's steely glare.

Talk about loose lips that could sink ships! I mean, let's face it. Great sex boils down to the gradual buildup of friction. Without something to work against . . . well, forget any fireworks. For all the friction these two have, they'd be better off trying to start a campfire by rubbing two bars of soap together. It's like diving into a sponge—no, worse, more like sinking into a platter of Jell-O.

Joe closes his eyes, tries to conjure up the face of the little nymphet in the skin flick he jerked off to last night. No good, his head is making him feel like the mattress is turning barrel rolls. She squeezes his ass, but I'm already in retreat. Joe slumps to the side with a groan.

"S'all right," she murmurs, rubbing his shoulder. "We'll try again in a li'l bit."

Luckily they curl up and let their eyelids shut. Within minutes they're snoring in each other's face.

By the time morning arrives, I'm ignored, quickly tucked away like some embarrassing old uncle who drools uncontrollably out of the corner of his mouth. They politely blow each other off and scurry to work.

I've got to do something. I can't go through that again. It's time to take charge, for Joe's sake as well as my own.

I wait until the following evening. Fortunately he didn't try to hit the bars; too much to do the next day. I let him drift into REM sleep. I despise looking in on his dreams; they're so predictable, I can't even get a Peeping Tom thrill out of them. Oh great—his mother, in a see-through negligee, pirouetting in front of him. Gimme a fuckin' break.

I begin forcing the tissue I'm made of—the *corpus spongiosum*—back up into the rest of Joe's body. The *spongiosum* contains cavities I can engorge with blood —that's how I pop a boner when I need it. I begin superseding—supplanting—the normal muscle tissue with my own.

It's easy as far back as the scrotum, the anus, and the seminal vesicles. But all that's familiar territory. It's more difficult once I reach the lower abdomen. The deep abdominal muscles set up some resistance. I realize I can't encompass them entirely. I'm going to have to settle for a less-than-total takeover.

Deep within his Oedipal fantasy, Joe feels something moving up inside him. His stomach churns, and he draws his knees up toward his chest. I have to be careful. I don't want to make him so sick he wakes up. All I need is for some doctor to discover penile tissue running throughout Joe's body. Joe groans low in his throat and turns to the other side.

It's slow going up through the chest cavity and along

the spine, but it gets easier with practice. By the time I'm spreading down through his arms and legs, I feel like an old pro.

It's a lucky thing the body works as a democratic unit.

I have the majority vote.

A week later. Joe's back at The Wall-Eyed. He tried to line up a date for the evening but hit bottom like a diver belly-flopping into an empty pool. I'm doing my best to keep him from drowning himself. He knows he came in here wanting to get blotto drunk. But now, three hours later, he's still on his second drink and doesn't even have a buzz on. He's been making eyes at this brunette, but she's hanging out with a bunch of her friends. Besides, she's not any better-looking than Miss Hand Job. As a matter of fact, I'm surprised she doesn't have a wheelbarrow beside her chair, to help her cart that ass around.

No, I didn't go to all that trouble so we could judge a dog contest. I'm more interested in the blonde in the corner booth. She's almost too beautiful to be in here. She's wearing a short floral print dress with a low scooped neckline. Her hair is piled on top of her head, with golden ringlets spilling down either side of her ears. Her legs look as if they were made just to wrap around Joe's waist.

Now, of course, Floral's playing footsie under the table with her date, the Missing Link. He's so broad, he nearly pushes her out of the booth. Joe took one look at him before and promptly filed Floral in the drawer labeled "Ones That Got Away," but I've got ideas of my own, and now I've got the means to carry them out.

The brunette is raising her glass. Joe is about to

walk in her direction. But Floral and her date are getting up, heading for the door. I have to make my first overt move. It might as well be here, in front of a crowd. This way, Joe can't afford to freak out. Since I now control the *spongiosum* tissue in Joe's body, I can make him walk wherever I want. He's the new Pinocchio, a marionette without strings. I swing him in behind Floral.

For a moment, Joe continues to face the brunette. He can't understand why he's walking toward her—yet her face is getting farther away. Then he realizes he's going in the opposite direction. "What the *fuck?*" You got it, Joe. He begins to reach for the bar, a table, to stop himself, but I force his arms to his sides.

We step outside, several yards behind the first pair. We've got to walk half a block to the municipal parking deck. Joe is swinging his head left, right, down, up, trying to make sense out of what's happening. *He's* not making himself walk, *he* didn't want to leave the bar, so what the hell is going on?

The parking deck is old, and the city fathers, in their infinite decrepitude, have never seen fit to install adequate lighting, which is just fine with me. The pair had to park their sports car in one of the shadow-cloaked corners. Joe's heels scrape against the concrete. I can't help it; I haven't had enough practice yet. The Missing Link looks up and squints. "Help you, buddy?" That's what he says, but what he really means is, "You wanna turn around and walk the other way fast, asshole."

Joe shakes his head. He still doesn't know what he's doing here. "I'm—uhhm—I'm sorry . . ." Let him mumble, I'm already moving. First I kick the car door. Its metal edges slam on either side of Link's fingers—those little bones just above the first joint.

Link bends and clutches his hand, howling (suitably enough) in primate fashion. I'm already lifting my foot again, catching the bridge of his nose with my boot's steel toe. There's the sound of a twig snapping. Stuff leaking from Link's face darkens the pavement.

Floral is screaming: "Non*ono!*" Joe's shouting too. "I'm sorry! I'm not doing this—I'm really *not doing this!*" I clamp down on Joe's jaw muscles. I don't want him alerting all downtown.

Floral hesitates. She isn't sure whether to check on the Missing Link or turn and run like hell. In that moment of indecision I have Joe grab her wrists. Her bones are thin enough I can grasp them easily in Joe's left hand. I pin her arms above and behind her, on top of the sports car's roof. With Joe's right hand, I reach into his coat pocket and withdraw a roll of electrical tape. Earlier that evening, while he was reading the newspaper at his desk, I made his hand reach into the side drawer and pull the tape out. He never even knew he put it in his pocket.

Floral manages to get out one or two good screams, but using Joe's right hand and his teeth, I get the tape around both her wrists and her mouth. She's wrenching her entire body from side to side, but I've got too good a hold for her to break free. I work her dress above her waist and yank down her panties. She tries to put a knee in Joe's face but only succeeds in grazing his temple.

All the while Joe's saying, "Please! I'm not trying to hurt you! I don't want to do this! I don't know what's happening to me!" I let him talk—but not too loud.

She doesn't listen, she can't be listening, she's tossing her head from side to side, her hair coming loose from its barrettes, whipping Joe across the cheeks.

"I can't help it!" he cries. "I can't make myself stop!"

I use Joe's hand to loosen his belt, his pants, tug down the Fruit of the Looms, and I'm driving between her legs, and I realize it was worth it, all of it was worth it, every second, she's already damp because she'd been anticipating the Missing Link's primordial prick but now she's got me, her cunt shudders with fear and revulsion, yes, all of them should be terrified of their lovers, I'm not gonna last long, but what it lacks in duration it's gonna make up in intensity, and anyway this is only the beginning because, because

Now I am not just Joe's penis.

Now I am Joe.

WHAT YOU SEE

Paul Dale Anderson

*W*ho do you want to be tonight? she asks herself. Sandra? Marsha? Cynthia?

Cynthia, yes. Cindy for short. Cindy is sexy, sinful. Full of fun. Tonight she wants to be Cindy.

Hurriedly stripping off her daytime persona to leave behind a scattered trail of discarded business attire and conventional undergarments—nylon half-slip, panty hose, bra, white cotton panties—littering the plush hallway carpet between master bedroom and bathroom, Cindy softly hums the theme song from *Gypsy*. She flings the brightly colored plastic shower curtain aside, her playful mood quickly escalating to near mania. She steps into the tub, adjusts the water temperature, yanks the curtain back into place, twists a plastic knob to divert the flow of hot water from spigot to showerhead, and luxuriates in the sheer sensuality of thousands of tiny needles pounding her shoulder blades and stinging her naked flesh like a cat-o'-nine-tails.

Her nipples instantly harden; her inner thighs become slippery and wet; a warm flush flutters her tummy as soapy fingers caress her tendermost spots.

After bringing herself to multiple orgasms with erotic daydreams of the night yet to come, Cindy shaves both legs and carefully trims scraggly strands of curly hair from her pubic thatch with her father's straight razor. She rinses off and towels herself dry.

Gaudy makeup comes next: eye shadow, eyeliner, and lipstick. Then she selects a long, blond fall, one of dozens of expensive falls and wigs that line her makeup table like trophies line the huts of South Seas headhunters. She expertly shapes and blends the soft synthetic human hair into her own closely cropped natural hair with the consummate skill of a professional hairdresser.

Nipple rings? Should she wear nipple rings?

She rummages through her jewelry drawer to find a pair of delicately crafted twenty-four-karat two-inch-diameter gold rings, pokes thin hypoallergenic wires through tiny holes piercing the center of both nipples. Delicious thrills sensitize her body as she tugs both rings to be sure the wires are securely seated.

On impulse, she spreads the lips of her vulva and attaches a third ring—this one a long, slender, razor-thin piece of jeweled metal that clamps tightly to her clitoris like the jaws of a vise.

The image that stares back at Cindy from the full-length mirror on the other side of the room is extremely beautiful, too beautiful to be believed. Didn't Mother always say Cindy was far too skinny and sickly looking for her own good? On closer inspection, she grudgingly admits Mother was right. Without an inch of fat to spare, her image appears delicate, fragile, easily fractured. Like a porcelain doll that will shatter to thousands of sharp shards if touched by human hands. Her skin, too, seems unnaturally pale; there should be telltale tan lines decorating her chest like military campaign ribbons, but there aren't. And her firm breasts, though more than ample for her height and slender frame, are neither as large nor full as the cover girls that pose for *Cosmo* or *Vogue*.

She makes a mental note to visit a tanning salon. A few more pounds might add an inch or two to her bustline, hopefully without ruining the rest of her figure. Why should she settle for anything less than perfection? Mother would insist she shouldn't.

And Mother is always right.

At twenty-eight, Cindy thinks she can easily pass for twenty-four—maybe even twenty-two, if the lights are right. She's young enough to be attractive, but experienced enough to know how to exploit a woman's hidden assets. Mother would say it's the best of all possible worlds.

She is the same age her mother was when she was born.

Toying with fabrics in the walk-in closet, she decides a red half-cup bra under a peach-colored silk see-through will be perfect tonight. A matching red garter belt, peach-tinted nylons, a magenta thigh-length leather skirt, and red patent leather pumps complete the outfit nicely.

Should she wear panties? Yes? No?

Wouldn't Mother be mortified at the thought? Not wear underwear? Mother would *kill* her if she knew.

But Mother isn't here now, and Cindy is a grown-up girl who can make her own decisions.

She decides to leave the panties at home.

* * *

"So this is where you live," Alex says. "Nice."

"I inherited this house when my parents died," Cindy tells him. "I've lived here all my life."

"Bet it costs a fortune to maintain a house like this and the grounds," Alex whispers appreciatively, strolling around the huge living room, examining the fine furniture, the glassed-in curio cabinets, original framed oils on all four walls. "How do you do it? Everything looks so neat, so clean, so spotless. So perfect."

"Why, thank you," Cindy beams, pleased he noticed. Most of the pretty boys she met tonight at the club wouldn't have. That's why she picked Alex: He has a certain sensitivity she finds attractive. "A landscaping service takes care of the yard," she explains, "but the house I do all by myself. My mother taught me that cleanliness is next to godliness. I've never forgotten a thing Mother taught me."

"No wonder I haven't seen you out on the dance floor before," Alex says, only half-jokingly. "You spend all your time cleaning."

"Not all my time," laughs Cindy. "I'm the chief executive officer and chairperson of the board of two international corporations my father founded. Most of my time, I'm sorry to say, is taken up by business. But I really don't want to spend all night talking about business or cleaning house. And neither do you." Cindy crooks a finger in Alex's direction. "C'mere, you gorgeous hunk, you. The bedroom's this way."

As Cindy climbs the carpeted stairs to an upstairs bedroom with Alex following closely behind like a lovesick puppy tied to a leash, she allows the short leather skirt to inch slowly up the backs of her thighs.

By now there should be absolutely no doubt in Alex's mind that Cindy isn't wearing panties.

Alex can't believe his luck. Not only is this prime-looking bitch horny as hell, she's also richer than Rockefeller.

A college junior, Alex was Friday-night bar-hopping with two half-drunk classmates—"looking *at* girls, not *for* girls," they lied to themselves as they put away beer after beer in bar after bar—when they discovered sexy Cindy gyrating on the crowded dance floor of an upscale nightclub out on the beltway.

Instantly smitten by the really seductive way this older woman's tight ass wriggled beneath her incredibly short leather skirt, the way her half-hidden breasts jostled the front of the see-through blouse, the way her piercing eyes scanned and measured each of them in turn—promising heaven on earth to anybody man enough to fuel the fire in those eyes—the boys picked a place at the bar where they could ogle the woman's every move without being obvious.

"She's not wearing panties!" Ernie relayed over the music, becoming so excited, he slipped off his barstool and nearly sprawled face-forward on the floor. "I swear she flashed me a live beaver!"

"Shut up and sit down," Alex shushed, embarrassed by his friend's drunken display. Alex was acting as the designated driver tonight, carefully nursing his own drinks to keep a clear head and stay within state-enforced legal blood-alcohol limits. "No need to blow your cool, Ernie. She's probably wearing flesh-colored bikini panties or a thong." Alex squinted his eyes, scrutinizing the hem of that short leather skirt bobbing oh-so-dangerously close to crotch level, a man might imagine almost anything. "You can't see well enough in this light to tell the difference," he concluded.

"I think I'm in lust," Ernie groaned, downing his nineteenth beer of the night, and immediately chasing that one down with a shot of Jim Beam. He signaled the bartender for another round.

"You're always in lust," Alex said disgustedly. *But then,* he mused, his eyes zeroing in on interesting shadows dancing around the woman's crotch, *so am I.*

When the dance ended, the woman excused herself to her dance partner—a muscle-bound thirty-something wearing a half-unbuttoned shirt that showed off his gold chains and steroid-induced pecs—and headed for the ladies' room.

"Show's over," Ted sadly lamented, killing his watered-down scotch and setting the empty glass on the bar. "You guys ready to move on to the next watering hole?"

"Not me, man," protested Ernie, beginning to look a little green around the gills. "The whole room's spinning around like the tilt-a-whirl at Kiddieland. I think I'm gonna puke."

"Warned you not to mix bourbon and beer on an empty stomach, didn't I?" Ted said knowingly. "Maybe if you eat something solid, you'll feel—"

At the first mention of food, Ernie lurched from his perch on the barstool and rushed straight to the john, a protective hand over his mouth.

"Guess *he's* done for the night," said Ted, shaking his head. "You wanna split before he comes back? Let the asshole catch a cab?"

"Here," said Alex, flipping Ted the car keys. "You go. I'll stick around and make certain Ernie gets home okay."

"You sure? The night's still young. We could always hit a few strip joints . . ."

"I'm sure," Alex said.

After Ted left, Alex asked the bartender to phone for a cab. Then he headed for the men's room to check on Ernie.

And bumped into the blonde.

Up close, he could see she was older than she looked on the dance floor. Suddenly he felt like an immature teenager with a crush on his eighth-grade English teacher. He couldn't move. He didn't know what to say.

"Do I have to crawl over you to get by?" she asked because Alex's solid bulk blocked the only way back to the dance floor from the rest rooms.

"You can crawl all over me anytime you want," he offered, surprised by the brazenness of the words coming from his own mouth. He couldn't believe he actually said that. He licked his lips, then literally bit his tongue.

Her eyes roamed his body from head to toe. "If I were to crawl all over you," she asked seriously, her voice indicating newfound interest, "what would *you* do?"

"I'd lick your pussy until you begged me to fuck your brains out," he said, still biting his tongue. It sounded to him like he said, "I dick yewsy ilew egg ilew uck ur ainsout."

"Think you're man enough to fuck my brains out?" she asked.

He reached for her hand and, without thinking of the consequences, moved her fingers straight to his fly. "Think you're *woman* enough to find out?"

Her eyes locked his in a battle of wills as two of her

painted fingers touched the tab of his zipper, tugging it down. Down past the dangerous snake uncoiling in his jeans. Down, down, all the way down. As far down as his zipper would go. A curious smile curled the corners of her eyes as the same two fingers slowly— oh, ever so slowly!—crept inside his open fly, around the elastic edge of his Jockey shorts, made intimate contact with his bare flesh. Made him jump. Made hot sparks shoot through his nervous system like fireworks on the Fourth of July.

"You'll do," she acknowledged, withdrawing her hand. "Let's go before I change my mind."

"Go? Go where?" Alex asked in a daze, awkwardly fumbling to zip up his pants before anyone else saw he was wide open.

"Why, my place, of course," the girl said, making him feel stupid for asking such a dumb question. "I'm going to give you a chance to fuck my brains out."

Cindy takes her time undressing.

She has already undressed Alex. He sits, completely naked, on the edge of the bed, watching her every move, a throbbing erection between his hairy legs.

Cindy loves the look of rapt attention fixing his face. He seems so young, so innocent, so expectant. So hopeful. So *perfect*.

He is the exact same age she was when her parents died.

She peels off her see-through blouse, drops it to the floor by her feet. Her full breasts, spilling over the tops of the half-cups, ache to be touched. She reaches up and touches her flesh herself, squeezes her own firm flesh as if she were kneading bread dough on a kitchen countertop. Alex is forced to watch all this from the edge of the bed. She has forbidden him to touch her until she gives explicit orders. The prolonged wait is meant to torture her as much as him.

She removes the confining material from around the bottoms of her breasts, drops the red half-bra to the floor next to the see-through blouse. She watches Alex's eyes widen in surprise and fascination as she slips her fingers through the golden rings dangling from her pierced nipples and *yanks*. An unsuppressible groan escapes her lips as exquisite thrills rip through traumatized nerve endings in both nipples, adding fuel to an already fierce fire blazing between her legs.

Bunching the short leather skirt up around her waist, Cindy slowly opens her thighs and allows a solitary fingertip to explore her moist crease from one end to the other. She licks her lips and imagines her finger has now become a tongue.

Despite strict orders not to move a muscle or she'll stop the show, she sees Alex can barely control himself. His hand goes to his lap and grips his erection like a vise. She can tell he is right on the edge.

She walks quickly to the bed, her fingers opening herself wide.

"Fuck my brains out," she orders, lowering herself atop his hard-on.

Alex awakens to bright morning sunlight spearing his eyes, temporarily blinding him.

He also has to pee something fierce.

Without realizing that he's not at home in his own room, he tries to roll out of bed and instantly discovers he can move no more than an inch or two in either direction. Then he remembers: Both hands and both ankles are firmly cuffed with police-style steel hand-cuffs; the handcuffs chained to iron eyelets anchored to ceiling beams above the bed.

He dimly recalls allowing Cindy, at some low point during their nightlong lovefest, to shackle and chain him like a criminal. Though it did seem a bit kinky at the time, he didn't voice an objection because beauti-ful Cindy had him so turned on, he would have agreed to almost anything.

Then she proceeded to test his sexual stamina until he fell asleep with the cuffs still fastened to his hands and feet.

Now, as he looks around for Cindy to free him, Cindy is nowhere to be seen.

Alex struggles with his bonds for what seems like hours, rattling the chains, rubbing his wrists raw, but neither set of cuffs wants to budge. He begins to panic. He shouts for help until he's hoarse. No help comes. His bladder lets go and he wets the bed.

Finally, when he's given up hope anyone will hear him, the door opens and an older woman—old enough, by the looks of her, to be his own mother or grandmother—enters the bedroom carrying a bundle of clean sheets. She walks to the windows and closes the blinds.

At first, as his eyes try to adjust to the changing light, Alex is absolutely certain this woman bears no resemblance to Cindy. This woman's hair is short and gray. Cindy's hair is long and blond. This woman appears old, tired, worn-out. Cindy is young and vibrant. Supersexy. Cindy, he's sure, would never dress in a frumpy pale green housedress that obscures her figure from neck to knees. Nor would she house her feet in brown, well-worn penny loafers a size too big. Nor wear ornate eyeglasses and no makeup.

"Where's Cindy?" Alex demands, thinking he's addressing a maid or cleaning woman. "Did she send you in here with the key to unlock these damn things?"

"Cindy . . . went . . . away," the woman replies, each word deliberately drawn out as if she has to think twice about what a word means before voicing its sound. "My . . . name's . . . Marsha. I'm Cindy's . . . mother. And . . . no . . . she didn't give me any key."

"You *can't* be Cindy's mother," Alex objects. "Cindy told me both her parents were dead."

"But I *am* her . . . mother . . . and I'm certainly . . . *not* dead," the woman insists, her voice beginning to sound more and more like Cindy's. "What's the . . . matter? Don't I look like Cindy's . . . mother?"

Despite her aged appearance and weird speech patterns, Alex now thinks he can recognize a certain familiarity in this woman's demeanor. Merely a family resemblance? Or is it possible he may be talking to Cindy in disguise?

"No," he decides. "You look more like Cindy in a cheap, gray wig than you look like Cindy's mother." He rattles his chains. "C'mon, Cindy, stop playing games. Get me out of these things."

"Oh, no. I couldn't . . . do that," says the woman, "even if I . . . wanted to. Cindy has the only key."

"Can the crap, Cindy," Alex shouts, angry at feeling toyed with. "Unlock these damn cuffs right now! I want to take a shower and go home."

"I can tell by your . . . lack of clothes, young man," the woman says sternly, glancing disapprovingly at Alex's nakedness, then quickly averting her eyes, "that you and my daughter have been very, very . . . wicked. I'll just have to . . . punish her for that . . . when she returns. I can't have Cindy bringing strange

. . . men into my house and doing heaven knows what . . . with them without . . . punishing her. Can I? I *always* punish Cindy when she's been wicked."

"You're . . ." *Crazy,* Alex starts to say, then quickly bites his tongue before the word can slip out. What if she really *is* crazy? Do crazy people turn violent, he wonders, when you tell them you think they're crazy? Alex is afraid to find out.

"What would be a suitable punishment for . . . my daughter . . . this time?" the woman asks herself aloud, momentarily ignoring Alex. "Should I beat her again? Lock her in a dark closet and feed her nothing but . . . prunes? Or should I make her lick the bathroom spotless . . . with her tongue? I've tried all those things, you know, and . . . none of them works. What can I do to make . . . Cindy obey me? What? What?"

Alex says nothing.

"Maybe I should punish *you,*" the woman suggests, returning her full attention to Alex. "Cindy seems to like you. Maybe if I were to punish *you,* it might hurt her worse than if I inflicted the same punishment on her directly. What do you think?"

"This isn't funny anymore, Cindy," Alex says, traces of fear edging into his voice. "Please. Just unlock these cuffs and let me go home. Play your mind games on someone else."

"I assure you, young man, this is no game," the woman says, laying the clean sheets at the foot of the bed and stepping to the doorway. "When I get back, I'll show you just how real all this can be."

"Oh, no," Sandra says when she opens the door to her bedroom and discovers a naked man chained to her bed. "Not again."

"Cindy?" the man asks hopefully. "Thank goodness, you're back, Cindy! Get me out of these cuffs before I go crazy!"

"I'm Sandy, not Cindy," Sandra quickly corrects the man, switching on overhead lights, casting out encroaching early evening shadows so the naked man can clearly see her raven-colored hair and baby blue eyes. "Cindy was my younger sister. Who the hell are you, mister? And what, pray tell, are you doing chained to my bed without any clothes on?"

"Alex," the man answers, hope draining from his voice when he sees that Sandy isn't Cindy. "I'm sorry. I thought you were Cindy. You look a lot like Cindy, except for the hair and clothes. And I thought this was Cindy's bed."

"It *was* Cindy's bed. Before Cindy died in it."

"Cindy died? In this bed?"

"Four years ago. I was away at college at the time, but when I came home for spring break, I found my father chained to the bed, Cindy tied up next to him, and my mother on the floor at the foot of the bed. All dead. According to the autopsy, Cindy and my father both died of starvation and dehydration after weeks without food or water. My mother died from a self-inflicted overdose of sleeping pills."

"Jesus," Alex says.

"I don't cry for them anymore," Sandy says. "I don't have time to cry, what with running my father's businesses and maintaining the house."

"I don't suppose you do," Alex says sympathetically. "And I really don't want to impose on your precious time at all, but do you suppose you might take just a *little* time to look for the key to these cuffs? I'd really appreciate it."

"I don't know where to start looking," Sandra says, wondering how this man got chained to her bed in the first place. Especially since the police took all the chains and cuffs away when they took her father's decomposing body away. Where did these new chains and handcuffs come from?

"Please," begs the man with tears glistening his eyes. "Look for the keys. *Please.*"

"Oh, all right," agrees Sandra. After all, it certainly wouldn't do if Mother were to come home unexpectedly and find a naked man chained to Sandra's bed.

It wouldn't do at all.

Can all three women be the same person? Alex wonders as he watches Sandra's shapely backside sashay from the room.

Is it possible?

Racking his brain for answers, he recalls something he learned during an intro psych class the spring semester of his sophomore year. "The victims of multiple personality disorder," his instructor had informed the class, "are almost always women, very often young and pretty women, usually in their mid-to-late twenties by the time symptoms manifest themselves for clinical observation.

"MPD is one of several mental disorders believed to be caused by severe emotional trauma during the identity realization phase of late childhood development or early adolescence. When a fragile undifferentiated preadolescent ego suffers an intolerable condition—such as repeated physical, sexual, or mental abuse—over an extended period of time with no end in sight and no possibility of escape in the real world, the human psyche's unconscious defense mechanisms take over and the damaged ego sometimes splits into separate personalities in a desperate attempt to fool itself. 'This isn't really happening to me,' the mind tells itself, 'it's happening to someone else.'"

So which personality is the someone else in Cindy's case? Sandra? Marsha? Cindy?

Which woman is real, Alex wonders, and which two women are figments of a warped imagination?

Sandra is obviously just Cindy with medium-length black hair, dressed casually in loose-fitting blue jeans and a patterned blouse, looking like your average graduate student or maybe someone's third-grade teacher. Marsha, too, is Cindy, shrouded in a shapeless shift that hides her figure, wearing ornate eyeglasses to disguise her face and a short gray wig to make her look twice as old as she really is. But Cindy herself is, he realizes too late to escape being trapped by the handcuffs, too fantastic to be real. Her long blond hair, fabulous body, and voracious appetite for kinky sex make her every man's wet dream come true.

While her Marsha personality is every man's worst nightmare!

And Sandra, who appears as nice and normal as the typical girl next door, is probably as crazy as an ax murderer.

Alex smells his fear. Tears run down his cheeks as he realizes the precarious predicament that thinking with his balls instead of his head has placed him in.

Next time—please, God, let there be a next time!—he promises he'll know better.

What are you thinking now, my beautiful blue-eyed boy? Have you figured it out yet?

Do you know what's going to happen next?

Cindy swivels around in her executive office chair, punches a button on an electronic control panel in front of her, and is able to view Alex's terrified face simultaneously in six live television monitors mounted on the wall. The hidden cameras—one concealed in the ceiling, one on the floor, and one in each of the bedroom walls—can zoom in on any part of Alex's anatomy she wishes to focus on at the flip of a switch.

A dozen other video monitors on another wall replay highlights from last night's hours-long fuckfest, more than enough footage, Cindy is certain, for three or four feature-length films. When she has time, she'll edit the tapes for content, develop a cohesive story line for each feature presentation, dub in additional dialogue as needed, then add scripted footage of herself in the roles of Marsha, Sandra, and Cindy to round out production values. After tightening each feature to ninety minutes, reproducible masters, digitally enhanced, will be distributed via modem and international phone lines to business associates in London and Bangkok. There her associates will inexpensively mass-produce videotapes for the booming billion-dollar porn markets of South America, Eastern Europe, and the Pacific Rim, where snuff films—real snuff films, not phony reenactments—are currently very much in demand.

Cindy expects to gross half a million dollars or more per feature, a mil and a half to two mil for the bundle. Not bad for a single night's work. Especially since her costar won't be alive to see a penny of the proceeds.

"The key to operating a successful business," her father taught her, "is to keep overhead low. Occupy a market niche that can command a high price for goods and services, and slice costs to the bone."

Her father had been her first costar, and she'd certainly sliced *him* to the bone.

Her mother had costarred in Cindy's second film.

Of course, Cindy isn't her real name. Nor does her real name appear in the phony credits of any of her feature films.

Cindy sees the growing fear on Alex's face in the monitor and knows it's time to end the charade. After all, it wouldn't do to have him die from sheer terror and ruin the bang-up ending she has planned, now would it?

Cindy picks up a twelve-foot braided rawhide bullwhip from her desk, coils it over her arm. The bullwhip is always a crowd pleaser. She'll start the next scene with the bullwhip biting into Alex's backside.

She slips on a pristine pair of white pumps with six-inch-high stiletto heels. The heels have been honed to fine points much sharper than nails. She'll end the scene by walking over Alex's groin, stomach, neck, and face with stiletto heels.

On her way from the office back to the bedroom, Cindy stops by a mirror, checks her makeup, and adjusts Marsha's wig so several strands of her own hair are visible at the edges.

The incongruity of the relatively young and well-proportioned naked female body in high heels she sees reflected in the mirror and the gray-haired granny wig slanted cockeyed on her forehead nearly makes her laugh.

But laughing is for later.

First she has to attend to business.

THE BEAST

Larry Tritten

*L*ewis woke to the sound of the animal breathing heavily, the gasped exhalations of its breath like those of someone sobbing, and they became steadily more excited as he lay alone in the darkness listening. It had reappeared again, after an absence of several nights during which he had dared to hope that the nightmare had finally come to an end, and as he lay quietly, paralyzed with fear, the familiar menacing sound overwhelmed him once more with a threat of terrible violence. As he listened, the gasping grew louder and more uneven and then broke as always into a protracted howling, the cry of a wounded or agonized thing.

The beast had returned. In a way it was a relief to have the tenuous thread of hope broken. There were times, now and then, when the beast would leave him alone for several consecutive nights, but after such an interim, it would always return, twice as fierce as before, growling and keening with such savagery that he could clearly picture for himself the manic gleaming of its eyes and the flashing of its teeth. He had only seen it once, a quick glimpse, but would never forget the sight, just as the beast would never let him rest. Except for its occasional absences, it prowled through the house each night, stalking him, endlessly, its presence a threat that dominated his thoughts by day as well as night. One day he was certain it would kill him and devour him, and on those nights when it didn't wake him with its wild cries, his dreams gave him dark visions of how this would happen, with the beast tearing the flesh from his struggling body. He had been born, he knew, to live indefinitely with this fear and to die after a seeming eternity of it when the beast decided it was time to feed. Perhaps a thousand nights from now, perhaps tonight.

Lewis began to weep, but soundlessly so as not to attract the beast to his door. Yet it was not that hard to cry soundlessly for someone who cannot even speak. Words were obstacles his tongue could not surmount, and his thoughts were themselves like tiny animals he had to struggle to control. What he perceived was a blurred and shifting montage of ideation illuminated by certain basic words and fragments of concept and guided by intuition. It was how he knew that his only real friend was dog, the good animal they allowed into his room sometimes to play with him. That was his only pleasure other than the customary one of eating and sometimes watching a little television. Beyond that there was only fear, his life an endless sequence of fear evolving into terror and devolving back into fear as he lived through blank days and dark nights waiting for the beast to come for him.

One night it would open the door, would come to feed.

Lewis wept soundlessly, his body shuddering with

repressed sobs, and watched the door in the darkness, waiting. After a long while he finally slept again, and so descended into a nightmare in which the beast devoured him alive and screaming.

Then it was morning and the cell of his dun room was bright with sunlight. He got out of bed and sat on the edge of it, staring at the pink bunnies on the sleeve of his pajama top. *Good* animals. In time Mother came and dressed him, neither of them speaking because neither of them had anything to say, and in any case Lewis knew that this quiet and gentle (if not loving) woman was something more than she seemed to be. It was why every touch of her fingers as she dressed him filled him with coldness, why he could never trust her. She was part of the conspiracy.

Father came and stood in the doorway. "Hey, Lewis," he said in a monotone. He was carrying a blue book. "Elaine," he said to Mother, "I'm going to be late if I don't haul ass. I've got to give that Chaucer exam and—" he glanced at his watch "—I don't want to emulate the White Rabbit."

"But you are rabbity in some ways," Mother said to him with a smile.

Father smiled back at her and crossed the room and put his arms around Mother and kissed her, and she put her arms around him and pressed her face to his throat. "I love you," she said. "Ummmmmmm, you're so good . . ." She reached to unzip his pants, but he pulled away, laughing.

"No more than thou," Father said. "As for Love . . . his wings will not rest and his feet will not stay for us; Morning is here in the joy of its might; With his breath has he sweetened a night and a day for us . . . but I must now haul ass . . ."

"Swinburne?" asked Mother.

"To a point," Father said. He kissed Mother again. Lewis saw the tip of Mother's tongue, like that of a serpent, wet with light, slip from her mouth to ordain a kiss unlike any she had ever given him before she stopped the charade of kissing him. "See you, love," he said. "'Bye, Lewis."

After Father was gone, Mother took Lewis into the kitchen and fed him. No communication passed between them and their eyes never met. Sometimes a vague sense of warmth emanated from her, but it was not even a flickering of the glow that she and Father exchanged, and Lewis sensed that it was because he knew her secret. He knew the horror that lurked within her. He lived in fear of her. He froze at her touch, and because of that, she cared little for him and he believed that she knew what he knew.

When Mother had fed him, she put him back in his room and closed the door. Lewis sat alone in the silent room with his brooding fear. A fly circled the room listlessly in the summer heat, returning again and again to the window to bounce buzzingly against the glass.

Lewis did nothing all morning and afternoon. It was his task. Nothing. He could hear Mother moving about in the house and his fear simmered within him. His thoughts moved like glacial ice floes in the deep gray tide of his consciousness. Could she know that he knew the evil she possessed? Or did she even know of the evil herself? Still, even in his fear, he relaxed somewhat because he doubted that she would kill him in the daylight. Only at night.

Early in the afternoon Mother fed Lewis again in his room and then admitted dog to play with him. She went away for a long while and when she came back the room was cooler, the sunlight had disappeared, and the sky through the window had gone from bright to gloomy. Now he believed that Mother was changing, too, by subtle degrees as the day waned and night, which was the habitat of the beast and the setting for his death, approached.

Mother smiled at Lewis and he cringed inwardly. She gazed at him but seemed to look unseeingly through him, and he could sense, the way an animal senses a subtle change in its environment, that she was beginning to change. The scent of it came from her like a warm fragrance. She looked at her watch.

"Lewis," she said, "I just don't know what to say. This way it's no good for any of us. I love you as much as I know how, but you're lost in darkness, we can't reach you, you can't reach us . . . We're going to take you to a place where you'll probably be more at home, if not happier, where there are others like you . . ." Her voice faltered and then she was crying the way Lewis did at night, silently, tears running down her cheeks. She came to him and embraced him, kissing the top of his head as her sobs became more audible, then burst from her in a welling up of stifled and confused love. But he couldn't discern the love and she couldn't see the look of terror on his face.

That night, after supper, Lewis sat alone in his room. Outside he could hear them talking and then the sound of their voices was absorbed by a lyrical stream of music that flowed through the house. Lewis saw that the fly was still at the window, its attempt to get outside reduced to a feeble straggling movement and intermittent buzzing.

He fell asleep, and when he woke the beast was in the next room, snarling, sounding crazed, and for some reason he was absolutely certain that tonight was the night it would come for him and would kill him. It had something to do with the speech Mother had made. He doubted that she understood this thing that happened to her any more than he did, and Father was just a helpless part of the terrible process.

In time the beast began to utter a loud cry that would normally have driven Lewis to the brink of collapse, but tonight to his surprise he discovered that his fear, so long pervasive and uncontrollable, metamorphosed suddenly and unexpectedly into a sort of wild anger. Uncaged, his fear, bestial in its own right, ran rampant. He found himself moving swiftly from the bed and into the hallway, an action so bold that he could never even have contemplated it on other nights. But this was different. This night was the night everything would be resolved.

Lewis half expected the beast to catch him in the hallway, but he could hear it behind the door of the room he ran past on his way to the kitchen. His thoughts reeled in a wet red medley in his maddened brain.

The knife, the knife! Lewis knew what it would do, had seen the way it cut smoothly and easily through a roast or a loaf of bread. He found it in its drawer and took it out.

Lewis opened the door quietly and firmly and looked into the room where, once before, late at night, he had glimpsed the beast, and there it was again. It reared up, staring at him with Mother's face, demonically transformed.

Like cutting bread, but wildly, fearfully . . .

At the end of a long tunnel of time the solemn men came for Lewis and found him triumphantly red with blood, the beast slain, Mother and Father freed from the bondage of bestial transformation, himself saved. But they were not pleased, these men like his father (teachers, they called themselves) who had been at the house before. Never at a loss for big words, they momentarily lost their gift of language and wailed and howled instead, acting like beasts themselves.

Lewis sensed that he would never understand. His perceptions of the things people did were constantly undermined by the paradoxes of their enigmatic behavior. An ape probably would have understood a play by Shakespeare as well as Lewis understood the world he had been born into. Shakespeare. There was a word, reiterated continually in Lewis's presence, that had no meaning whatever to him. He barely understood simple words and concepts. Beast. Animal. Bad. Good. Mother. Father. He sensed that Mother and Father were broken now, like many of the moving dolls they had given him and which he had eventually broken, but on the dim stage of his mind he would always see them, again and again, turning into the raging and screaming beast with Mother's face, and would always hear Father's harsh words as he pinned her to the bed, biting her and being bitten in turn until they moaned and writhed, "Come, now, milady, animal, sweet animal, let us make the beast with two backs, let us make the wild beast and howl at the melting moon!"

SEE MARILYN MONROE'S PANTIES!

Bentley Little

*W*e'd been seeing the signs for the past hundred miles:

SEE HITLER'S SS UNIFORM!
SEE JOHN LENNON'S GUITAR!
SEE ELVIS'S TOUPEE!

They were spaced twenty-five miles apart, the only man-made objects on this godforsaken stretch of desert highway, and as advertising, I had to admit, they were pretty damn effective. There was nothing else to focus on, nothing else to remark upon, and without any visual competition, the signs captured drivers' undivided attention. The space between them gave them time to be discussed, the next one antici-pated, and that only increased the attention they received from motorists.

As a communications major with an emphasis in

advertising/public relations, I admired the billboards and their ability to intrigue and involve, in a crudely simplistic way, their captive audience. At the same time, I knew that the audience was small—most people preferred to fly to their destinations these days rather than drive—and that, as effective as they were, the signs were little more than quaint relics from an earlier marketing age.

I stared through the front windshield. Another sign was coming up, the bright red rectangle growing as we sped toward it.

SEE MARILYN MONROE'S PANTIES!

Ray looked over at me. "What kind of place is this?"

I shook my head. "How would I know?" I took a sip of warm melted ice from the McDonald's cup between my legs.

Another billboard was already visible a mile or so ahead. Whatever it was, we were getting close. I realized that we still did not know the name of the museum, store, or tourist trap whose wonders had been spelled out for us. Clever hook.

FIVE MILES TO
THE PLACE!!

" 'The Place'?" I said. "Is that what it's called?"

Ray grinned at me. "How would I know?"

Ahead, we could see a series of signs, spaced approximately a mile apart. The signs counted down the distance to The Place. Four miles. Three miles. Two. One.

"Let's check it out," Ray said as we passed the last sign.

I nodded. "Sure."

I could already see a small run-down building by the side of the highway. A final billboard stood directly in front of the short drive, this one with an arrow pointing toward the building and the words THIS IS THE PLACE!! printed in huge letters. Ray slowed the car, pulled in.

I don't know what I was expecting, but it sure wasn't this. We parked in the dirt lot next to the only other vehicle there, a dusty red pickup. At the very least, I'd assumed that The Place would be bigger. I'd known that the trail of billboards was meant to lure in suckers, but in my mind, the building had been larger, gaudier, in keeping with the signs. The ramshackle wooden structure before us was definitely not what I had been led to expect from all the hype and buildup.

I guess I was one of the suckers.

I got out and stretched my legs. Ray did the same. We looked at each other over the roof of the car. "Still want to go in?" I asked.

"Might as well. We're here. Besides, I gotta take a whiz."

The front door was mirrored glass, reflecting the highway and the desert beyond. We pushed the door open and walked inside.

The interior of The Place was dark, lit only by a single bar of fluorescent light and the filtered sunshine that was strong enough to penetrate the dust on the skylight. The air was humid and only marginally cooler than the air outside, circulated by an ancient swamp cooler I'd spotted on the roof. It looked like a gift shop, the type of slightly seedy tourist trap usually attached to gas stations in towns that had been on the main highway before the newer freeways had passed them by, and on the shelves and counter I saw cut geodes, fake Indian jewelry, assorted candy bars, and the type of novelty items that were mass-produced in Asia but had local names added on in an attempt to make them seem like legitimate souvenirs. An old man who was probably in his sixties but whose sun-leathered face made him look more like he was in his eighties stood behind the cash register, smiling at us.

"How do today," he said. "Welcome to The Place."

"You got a bathroom here?" Ray asked.

"Public facilities are outside and around to your left."

Ray looked questioningly at me.

"I'll meet you back in here," I said.

He went back out the front door, and I turned toward the old man. "I thought this was, like, a museum."

"Oh, it is," the old man said. "This is just the gift shop. Museum's through that door there." He gestured over his shoulder at a doorway behind him. "Admission's a dollar."

"A dollar, huh?"

"Can't beat that price," the old man said. "Not out here." He laughed wheezingly.

Why not? I thought. I dug through the wad of bills in my pocket and pulled out a one, handing it to the old man. "Here."

He took the bill, stepped aside, and flipped a light switch next to the doorway. A series of low lights flickered on in the museum behind him. He motioned toward the entrance. "Step right in. We don't have a guided tour, but all of our exhibits are pretty well marked. If you have any questions, give me a holler."

I nodded and stepped past him into the museum.

It was bigger than I thought it would be. The gift shop was small, and I guess I'd assumed that the museum would be equally tiny, but though it was narrow, it stretched pretty far back. In contrast to the rough exterior of the building and the cheap paneling of the gift shop, the museum's walls were finished white, more suited to a metropolitan art gallery than this collection of kitsch in the middle of the desert.

I walked up to the first exhibit, a large glass case housing an electric Gibson guitar. A low spotlight in the ceiling directly above the case was trained directly on the instrument, dramatically highlighting it. A simple sign on the side of the case read: "John Lennon's Guitar." There was no other description, no explanation, only those three words.

I didn't know if the guitar really had been Lennon's, but I wasn't quite as skeptical as I had been earlier. Something about the museum and its layout bespoke authenticity.

I glanced around the room, not certain where to start, and decided to tour the room clockwise. I walked over to the next case on my right and read the sign.

"Marilyn Monroe's Panties."

I looked through the glass. On the floor of the case was a grayish greenish clump of what looked like mold on wadded cloth. I blinked, stared, moved around to the side of the exhibit. The disturbingly fuzzy material in the case could have conceivably been moldy panties, but the sight was so unexpected and so bizarre, so at odds with my perception of Marilyn Monroe, that it startled me. I had been expecting exotic lingerie, satin or some sort of frilly lace, not this disgusting wad of filth, and I couldn't take my eyes off the object. If these really were Marilyn Monroe's panties, how had they gotten to the state they were now in? Had they been tossed in some dump or garbage can? Had they sat for years next to rotting food? They had to have been moist to become moldy.

Moist from her?

The thought aroused me. No matter that the mildewed wad of material in the middle of the case looked like it was putrifying, the idea that the mold was growing from Marilyn Monroe's lubricating juices stimulated me. I stared into the case.

And the clump moved.

It did not move a lot, did not crawl around or jump against the glass. But there was a definite shift in the material, almost a shrug.

And there was something exciting about it.

I felt a stirring in my groin.

Another shift. I breathed deeply, continued to stare. Were the panties . . . beckoning to me?

I touched my hand to the glass and the illusion was gone. There was only a dark fuzzy clump of wadded cloth in the bottom of the case. It had not moved. It could not move.

Still, the attraction had not gone away, and an erection pressed hard against the denim of my jeans as I looked in at the panties.

"Dude!"

Ray's voice carried across the silent room, and I turned to see him standing on the other side of the counter back in the gift shop.

"Anything worth seeing in there?"

I hazarded one last look at the panties, then shook

my head and walked toward the museum entrance, surreptitiously pressing down on the front of my pants. "Not really."

"Ready to hit the road, then? We're losing time."

I nodded, walked out of the museum. For some reason, I didn't want Ray to see the panties. I felt protective, almost jealous, of what I had seen, and I didn't want to share it. I glanced behind me, at the other cases I hadn't yet viewed, but I realized that I didn't care what was in them. Whatever curiosity I had initially felt had fled.

I stepped around the counter to where Ray was drinking a Coke he'd bought. The old man grinned at me as I passed by him, and though it might have been my own paranoid imagination, it seemed as though he knew what I had experienced in there, what I had felt. "See anything you like?" he asked.

My answer came out harsher than I intended. "No, your mama's vibrator wasn't in there."

He laughed, a high harsh cackle, and I did not look back as I followed Ray out of the building into the parking lot.

"See any of that stuff they advertised on the signs?" Ray asked. "Hitler's toupee, Elvis's uniform, Marilyn Monroe's panties?"

I shook my head. "It was all fake."

"That's what I figured."

I did not feel like talking, and once in the car, I leaned my head against the passenger window and pretended to fall asleep. I tried not to think of what I had seen in The Place, but I could think of nothing else, and I kept my hands in my lap, pressing down on my erection, hoping Ray wouldn't notice. Eventually I did fall asleep.

I dreamed of Marilyn Monroe's panties.

Phoenix was where we were to part company, and we reached the city three hours later. I was going to stay at my brother Jim's house there for spring break, while Ray was going on to Palm Springs, where he hoped to get into some serious partying. He'd come back through in six days to pick me up, and then we'd drive back to Albuquerque together.

I was silent as I unpacked my bag and suitcase from the trunk, and Ray looked at me strangely as he helped me carry the ice chest into my brother's house. "Are you okay?"

"Sure. I'm fine."

He nodded, but I could tell he didn't believe me, and he still looked uneasy as he said good-bye and pulled away ten minutes later.

I had been looking forward to staying at Jim's ever since the semester started. I hadn't seen him for a while, and I figured we could hang together, maybe get in a little hiking, hit some of our old haunts. But I felt restless, and as I sat there in my brother's living room, drinking a beer, listening to him tell me about his job, about the babes he'd gone out with since the last time we'd spoken, I found myself tuning him out.

And thinking about The Place.

There was no doubt in my mind that the dirty mildewed material I had seen really had been Marilyn Monroe's panties, but I could still not figure out how they had ended up there, in the middle of nowhere, in the hands of that old man. The whole thing seemed creepy to me, unsettling, and the fact that I could not stop thinking about it—and that every time I did recall what I had seen, I became aroused—frightened me.

"So what do you want to do tonight?" Jim asked. "Want to hit some of the clubs?"

I didn't really feel like doing anything, but I found myself nodding. "Sure," I said. "That'd be great."

The hip nightspots had changed in the two years I'd been gone. Jim took me to the newest meat markets, and he met a tall blond bimbo while dancing who was more than willing to come home with him. I was sitting alone at the bar, trying my best not to meet or talk to anyone, and he sat down on the stool next to me and asked me if it was okay if the woman spent the night, and I said I didn't care and was ready to head back whenever he was.

I sat in the back of the car on the way home, with the two of them up front, and as soon as we reached Jim's house, I said good night and locked myself in my bedroom.

I awoke sometime in the middle of the night to take a piss, and I pulled on my jeans and walked down the hall to the bathroom. I turned on the light, closed the door, and saw, on the shower rug next to the tub, clothes. Jim's and the woman's. I stared down at the black satin panties lying atop the wrinkled minidress. I bent down and slowly picked them up, running my fingers over the smooth material. It had been a long time since I'd had sex, over a year, and this woman's underwear should have been exciting to me. But I felt nothing as I rubbed the soft panties over the skin of my face.

I kept thinking how much sexier these panties would be if Marilyn Monroe had worn them.

If there was mold growing on them.

I dropped the panties, my erection springing to life as I thought of the grayish green fuzz on that wadded clump in the museum case.

What the hell was wrong with me?

I hurried back to my bedroom.

I tried to fall asleep, but I was wide-awake, thinking, my brain unable to concentrate on anything other than what I'd seen in The Place, and finally I succumbed, pulling down my underwear, grasping my erection and stroking it as I thought of the sensuous way in which the moldy panties had shrugged at me, beckoning me. I came violently, the biggest orgasm I'd ever had, so much semen pumping out onto my chest that I thought it was never going to stop.

I cleaned it up with Kleenexes, dumped the Kleenexes in the trash can, and lay there breathing deeply until I finally fell asleep.

In the morning, I knew what I had to do.

I asked my brother if I could borrow his old Dart. He was reluctant at first and asked what I wanted it for, and I said that there was an old girlfriend I wanted to look up. I pointed out that he would still have the Lexus to drive around in, and he said okay, he'd let me borrow the Dart, but I had to promise to bring it back before nightfall because the taillights didn't work.

I lied and said I would.

I reached The Place just after noon.

The old man was again behind the counter, only this time he looked at me more suspiciously when I paid my dollar and walked into the museum. Or maybe I was just being paranoid.

The panties were as filthy and disgusting as I remembered. Green and gray and black and fuzzy. The allure was there, though. Stronger, if anything. My penis grew, the erection straining against my pants. More than anything, I wanted to smash that glass so that there was nothing between the panties and myself. I examined the case and saw that one of the glass sides, the one opposite the identification sign, was hinged. There was no lock on it, and I touched it and it swung outward.

I glanced quickly toward the door, to make sure the old man hadn't seen me, but I could only see the back of his head and the right half of his body. I quickly closed the door to the case and glanced around the museum. There were two doors other than the entrance through which I'd come, and I gave Marilyn's panties one last loving look, and then walked over to the door on the side wall. Again I looked toward the entrance to make sure the old man wasn't watching me. I didn't see him at all, and I quickly turned the knob and opened the door.

I closed it just as quickly. It opened onto the desert on the side of The Place.

A possibility.

I walked to the rear of the museum, glanced up front, then tried to turn the knob on this door. It was locked.

That settled it. If I was going to break in, I would do it from the side.

I glanced around at the museum's other exhibits, then moved back over to the case with Marilyn's panties.

"Time's up."

I looked toward the entrance to see the old man staring at me.

"Your time's up," he said.

I walked toward him, reaching for my wallet.

"I don't want your money," he said. "I want you out of here."

I looked at him. "What?"

"Out." He stood next to the door, and I hurried past him, walking around the counter into the gift shop.

"I don't—" I began.

He pointed to a sign above the cash register: *We reserve the right to refuse service to anyone.* "I don't ever want to see you again," he said.

My face was flushed. He must have seen me, I thought. He must know. I looked away, started toward the door.

"And don't come back!"

"Fuck you!" I yelled over my shoulder.

I walked across the dirt to the Dart, my heart pounding in my chest. Ordinarily I was not the type of person to engage in any sort of altercation, verbal or otherwise. I always tried my best to avoid confrontation. But I felt a strange sort of defensiveness at the thought that the old man might have seen me looking at the panties, and I was angry enough that if he had responded to my epithet in any way, if he had come out of the building and come after me, I would have punched him.

I got into the Dart, drove out of the parking lot, pulled onto the highway. I drove five miles east until I saw the back of the billboard that I was looking for on the opposite side of the divided highway. I slowed, looked in my rearview mirror to make sure it was the right sign, then drove over the dirt of the center divider and parked underneath the words "See Marilyn Monroe's Panties!"

I waited there until dark.

I had not checked to see what time The Place closed, so I drove closer, until I could see the building. The lights were still on in the gift shop, so I pulled off the side of the road and waited.

The lights went off at seven. I waited another hour, but the pickup in the parking lot did not move, and I assumed that the old man lived somewhere on the property and did not have to drive anywhere to go home. I gave it until nine, just to be on the safe side, then pulled forward to the arrow billboard, turned off my lights, and coasted to a stop in the parking lot. I waited a few moments to see if I'd been spotted, if the old man was going to come out, then took the flashlight from the glove compartment, got out of the car, and quietly hurried around to the side of the building where the door was. As I'd feared, the door was locked, but I knew there were no dead bolts or anything, just the knob lock, and I took out my Texaco card, pushed it in the doorframe, slid it down, and was gratified to hear a click and see the door move outward.

I pulled open the door and stepped inside.

My heart was pounding, my hands shaking with the rush of adrenaline. Turning on the flashlight, I walked quickly across the room to the case housing Marilyn's panties. I stood there and shone the light through the glass. The beam of illumination highlighted the dark fuzziness that coated the material.

And the panties moved.

I stopped, the flashlight shaking in my hand. I held my breath, forced myself to exhale. This was stupid. The light had jiggled in my shaking hand. Or my perception had been off. The panties themselves had not moved.

They moved again.

I stepped forward, peering through the glass, terrified and at the same time fascinated. The panties were definitely moving now, inching across the bottom of the display case in a wormlike crawl that was sickening and unnatural and . . . and somehow arousing.

I was already hard, and I unbuckled my pants with my left hand while my right trained the flashlight on the crawling panties. I yanked open my button fly, pushed down my jeans and underwear. My penis was firm and rigid, harder than it had ever been before, and I reached out and opened the back of the case.

I smelled mildew and dirt, rot and decay, and I wanted to touch myself, to stroke myself, but I was already coming, and my hips thrust convulsively in the air as my semen shot into the case, the thick white liquid spurting onto the panties, the panties moving back and forth across the floor of the case to catch every last drop of my randomly pumping sperm.

It went on for what seemed like minutes, until my penis was hurt and sore, still throbbing in time to spurts that were no longer coming. I was out of breath and shaking, and I stared into the case, holding weakly on to its frame, watching as the whiteness grew dark, hardening, solidifying, developing what appeared to be an outer covering of mold and mildew. The individual pools and puddles and drops and droplets slid over the irregular surface of the panties, meeting in the middle, becoming one unified mass that pulsed and undulated in a rhythm so alien that even in the aftermath of my ecstasy, I was frightened by its strangeness.

The wadded panties jerked once, throwing off the hardened lump of darkening sperm, which landed on the floor of the case next to it, still pulsating. The mound of sperm stretched, twisted, grew, and underneath the moldy surface, I thought I could detect a vaguely humanoid form.

The lights in the museum switched on.

I jumped, looking immediately toward the door to the gift shop. The old man was standing there, staring at me, his hand on the light switch. I'd half expected him to be holding a shotgun, but he was unarmed. I quickly reached down, pulled up my pants.

"I figured you might be back," he said. "I was hoping you wouldn't be, but I figured you might."

I licked my lips, not knowing what to say.

He walked into the museum. "I know how it is, boy. I know how it gets."

He looked into the case, and I did too. My moldy sperm was now the size of a hardback book, and pale protuberances that definitely looked like arms stretched out from the fuzzy darkness. I swallowed. "What is it?" I asked. My voice was quiet, barely above a whisper.

"It's yours. Yours and Marilyn's."

"This . . . this has happened before?"

The old man nodded. "You could say that."

I looked at him. "Are you . . . are you going to have me arrested?"

He shook his head. "Wouldn't make much sense. You didn't have no more control over it than I did. It's not you. It's her." He motioned toward the panties, now hunched in the corner opposite the open door of the case.

The pulsating mass was now obviously humanoid in shape, pieces of hardened mold and gelatinous blackness cracking and sliding off from the small figure as it struggled to right itself. I saw a head, eyes, mouth.

The old man cleared his throat. "I can help you dispose of that," he said.

I looked at him, not certain what to say, not certain of what I was feeling.

"Come here," he said. "Follow me."

I hazarded one last look at the twisting creature, at

the panties in the corner, then followed him to the rear of the museum. We walked through the back door and out behind The Place. There was a full moon, and though no lights were on in the back of the building, I could see clearly and did not need my flashlight. I followed the old man down a barely extant dirt path, behind a stand of ocotillo and over a small rise.

And looked into the pit.

It was easily as big as a football field, sunk some twenty or thirty feet down in the desert. He obviously used this as his landfill. There were sacks of groceries, pieces of broken bric-a-brac, a couch, a car door, lying in the dirt.

But there were other things as well.

I felt sick to my stomach as I looked at the dried vaguely humanoid forms piled on the sloping sides of the pit, as I saw the small bones protruding from the dirt.

"Ten bucks," he said. "No one'll ever know."

I don't know what shocked me more, the fact that he had a killing field in his backyard and was willing to kill my . . . creature for me, or the fact that he wanted to charge me for it.

He must have guessed by my silence what I was thinking, because his voice, when he spoke, was softer. "It's not human," he said.

I nodded.

"Do you want me to dispose of it for you?"

I shook my head, staring at the overlapping forms in the pit.

"Well, then, we'd better get it into your car."

We walked back into the museum, and he grabbed a large box from a pile outside the rear door. I walked back over to the case and was shocked to see that the creature had jumped or fallen out and was now on the ground in front of the exhibit. It was now the size of a medium-sized dog.

"How—" I began, but my voice cracked. I cleared my throat. "How big is it going to get?"

"How tall are you?"

I frowned. "Six feet."

"It'll be six feet tall."

I watched as the old man gingerly picked up the creature and placed it in the box. Its mouth opened as he did so, as though it was trying to scream, but no sound came out. Its eyes, black and white, rolled strangely.

"Take it," the old man said.

I was frightened, but I forced myself to pick up the box. It was lighter than I'd thought it would be. I stared down at the creature. It was not human, but . . . but it looked like me. It also looked a little bit like Marilyn, and I was instinctively protective of it. Part of me was repulsed by the creature, but another part of me wanted to take care of it.

The old man held open the side door and walked with me as I carried the box out to the car and placed it in the backseat.

"Remember," he said. "I can get rid of it for you."

I shook my head. "No, thanks."

He held out his hand. "That'll be five dollars."

I blinked. "What?"

"Five dollars."

"For what?"

"That's half Marilyn's," he said.

I didn't want to argue, so I took out my wallet and gave him a five.

I got into the car, backed up and pulled onto the

highway, heading toward Phoenix. I saw no other cars on the highway, no other lights, and I could hear the . . . thing on the seat behind me, making strange mewling noises, as well as sounds like crackling cellophane and breaking twigs issuing from somewhere within its still-growing body. The noises sent a chill through me, and I turned on the radio, cranking it up. The only station I could get out here was a gospel station, but I didn't care, and I tried to focus on the music, tried not to hear the noises on the seat behind me.

Ten minutes later, I heard it move out of the box.

I kept expecting at any minute to feel cold slimy hands touch the back of my neck, but I was afraid to look behind me, and I didn't want to pull off the side of the road because I knew I might never get back in the car, so I kept driving.

By the time we reached Phoenix, I could see the thing in the rearview mirror, sitting up on the seat. It was as tall as I was. It had Marilyn's face.

It smiled at me in the mirror, and against my will, I felt myself becoming aroused.

I pulled into the parking lot of a twenty-four-hour supermarket. I was no longer frightened of the creature, but reality had set in. How was I going to bring this thing into my brother's house? I wondered. What was I going to say? How was I going to explain it?

I parked the car beneath one of the lights in an empty section of the parking lot and turned around to look at the creature.

It was male.

The sight of the penis, long and gracefully slender, shocked me. The face was Marilyn's, as was the hair, and I had automatically assumed that the creature was a female. I had seen no breasts, but I had not been able to see that low in the mirror.

Now I saw everything.

And I felt attracted to it.

The creature smiled at me.

And its penis stiffened.

What the hell was happening? My own erection was growing, even though I didn't want it to, my body responding to this monster even as my brain was disgusted by it. It wasn't even human, I told myself. Three hours ago, it had been a puddle of my sperm that had landed on Marilyn Monroe's moldy panties.

The creature leaned forward, puckered its lips, and though there was no lipstick around its mouth, it looked exactly like one of Marilyn's classic poses.

My penis hurt, it was so hard. I didn't want to insert my penis in the creature, didn't want to stick it in its mouth or in its ass. I wanted to do what I'd done with the panties: spurt on it.

But what would happen to that sperm?

In my mind, I saw it blackening, moldering, combining with the flesh of this monster to create yet another monster.

The protective feelings I had originally felt for the creature were gone, replaced by this unnatural lust. The disgust was still there, though, augmented by an unfocused rage. I got out of the car, opened the back door, grabbed the creature's arm, and yanked it outside. Its skin was soft, erotically smooth to my touch, and I could not help looking down at the erect organ pointing outward from between its legs as I pulled it from the car.

I hit it over the head with the lug wrench I took from the Dart's trunk. It did not bleed, but it fell down in a crumpled heap on the parking lot. It had not even tried to avoid the blow, and though a brief flicker of that initial protectiveness returned as I hit it, the feeling was overpowered by my rage and fear, and I hit it again.

And again.

I glanced around the parking lot to see if anyone had witnessed this beating, but the lot was empty save for a few cars near the supermarket entrance, and there was no sign of any people.

I picked up the creature and put him in the backseat.

I drove at an even seventy miles an hour once I got past the outskirts of the city, but it was still close to dawn when I reached The Place. I skidded into the parking lot, braked to a halt. I opened up the back door and looked down at the form of my son. I didn't know if he was dead or merely unconscious, but I didn't really care.

I picked him up. He was warm, still alive. The sensuous smoothness of his skin aroused me again, and I glanced involuntarily at his slender penis and I felt myself becoming hard.

I kicked shut the door of the car and carried him into The Place.

The front door was open, the old man waiting for me. He looked at me and there was neither horror nor humor on his face, no look of I-told-you-so in his eyes. He merely looked at the form in my hands, nodded at me.

"Want me to take care of it?" he asked.

I nodded. I could not even bring myself to speak.

"Ten dollars," he said.

I took out my wallet, handed him two fives.

He accepted the money, pocketed it.

I glanced toward the museum entrance, thought of Marilyn's panties, then forced myself to turn and walked out of The Place. I pressed down on my erection.

I did not look back.

DEVIL WITH A BLUE DRESS

P. D. Cacek

You wan me suckee you good, GI?

Gil Thornton's elbow slammed into the side of the restaurant's neoclassic facade as his hand reached for the side arm that should have been caressing his hip like an enamored lover.

That *should* have been there.

But wasn't.

Hadn't been for twenty-plus years.

You wan me suckee you good, GI?

Gil pushed away from the thin sheet-marble column and ran a shaky hand through thinning hair. Tried to force an even shakier smile to his lips, but found that particular action as impossible as trying to draw a long-forgotten gun.

To shoot a long-dead whore.

watching him

He would have laughed out loud if he'd been able to

264

stop panting. The reaction and the (*fear*) memories had undoubtedly been the direct result of the "182nd Point 5" reunion dinner he'd just suffered through.

And wondered, again—for the hundredth time that evening, actually—why the hell he'd suddenly felt obliged to sit through an overpriced meal and down watery scotch alongside men whom he shared nothing in common with except the number *182.5.*

The exact middle of the summer of '69 *draft* choice.

If you didn't count leap year.

Which Uncle Sam didn't.

Why after all these years? was still playing like a broken record in his mind when the evening's "Reopening of Old Wounds" had drifted away from firefights and cheap pussy and focused on the current administration's brownnosing attempt to reestablish trade agreements with the Nam.

The boys of the "182nd Point 5 Club" thought that was a *bad* idea.

And Gil had kept quiet, sucking down three times his usual two-drink limit and making himself a promise he intended to keep *this* time: No more reunions with men incapable of putting the past behind them.

Like he'd done.

At least until tonight.

"So ya wanna *suckee* or not?"

Gil lowered his hand slowly, remembering the side arm at the last moment, and quickly grabbed the restaurant's brass handrail instead.

still watching him

"What?"

The vague female shape stepped away from the line of parked cars and started a slow, cautious advance— high heels clicking against the sidewalk like bamboo chimes, her body moving beneath the minidress like a snake trying to shed its skin.

Gil enjoyed the show until she stepped into the light and tossed her head. A flash of bright blue (*the color of a peacock's breast*) stabbed him in the gut.

You wan me suckee you good, GI?

"What?"

The heart-shaped face he remembered (*expected*) melted under the light into a haggard scowl topped with a Raggedy Anne fright wig. Sighing, the hooker tossed the fringed blue scarf back over her shoulders, exposing tired-looking breasts that had been cinched into a black leather vest, and stared up at him. Ran a jaundiced tongue over corpse-pale lips as she rolled nearly colorless eyes.

You wan me suckee you good, GI?

Gil felt his backbone mold itself to the smooth marble sheeting.

"Shit, man," the hooker hissed at him, "you from outta town or sumthin'? You wanna blow job or not?"

He couldn't tell her age—somewhere between twenty and death was as close as he could come—but the streets had already done a number on her. Gil could almost smell the coppery sweet stench of decay rising from beneath the short skirt.

Could almost hear the skin on his balls go *snap crackle pop* as they shriveled at the thought of her tongue and teeth closing over his—

"I'll do it for twenty-five," she said, taking a step closer, running knobby-fingered hands down the front of her thighs. "What'dya say?"

Gil shifted his weight, feeling the solid wall of protection at his back give way to a sweating chill as he focused on the bright

sun-faded palms already dripping onto the tin-roofed

plywood stalls where bird-legged children ran between the coils of barbed wire and a heart-shape-faced whore in a blue dress walked past a stinking, dilapidated bar called the

San Francisco skyline towering overhead . . .

. . . as he tried not to breathe in air that suddenly seemed thick, heavy with the stench of urine and burning shit and fish drifting in from the Bay . . .

. . . as he rushed down the polished marble stair, ducking at the last moment to avoid the outstretched claws.

As he listened to another voice whispering seductively in his ear.

you—wan—me—suc—kee—you—good—G—I became Gil's marching cadence as he crossed against the light and turned in to the deeper canyons of the Financial District.

He didn't even stop at the opposite side of the street to hail a cab—something he *never* would have done (considering the five-block technical climb back to his apartment) if it hadn't been for the booze . . . and the reopened wounds his "buddies" of the *182nd Point 5* had picked at all night.

"You remember those friggin' 'bars' down on Plantation Road?"

"Man, oh man . . . my wiener never ate so good."

"Shit, yeah—them B-girls were the best, man. You remember, Gil?"

I remember.

"You remember, Gil?"

"I remember."

"But ya gotta be careful, pal . . . 'cause you never know which one could be workin' for ol' Charlie. Right . . . gotta watch their eyes, man."

"Right. Gotta watch their eyes," he whispered, and

caught the reflection of his own eyes in the subdued, night-lit windows of the district's "trendier" boutiques and storefront offices.

eyes watching

God, he was getting old.

Getting? Fuck, he *was* old. Despite the hand-tailored suits ("customized" to hang loose around the softness at his belt line and wide over his stooped shoulders) and weekly salon trims, Gil could see his father and grandfather where there had once been a hard-muscled, hard-assed boy who always thought he'd be that way.

Back when "getting old" meant surviving your tour of duty.

The *good* ol' days.

Gil made a sound in the back of his throat that might have been a laugh if it had been any other night and he hadn't downed quite so many waterlogged whiskeys and smiled. Flipped his reflection the single-digit salute.

And momentarily forgot how to breathe.

you wan me suckee you good, GI?

The large poster dominated the travel agent's window, its young Vietnamese model—complete with straw "Ah so" hat and white silk *ao dai* pajamas—holding a bouquet of jungle orchids: half-turned toward the camera. A shy smile on her lips. The pale green cast of her eyes a silent indictment to her racial impurity. Either Amerasian or Eurasian.

Gil was surprised the gooks had let her live, let alone become their country's poster child.

She looked about the right age, probably no more than

eighteen, GI . . . and she no do this much like other

girls . . . I keep her special for you, GI . . . just eigh-teen

GI

twenty, and twenty years ago there was more than enough American DNA swimming in the ol' gene pool to produce a whole generation with shit-green eyes.

Gil let his own eyes drop to the caption just below the half-caste's tiny breasts: *Come Back to VIETNAM.*

Come back.

Come *back.*

Come back, GI . . . I no bite

She was standing next to him in the glass, wearing the same bright blue *ao dai* she'd been wearing the day Gil killed her.

Watching him.

You wan me suckee you good, GI? she asked, her voice a whisper as she slowly lifted her hand to his shoulder. *I be your numbah one girlfriend Vietnam.*

Gil was shivering even before he felt the coldness of her hand through the thick layers of tailored wool. She was just as lovely as the last time he'd seen her.

And just as dead.

You wan me suck—

"—ee you good, GI?"

Gil tightened his grip on the limp rice-paper bag he was carrying and rolled his shoulders beneath the sweat-soaked uniform tee. Ignored the sweet-soft voice as he forced himself to take another step through the morning's almost liquid heat.

When he got to the next stall—a seller of plaster *Buffies* and other objets d'art—Gil wiped the drip-ping skin below his boonie hat and cursed softly to himself. *Seven-fucking-*A.M. and he already felt like a used rubber . . . wrinkling into himself and leaking juice like a sieve.

"You wan me suckee you good, GI?"

Jesus, didn't whores take ANY time off?

Gil quarter-turned again and thumped his boot-heels hard against Duong Cong-Ly's rutted, monsoon-pitted asphalt; ignoring the muffled squawks of a half dozen dusty chickens the same way he'd ignored the whore's "come-on" line.

The *first* time.

Halfway around the plywood and hammered-tin stalls that made up Centertown's "business district" and Gil could still feel the silent, angry stares collecting along his backbone like starving leeches.

Had been collecting there from the first moment he stepped foot in country.

He knew no amount of shoulder rolling would detach them.

That no amount of *bug juice* would keep them off him.

For long.

Gil didn't like being stared at. Never had. But now it was worse. Now his life might be threatened by one of those stares.

Because you never knew.

Never knew when Charlie might be the one staring.

never knew

He'd even heard about whores with glass up their snatches just waiting for horny GIs.

They were still watching. He could feel them.

Didn't they know he was one of the GOOD GUYS? Didn't they know he was there to try and save their fucking country for them? Why the fuck did they have to WATCH him all the time?

To keep himself from drawing the service "piece"

on his hip and taking out a few of the WATCHERS (*because you never knew when Charlie might be one of them*), Gil ran a greasy hand over the back of his neck and took a deep breath . . . almost gagging on the combined stench of his fear sweat and Vietnam's pungent ambience.

Something had died nearby. Either that, or the wind had shifted and was blowing from the direction of the *nuc mam* seller. A thin-legged boy pulled down his shorts and added to the overall olfactory effect.

Watching him. Watching Gil with hate-filled eyes.

The gun would have felt so good in his hand.

Rolling his shoulders, turning away from the (*eyes*) child, Gil opened the soggy bag and looked inside— reassuring himself that it was still there.

It was.

Although the humidity had already gotten to the plastic (unbroken) shrink-wrap covering the jacket, fogging over the full color photo, Gil could still make out some of the lettering: *Mitch Ryder and the Detroit Wheels.*

Featuring their hit single: "Devil with a Blue Dress."

Gil sighed and nodded, carefully folded the bag closed and tucked it under his arm. Felt better knowing it was still there, even though it was the reason he was out wandering the marketplace; collecting hard-edged stares the way a turd collects flies.

But that was okay, he reminded himself, because *he* had the record.

The night before he and seven of his barracks-mates had each pitched in twenty-five cents for the weekly "record run," then drew straws to see who the runner would be.

Gil made sure he lost.

Almost ten months in country and he hadn't realized how much "Devil with a Blue Dress" had meant to him . . . *back in the "World"* . . . when he still had a future that wasn't measured in firefights and hostile stares.

The rest of the "record runners" would probably be pissed when he got back with the *classic,* but fuck 'em, he sure as hell wasn't going to tell them the reason behind it. *Couldn't* tell them that it was the song blaring on the radio of his dad's Chevy the first and *last* time he'd had sex.

Made love.

Screwed.

Fucked.

Gil hugged the record to his chest and found himself stopped in front of a fruit stall, staring at flat-topped green coconuts.

They were the only things in the display he could recognize.

Something familiar . . . like the constant bulge straining against the front of his fatigue pants.

Both his family doctor and the 90th Repo'-Depot's medic had warned him about "sticking his pecker where it don't belong."

Gil shook his head when the fruit seller lifted one of the nuts and heard his dog tags jingle—in three-part harmony. Two STANDARDS, dull tin gray, and one NONSTANDARD. Blood red.

If, however, he did "stick his pecker where it didn't belong" and caught something "more aggressive than crotch rot," the NONSTANDARD tag would tell the medic in charge to avoid the rush and just hand him a body bag. Because he was gonna die.

Allergies to penicillin and most sulfa drugs did not a "happy soldier" make.

Especially when pussy came cheaper than a crew-cut coconut.

Especially when his "buddies" back at Tan Son Nhut would be keeping time to the Wheels' driving beat between the legs of some hooch maid while he, Corporal Gil "Can't Get No Satisfaction" Thornton, humped the barracks' communal stereo system.

And watched.

"*Fuckin' shit!*" Gil snarled, waving aside the seller's jabbering *makee deal makee deal,* and spun on the balls of his feet. The lug soles of his boots made soft crushing sounds as he turned.

She was standing directly behind him; black-almond eyes smiling up at him.

watching him

"You wan me suckee you good, GI?"

Gil felt the front of his pants shrink another size.

She was young and beautiful. Her black hair gleaming under the relentless sun. Her eyes clear and bright.

And watching him.

Gil's fingers dug into the bag, striking plastic wrap.

"You wan me suckee you good, GI?" she asked again as if he hadn't heard.

While she waited for his answer, she tossed a thick black braid over the shoulder of her blue *ao dai.* A bright blue *ao dai* . . . the "Devil with a Blue Dress" brought to life.

Halfway around the world from where they first met in the backseat of his dad's car. But this time she wasn't blond.

And this time what was between her legs could kill him as surely as a VC's bullet.

Not as quickly.

Not as cleanly.

But just as dead.

One more grunt for Charlie's body count.

One less grunt to watch.

"You have girlfriend Vietnam?" she asked when it became apparent Gil wasn't going to answer.

Her skin, without the usual scabbed-over lesions and pustules he'd seen on some of the camp's other "girlfriends," was stretched tightly over her heart-shaped skull; and Gil could see the sharp edge of one collarbone as she fingered the high silken collar.

In fifteen months he hadn't seen one fat dink whore.

Hell, he hadn't seen one fat dink *anything*.

"I be your girlfriend Vietnam," she said, and gave one *case closed, end of discussion* nod.

The Regulation Hustle: as STANDARD as the two tags hanging around his neck; and as obvious as the NONSTANDARD tag.

Gil shook his head, usually all the discouragement they needed, and checked the Seiko he'd picked up his first week in country. Frowned. The dubbing/screw 'em if you can "party" wouldn't start until the evening's torrential rainstorm, around seven.

That left him twelve full hours before he had to become Gil the Geek—master deejay and part-time voyeur.

watching

Twelve hours to kill.

Gil could feel her eyes on him. Leeches. But hungrier than the rest.

"I be your girlfriend Vietnam." Stepping closer, she laced one blue-draped arm though his and began pulling him away from the still-babbling fruit seller. "You buy me tea, then I suckee you good."

Gil put a stranglehold on the bag containing the imaginary *devil* while he followed the real one, the one wearing the *blue dress,* through Centertown's semicircular heart toward the "bars" on Plantation Road.

And kept following her even as they began passing the plywood-and-pressed-beer-can establishments. When an even thinner whore in a bright red miniskirt and UCLA T-shirt darted out of the *San Francisco* and made a snatch at Gil's hat, the Blue Devil at his side made her own snatch and came back with a tiny fist full of greasy black hair.

"I know beddah place," the Blue Devil said, ignoring the screeching, scalped whore behind them. "More beddah this place, for sure. No worry. We go."

Gil knew the "place" wasn't any "beddah" than any of the other prefab bars they were passing, but he went—following after her like a dog after a bitch, listening to her jabber away in a fast-forward version of pidgin English Vietnamese and trying to negotiate cobblestones thick with liquified human waste.

"You see," she said, turning to look into his eyes as she stopped and began pulling him through a doorway hung with blue and crystal plastic beads. "Much beddah place. You see."

you see

But he hadn't. Didn't see the door until the beads *clicker-clacked* behind him. And by then he was too late.

The verbal horseshoe ambush caught him from all sides as floor-to-ceiling curtains were pulled aside, bamboo rings chattering, and the tiny "outer" room was suddenly filled with smiling, *ao dai*–clad whores.

But *his* was the only one wearing blue, Gil noticed. *He* had the only *blue* devil.

Four pair of dark eyes locked onto his as lips smiled and heads nodded. Gil felt his balls pucker up into his belly. Felt their stares latch on to his flesh and start feeding.

felt Charlie watching

When the *mammasan* in black pajamas shuffled out from behind a painted bamboo screen, his little Blue Devil raced forward, arms outstretched, jibbering like a monkey.

One of the curtains fluttered in her wake, exposing the cramped interior. An American GI, his sweat-slick Afro pressing into the filigreed back of a bamboo *papasan* chair, eyes rolling white, groaned while a half-naked woman kneeled between his spread legs, her shining black head nodding slowly.

Gil could still see their images, in reverse color— the man white, the woman's silken pants dull green— superimposed on the curtain as it fell back into place.

could still see

It wasn't much different than the (*few*) parties he had attended his last year in high school . . . back when free love was, and Vietnam was just something you heard your parents talk about in hushed tones and Canada was still just a plane ticket away.

Back when he *thought* he'd live forever.

Gil looked down at the soggy bundle in his hand. One plastic-sheathed corner had worked its way through the rice paper. Beads of condensation, like sweat, gathered and disappeared beneath the matted paper. He could almost feel the LP getting softer in his hands. If he didn't get back to base and start transferring Mitch Ryder to cassette tapes, he might lose the "Devil" for another God-knows-how-long.

Except that there wasn't any real danger of that happening. Not now. Not really. Not in *real* time.

Gil looked up as the living Devil rushed back

toward him, the ancient *mammasan* in tow. Smiling, nodding,

watching

"This be numbah one GI, *Ba,*" the girl said as she laid a surprisingly cool hand against Gil's chest. He shivered under its pressure. "I be his girlfriend Vietnam."

The old woman nodded her sparsely covered head and smiled. Worn, betel-stained teeth gleamed at Gil in the murky half-light.

"You like, you like," she hissed at him, "you see, she numbah one suckee girl. How old you, GI? How old you?"

"What?" *Was there an AGE requirement?* "Nineteen. And a half."

The *mammasan* hooked a gnarled finger under the whore's chin and lifted the perfectly heart-shaped face.

"She eighteen, GI . . . an' half, like you, GI. She no do this so much like other girls. I keep her special for you, GI. I keep her clean. Just for you, GI."

And it's not even my birthday.

"An' she virgin . . . just like all girls here. She suckee you good, GI, but no fuckee. She *virgin.*"

That must have been a major problem, Gil thought, considering that every woman he'd met in Nam was—by her own admissions or those of her pimp—a virgin. Gil wondered if Uncle Sam knew he was waging a war against immaculately conceived VC.

Still nodding, the *mammasan* grabbed Gil's arm just above the elbow and began leading (*dragging*) him toward one of the closed curtains. The exposed corner of the record bumped against the dog tags hanging at his throat. Rattling them. Reminding him.

The *mammasan* heard the noise and turned without stopping, fingered the bright red one and smiled.

"Pretty, pretty . . . you like, for sure. Virgin girl know how to make GI plenty happy."

Gil felt the blue-dressed "virgin" brush past him and push the curtain open. Another bamboo chair, identical to the one he'd seen holding the black grunt, sat in the middle of the tiny room. Although *room* was too big a word for the space he was looking at.

There was just enough room for the chair and a woman kneeling in front. Watching.

Gil took a deep breath and watched the girl bend down and fluff the thin pillow in front of the chair. As she straightened, she began slipping the tiny covered buttons on her shirt through the silken loops. In less than a minute she shrugged out of the knee-length top and draped it over the fanned back of the chair. Her tiny, rose-nippled breasts trembled with the motion . . . begging for his tongue . . . his fingers . . . his . . .

"A . . . *virgin?*" Gil whispered without benefit of spit. Every drop of moisture in his body, except for that oozing out through his pores, was currently filling the Full Military Erection jutting out the front of his pants.

"Sure she virgin," the old woman growled, "what you think? She some goddamned bar girl? She virgin . . . like all others virgin."

"*Why?*" Gil heard himself ask.

"Must eat," *mammasan* said, "and war not last fo'eber. When war end I sell *real* virgins for beaucoup bucks to good family. Make plenty money. She suckee only, no open legs . . . no fuckee. She virgin."

Gil suddenly felt like he *was* back in high school, about to go out on his last (*first time*) date; standing with his hands clasped over the pathetic throbbing in his jeans while he listened to the girl's father explain the facts of life (everlasting) to him—that his daughter was a virgin and he expected for her to come home in the same condition.

Which she hadn't.

Neither of them had.

Gil pulled his arm out of the old woman's grasp and laced both over the record.

"So how much are virgins going for *these* days?" he asked.

Twin smiles beamed at him.

"Five dollah American."

"Five—"

For that amount he could probably buy Ho Chin Minh's daughter. Or a water buffalo. And still get change back.

Gil shifted the record to one side and shook his head, waving away the offer with his free hand. "Too beaucoup much. I'll give you . . ." Pause. ". . . twenty-five piastres. That's more than most bar girls get."

The *mammasan's* black eyes disappeared beneath wrinkled flaps of skin as she puckered up and deposited a wad of cocoa brown phlegm an inch from the toe of Gil's right boot.

"You wan spend twenty-five p, you go get goddamned bar girl. This numbah one virgin girl give you good suckee, no disease. No nothing bad. She be worth five dollah American. Worth more, for sure."

Gil shook his head in time with the throbbing in his groin (*please, Daddy? Please?*). Five dollars American could buy a whole hell of a lot of things more important than a quick blow job . . .

. . . but for the life of him, he couldn't think of any at the moment.

Grumbling under his breath to let the *mammasan* think her lie about the "virgin whore" had caught yet another oversexed grunt, Gil reached into his back pocket and pulled out the thick wad of MPCs. Kept on grumbling while he peeled off the military scrip. Stopped when he reached five and held them out.

The old woman spit again.

"No wan Mickey Mouse money . . . that not good for nothing." She held out a scarred palm and slapped it with the fingers of her other hand. "Five dollah American. Real money."

"It's worth it, man," a husky voice said.

Gil turned to watch the black grunt, chest glistening with sweat beneath his web gear, arm tossed casually over the bamboo curtain rod less than a foot above his flattened Afro. His eyes were half-closed beneath chocolate brown lids, thick lips hanging open in a loose smile.

He looked more stoned than fucked over.

"Five dollars worth?" Gil asked.

"Fuckin'-A, man." Tipping forward at the waist, the grunt planted a sloppy, openmouthed kiss on his whore's puffy lips. "An' I was even in *Vung Tau*. Shit, these ladies could suck the eye out of a needle. *Damn!*"

"Five dollars."

The black grunt shot Gil a thumb's-up, then staggered to and out the beaded doorway. The flat rattling sound continued as Gil flipped back the pay certificates to the *real* stuff. He, like every other grunt who'd passed the Turtle Test, and lived to see his dark OD fatigues fade, always kept at least a cool hundred in U.S. currency.

For emergencies.

like this one

"She'd *better* be worth this," Gil snarled, taking a relatively crisp five-dollar bill and dangling it before the *mammasan's* jaundiced eyes like a baited hook. Her stares were more like grubs than leeches. "If she's not, there's going to be beaucoup hell to pay. You understand?"

"Yes, yes, understand good. She berry, berry good, GI, you see. If no think so, you can beat. Beat, just no fuck. She virgin, worth more than five dollah American when war finished."

Gil could almost feel the steam rising as she pulled the bill from his fingers.

"You see, she numbah one girlfriend. If you like, I no let her give suckee any other GI but you. You see, you like whole hell'a lot. Come, you sit . . . she suckee you good."

Gil let himself be steered toward the chair and sat down, the woven bamboo squeaking beneath his ass in protest.

"You wan me take that? Keep it plenty safe, for sure."

Gil followed the *mammasan's* hand to the record clutched to his chest and shook his head.

"No. I'll keep it. Here. With me."

"No worry, GI," the old woman said as her fingers closed over the record and pulled it from his grasp. "This be plenty respectable place. We no steal. Oh . . . record. You like me play?"

Gil watched the old woman slice the plastic cover with a ragged nail and slide the real virgin out of its tissue paper protector.

"Have plenty good record player, GI. You like play?"

She turned without waiting for him to answer, shuffling away from the curtained cocoon as fast as her bandy little legs would carry her. Gil stood up and took a step forward when he saw that the *plenty good record player* was one of those claw-lidded things he'd had as a kid. The kind that left scratches the size of the Grand Canyon.

oh shit

Gil took another step when Mitch Ryder's voice (sounding a little like Donald Duck) filled the room, singing about the *Devil with a Blue Dress*. The *mammasan* looked up from the phonograph and nodded as the other whores clapped happily.

shit shit shit

"You wan suckee now, GI?"

Gil glanced back over his shoulder. She was standing next to the chair, the blue pants bunched around her ankles.

"You come back, GI. I no bite."

The curtain *swooshed* closed as he sat back down. Gil thought he heard a soft chuckle as she kneeled in front of him but wasn't sure. Couldn't be sure of anything but her cool fingers moving swiftly to his belt buckle . . . to the buttons of his fly.

"I be your numbah one girlfriend Vietnam, okay?" She was watching his face as her hands parted the heavy cotton and lifted him out. "You see, I give good suckee . . . make you forget. You not want me do this with other GIs, I not do.

"Just you, GI.

"I be just for you. You see."

you see

Her lips went taunt as she slipped down over his engorged prick. Every muscle in Gil's body tightened. It was unbelievable . . . a feeling like cold fire sweeping upward from his cock and engulfing him . . .

. . . swallowing him . . .

. . . eating him . . .

watching

Gil felt his pubic hairs twitch as he opened his eyes.

She was staring back at him—black-almond eyes wide and locked on to his face. Studying him. Filled with hate. A wave of heat raced down his spine, meeting the cold fire somewhere near his belly.

And turning it to steam.

"You *like* to watch, don't you?"

Without waiting for an answer, Gil arched his back and forced more of himself into her waiting mouth—digging his fingers into her thick black hair, rubbing his thumbs against her sweating temples. She grabbed his wrists and pulled away, exposing the purple heart-shaped tip of his cock.

"No do . . . too beaucoup big . . . you choke me. Too big."

"Liar," Gil whispered, and moved his thumbs closer to the epicanthic folds that shaped her eyes. "I'm not any beaucoup bigger than any other grunt, am I?"

She smiled up at him and ran her tongue slowly over her lips. How many other grunts had she smiled at like that? How many others had she *watched. Like that?*

Like *they* were the enemy?

Like she was watching him right now.

Gil felt the steam inside his gut reach his brain. He'd fucking had enough.

Scooting forward, he grabbed her chin, wrenched it to one side, and thrust himself back into her mouth.

She gagged and pulled back, her black hair shimmering as she began to shake her head—back and forth, back and forth. Gil felt her teeth rake the tender flesh of his cock.

"You trying to *bite* me, bitch?" he screamed, grabbing and jerking her chin down toward her quivering breasts. "You said you wouldn't bite!

"What are you lookin' at, cunt?"

Her eyes widened an instant before Gil raised his free hand and jammed two fingers into them, popping them while Mitch Ryder howled in the background about a blue-dressed devil.

Setting the beat.

"Yeah . . . you ain't gonna bite and you ain't gonna *watch*. Your whole fucking country likes to watch, don't it, cunt? You gonna watch me now, dink?" Gil hissed as he tightened his grip and scooted to the edge of the chair. "That's what you people like to do, isn't it? Watch GIs until you think we don't see you anymore and that's when you get us, isn't it?

"Well, watch *this*." Gil shoved himself still deeper and felt the tip of his cock slide down into her throat. "Watch it all, bitch. Watch it! WATCH IT!"

Forgetting, for the moment, that she had nothing left to *watch* him with. But that was okay . . . that was fine . . . that was fuckin'-A, man!

Because she wasn't nothin' but a dink, anyway.

Blood-tinted goo dripped down the sides of Gil's hands as the *Devil* pummeled his thighs, his belly, his chest, with her fists; losing the music's beat as pink foam bubbled around the inch of his shaft that still protruded from her mouth.

As Gil worked on her . . . still shouting *watch me, you goddamned whore, watch me NOW!* until he felt her body go limp.

one less gook to watch

"What you do?" someone yelled. "You *dinki dau* GI? Crazy? You stop—*dung lui*. No do this."

The fire continued to build, destroying the fear that had been building in his belly since the moment he'd felt the first stares burrowing under his skin.

"I call MP! They come quick, shoot you dead! *Dung lui,* you summa beech!"

The orgasm tightened, pulling him forward, driving him down to the hilt. Gil felt the sides of his cock scrape against her back teeth. Felt her body match his shudders as the cold fire exploded like a Claymore.

This side toward enemy.

Panting, sweat burning his eyes, Gil scooted back in the chair and let the dead whore collapse backward onto the mud-streaked floor. At his feet. As flaccid as his spent cock.

"That really was great," he said, nodding to the gaping *mammasan* as he reached for the side arm and licked his lips. His mouth tasted like the whorehouse smelled.

"Really numbah one." Gil nudged the *virgin's* naked thigh and watched her head loll back over her shoulder. Empty, blood black holes staring up at him.

Still watching him.

Gil tried to stand and felt the chair slide backwards under the weight of his frantic shuffling until it collided with the wall. And propelled him up and out.

Toward the dead woman on the floor.

watching him

The Wheels broke into another driving piece, but Gil didn't notice it any more than he did the whimpering screams from the other virgin whores or the *mammasan's* threats.

"You crazy man," the old woman screamed at him, clawing at the front of his fatigues. "You *dinki dau! Dinki dau!* I call MPs . . . I call MPs make plenty trouble. You wait, you *dinki dau* crazy American GI, you wait and they come, make plenty beaucoup trouble. For sure!"

Gil stuffed himself back into his pants with one hand as the other pulled out the money clip. Began pulling off the *real* bills until the old woman stopped screaming.

The going price for a dead *numbah one suckee girl* was twenty-six dollars.

American.

Gil left Mitch Ryder to the purgatory of a cheap turntable and 98 percent humidity . . . knowing that in a few weeks both the musical version of the "Devil with a Blue Dress" and its human counterpart would be unrecognizable lumps of melting goo.

Knew it.

But could still hear the song playing over and over and over in his ears.

The way he could still feel her empty eyes staring at him

in the reflection of cool San Francisco glass.

Come Back to Vietnam

Come back.

Gil watched the dead whore slide her hand into the crook of his arm, trembling when the cold seeped through the layers of textured fabric and years.

"You wan me suckee you good, GI?"

Her voice suddenly had a soft, mushy quality to it . . . like fruit that had been left out in the sun too long.

"I be you numbah one girlfriend Vietnam. Come back, GI. I no bite."

She smiled at him from the glass—the empty eye

sockets deep shadows in the reflected streetlight . . . receding gums black against strong, white teeth.

Gil heard them clicking together as she tightened her grip on his arm.

"I not finish last time, GI . . ."

She smiled and twin blue flames, like misplaced gaslights, suddenly glowed from the depths of her empty sockets.

This time be more beddah, GI . . . this time I suckee you good.

You *watch,* GI. This time gonna be more beddah, for sure!

The sound of tires hissing against damp asphalt snapped Gil's attention to the street. A three-wheeled, surrey-fringed Lambretta "taxi" whispered past, the American-made transistor radio hanging from the motorcycle handlebars bouncing against the driver's bare knees as it played something soft.

Something familiar.

Something about a devil in a blue dress.

And he ran to it.

Gil saw the driver's eyes through the windshield an instant before the cab's right bumper crushed his rib cage . . . heard the "What the FUCK?" a moment before he slipped beneath the good Detroit wheel.

He came outta nowhere, someone was shouting over him. *Just run right out in front of me like he was crazy or something.*

Musta been drunk, another voice said.

Or high.

Anyone know who he is?

Seen 'm come out o' that fat-assed restaurant—guy was a real pervert, y'know.

The last voice was familiar and Gil wished he could

open his eyes to make sure. But it really didn't matter because he knew she was still there.

They were *all* still there.

Watching him die.

watching

forever

THE CONTRIBUTORS

Paul Dale Anderson

Anderson is the author of *Claw Hammer, Superstitions, Daddy's Home, Effigies, Games, Sidewinders,* and *The Devil Made Me Do It*. The Illinois resident's short stories have appeared in *Shock Rock, Hotter Blood, Masques III, Best of Horror Show, Deathrealm,* and *New Blood,* among others.

P. D. Cacek

Colorado's Cacek is an active contributor of short fiction to small-press magazines, as well as *Pulphouse, Deathrealm,* and *Bizarre Bazaar*. Her anthology story credits include *Deathport, Newer York,* and *Journeys to the Twilight Zone II*.

J. L. Comeau

Comeau is a writer and writing instructor whose work has appeared in *Hottest Blood, Women of the West, Borderlands 2* and *3, Year's Best Horror XIX, Best New Horror 2, 3,* and *5,* and others. The District of Columbia resident is currently working on a novel.

James Crawford

New Yorker Crawford has been writing since he was very young, with earlier material appearing in comics fanzines and *Vampirella.* This is his first professionally published prose fiction.

Michael Garrett

Michael Garrett is coeditor of the *Hot Blood* series and author of the suspense thriller *Keeper.* His work has recently appeared in *Shock Rock II* and *Fear Itself.* He is an instructor for the Writer's Digest School and teaches writing seminars at college campuses across the Southeast. He resides in Alabama with his wife and children.

Jeff Gelb

Gelb is a California-based editor of the *Shock Rock* and *Fear Itself* anthologies, and coeditor of the *Hot Blood* series. He is the author of the horror novel *Specters,* and, as a rabid comic book collector and historian, is a frequent contributor to magazines about comic books such as *Comics Buyers Guide, Comics Interview,* and *Overstreet's Gold & Silver.* His short fiction has appeared in such anthologies as *Scare Care* and *100 Vicious Little Vampires*.

Stephen R. George

Canada's George is the author of a dozen novels, including *Torment, Bloody Valentine, Deadly Vengeance, Nightscape, Near Dead,* and *The Forgotten*. His most recent novel is *Seeing Eye*.

Ronald Kelly

Kelly, a native of Tennessee, is the author of eight novels, including *The Possession, Fear,* and most recently, *Blood Kin*. He has been published in numerous anthologies, and his short fiction has been featured in his audio collection, *Dark Dixie: Tales of Southern Horror*.

Edward Lee

Lee is the author of nine horror novels, *Ghouls, Succubi,* and *Creekers* among them. His most recent novel is *Sacrifice*. His short fiction has appeared in *Cemetery Dance, Bizarre Bazaar, Dark Seductions,* and *Voice in the Night,* plus a chapbook called *Sex, Truth & Reality*. The Maryland resident is currently writing an SF novel, *The Epicycle,* a collaborative horror novel with t. Winter-Damon called *Shifters,* and a horror epic called *The Bighead,* which he says he hopes will be the grossest book ever written.

Bentley Little

Californian Little is a respected D. H. Lawrence scholar who claims to have worked in various carnivals and strip clubs throughout the Southwest. He is the author of *The Mailman, Death Instinct, The Summoning,* and the Stoker award-winning *The Revelation.* His latest novel is *University.*

Rex Miller

Butcher, next in the series of Chaingang novels, was published in December '94. Missouri's Miller is the author of eleven novels, two nonfiction books, two teleplays, and some fifty short stories, including ones in *Fear Itself,* the *Hot Blood* books, *Shock Rock II, Forbidden Acts,* and a forthcoming anthology featuring Will Eisner's *The Spirit.*

Billie Sue Mosiman

Mosiman, a Texas resident, is the author of five novels of suspense, including *Night Cruise, Slice,* and *Deadly Affections.* Upcoming are *Widow* and *Suddenly.* She is the author of upwards of seventy short stories in *Ellery Queen Mystery Magazine, Hardboiled, Pulphouse, Horror Show,* and more. Her anthology sales include *Invitation to Murder, Psycho-Paths, Dark Crimes 2, Predators, Monsters in Our Midst, Frankenstein: The Monster Wakes,* and *Santa Clues.*

Michael Newton

Michael Newton has published 112 books since 1977, with eleven more "in the can" and pending release from various publishers by 1996. His work includes fifty-two episodes of the Mack Bolan series, plus nonfiction volumes like *Raising Hell* and *Silent Rage*. Newton lives in Indiana.

Kathryn Ptacek

Kathryn Ptacek has written eighteen novels, edited three anthologies, including *Women of Darkness,* and has published two dozen stories. She is also the editor of *The Gila Queen's Guide to Markets,* a comprehensive market newsletter for writers and authors, and works full-time at the *New Jersey Herald.*

Wayne Allen Sallee

The fiction of Illinois resident Sallee has been reprinted in *DAW's Year's Best Horror Stories* annually since 1986. He's won Stoker awards for novelette, short story, and for his first novel, *The Holy Terror.* His fiction has appeared in such anthologies as *100 Vicious Little Vampires, Love in Vein,* and *Nightmares on Elm Street.* Sallee is currently at work on several novels, including *Marnie's, Near Morning,* and *The Skull Carpenters.*

Brinke Stevens

California's Stevens is a world-renowned Scream Queen who's starred in over two dozen horror films, including *Teenage Exorcist,* for which she wrote the screenplay, *Slave Girls from Beyond Infinity,* and the upcoming *Mommy.* She has been a production executive for *Weird Tales,* staff writer for *Monsterland,* and correspondent for *Femmes Fatales.* She is the heroine of her own comic book series, a star of trading cards, and has several model kits based on her various horror personae. She's currently writing erotic horror short stories, a new movie script, and a children's book.

John F. D. Taff

Taff has been published in *Shock Rock 2, Cemetery Dance, Eldritch Tales, 2 AM, Midnight Zoo,* and *Aberrations.* His first published short story was awarded an honorable mention in the *Sixth Annual Year's Best Fantasy and Horror.* He lives in Missouri, where he is working on his second novel.

Larry Tritten

California's Tritten is a veteran magazine editor and writer whose credits include *Amazing, Azimov's, Cosmopolitan, F&SF, New Yorker, Harper's, National Lampoon, Playboy, Redbook, Twilight Zone, Spy,* and *Vanity Fair.*

Scott H. Urban

Urban's stories, poems, and commentaries have appeared through the dark fantasy small press in publications like *After Hours, Doppelganger, Fantasy and Terror,* and *Thin Ice.* His paperback appearances include *Fear Itself* and *Shock Rock II.* The North Carolina resident is at work on his first novel, *Crevices.*

J. N. Williamson

Indiana's Williamson is a veteran horror novelist whose fifty-three works include *Don't Take Away the*

Light, The Book of Webster's, and *Bloodlines.* He is no less prodigious in short stories, with over 140 works appearing in anthologies including *Hot Blood, Hotter Blood, Werewolf,* and *Vampire Detectives,* along with magazines like *Twilight Zone, Weird Tales,* and *Night Cry.*

Feel the Seduction Of
Pinnacle Horror

When Darkness Falls
Grab One of These
Pinnacle Horrors

BOOK YOUR PLACE ON OUR WEBSITE AND MAKE THE READING CONNECTION!

We've created a customized website just for our very special readers, where you can get the inside scoop on everything that's going on with Zebra, Pinnacle and Kensington books.

When you come online, you'll have the exciting opportunity to:

- View covers of upcoming books
- Read sample chapters
- Learn about our future publishing schedule (listed by publication month *and author*)
- Find out when your favorite authors will be visiting a city near you
- Search for and order backlist books from our online catalog
- Check out author bios and background information
- Send e-mail to your favorite authors
- Meet the Kensington staff online
- Join us in weekly chats with authors, readers and other guests
- Get writing guidelines
- AND MUCH MORE!

**Visit our website at
http://www.kensingtonbooks.com**